The Girl Under the Flag | Alex Amit

Copyright © 2020 by Alex Amit
All rights reserved. This book or any portion thereof may not be reproduced or used in any manner whatsoever without the express written permission of the publisher except for the use of brief quotations in a book review.

Printed in the United States of America

First Printing, 2020
Line Editing: Grace Michaeli

Contact: alex@authoralexamit.com
http://authoralexamit.com/

ISBN: 9798678218247

The Girl Under the Flag

Alex Amit

Paris 1942

Top Secret

7/2/1942

From: Western Front Wehrmacht Command

To: Gestapo Headquarters, Paris

Operation Spring Breeze

Purpose: Purge of Jews from Paris.

Method: Arrest all Jews of Paris and concentrate them in the Vélodrome d Hiver winter sports stadium, in order to cleanse the Paris area of Jews and send them to resettlement in eastern Poland.

Forces and missions: For the benefit of the operation, cooperation will be coordinated with the Paris police headquarters, which will allocate police forces to the operation. Supervision of the Paris Police is the responsibility of SS Regiment 1455.

Division 381 will serve all logistical needs during the operation.

Locomotives and train carriages for transport to eastern Poland are the responsibility of Western Front Railway Command.

Schedules:

Operation start time: 7/16/1942 at H − 04:00

SS. Telegram 344

Paris, Fourth arrondissement, July 16, 1942, 6 am.

"According to our records, there is a missing person here. A girl, Monique, seventeen years old."

I cling as close as I can to the wall, feeling the roughness of the bricks through my thin nightgown. It seems to me that the cracks in the wall are slitting and injuring my back, but I keep myself quiet. My palms cover my mouth so I do not cry out in fear, and my eyes are wide open in panic, but it does not matter, I cannot see anything in the dark.

"I sent her early to go stand in line for flour and oil at the grocery store on Capone street," I hear my mother's voice answering the stranger through the small wooden door that hides me.

Only a few minutes, or maybe more, have passed since the loud knocks on our apartment door and the shouting: "Police, open the door!" I ran barefoot down the hall, watching Dad come out of their bedroom walking slowly, wearing his brown robe, and giving me a soothing look.

"Quick, take Jacob," Mom shook me from my standing in the hall, holding my hand tightly and whispering for me to take him and hide.

"What about the boy, Jacob, eight years old?" There is another foreign voice, as if passing by and reading from a pre-made list, and I cling even more to the small place.

"He's in the other room with his Dad, they are packing the suitcase, tell them to speed up."

He wouldn't come with me. I rub my arm where mom held me and feel a tear running down my cheek. He'd clung to her tightly, refusing to leave her, and began crying as the knock on the door got stronger, until I had no choice but to run down the hall, leaving him hugging her leg while she tried to calm him down.

The noise of the opened door and the voices of the men

at the entrance echoed in my ears as I entered the pantry, bending down and crawling into the corner of my childhood hiding place, carefully closing the wooden board behind me and resting my head on my knees in the dark. My fingers are constantly rubbing my nightgown, I mustn't make any noise.

"When will she return?"

"After she's finished, I asked her to go to my sister in the second arrondissement, so she will only be back in the afternoon."

"Do you believe her?"

Why us? Get out of here, go get another family, not us, you can go to the Jacques family, they live in the building next door, number 41, third floor, why did you choose to take us? For a moment I'm afraid I'll start screaming and I shove my palm back into my mouth, turn it into a fist and bite it until I bleed. Go to them, we have not done you any harm.

"You can ask the neighbor next door. Go knock on her door and ask if she saw the girl coming out." The stranger continues with his horrible words.

She will protect me, she must protect me, she always allows her son to study with me, even though we are Jews and I no longer go to school. She even says that it is terrible, and that this war has been going on for too long.

I breathe quietly, another breath and another breath.

"I asked the neighbor, she says she did not see her go out this morning, and that she never sends her out so early."

Please do not search for me, please don't. My entire body cramps as I cover my ears with my palms, trying to keep the horrible sounds away as they penetrate the thin wooden board that separates me from them. For several days now, Mom has been telling Dad that there are rumors the Germans intend to send the Jews to the East, talking in whispers at the family table after dinner, making sure Jacob does not hear and start asking questions. And Dad answers in his authoritative voice that these are just rumors and that it will not happen, that we are French citizens and the Germans would not dare to do such a thing. I don't want to travel east. My fingernails grip my folded legs tightly, scratching them as I cling to the wall harder, wanting to disappear inside the wall cracks.

"Search for her."

Do not breathe, they will hear my breaths, do not move, close your eyes tightly, think about the pre-war summer, how beautiful it is in the sun. Do not scream, put your hand in your mouth again, do not shake, they will hear the tremors.

"Aren't you going to help him pack the suitcase? Only one suitcase for the family, in the East they will provide you with everything you need."

"No, I want to look after the family's silverware." I hear Mom's voice and the click of her shoes on the wooden floor in the kitchen, next to my hiding place.

"Did you find her?" The stranger raises his voice.

"She's not here and the neighbor is wrong. I sent her early in the morning. Ask the doorwoman at the entrance to the building."

"Go down and bring the doorwoman, but hurry."

Just not Odette, the doorwoman of the building. I've been scared of her since I was a kid, she's always yelling at Jacob and me. Like a tiger she lurks for us in her little room at the bottom of the stairs, where she lives, leaping towards us as we enter the big door laughing, or playing catch in the courtyard, berating us that we are not educated and making noise. To avoid shaking, I have to think of something else, not about this dark place, please don't find Odette.

"Aren't you getting dressed? Go get dressed." The voice of this terrible stranger does not stop.

"I'm waiting for them to finish packing, one more minute. Please."

A mix of footstep noises in the house, hitting the wooden

floor, approaching and moving away, as though passing between the rooms. With every door slam I cringe a little more, waiting for the creak which will open the little wooden door that protects me.

"Whose shoes are these? Your daughter's? How did she go without shoes?"

The sound of something hits the floor.

"She took my shoes. Those shoes already squeeze her when she has to stand for hours."

"It's because she's a spoiled Jew."

Another sound of footsteps and another door slam and I cringe more in the dark.

"Did you see our Monique leave the building early this morning for the grocery store on Chapone Street?"

"Do not ask her, I'm asking her, have you seen the Jew girl going out? We are evacuating them."

Tears drip down my cheeks, I don't want them to look for me, I don't want to be Jewish, I want to be just an anonymous girl, why did they come at all? Why are they taking us? My body is shaking and I'm so cold.

"The rude Jewish girl? Yes, she went out this morning. I was angry with her, the little brat did not want to tell me where she was going."

Return to breathing, small breaths.

"What should we do, keep searching for her?"

Breathe quietly, do not move.

"No, we have to hurry. We have another whole truckload of Jews for evacuation. Later they will pick her up off the street and load her."

Mom's footsteps walk away from the kitchen, becoming weaker and weaker.

"Give the neighbor the key to the apartment. She'll keep it until we get back." I hear Dad say to Mom before the door slams shut. And even though I keep listening from my hiding place, I hear no more noise inside the apartment, only Jacob's cries from the staircase and Mom's soothing words until they are no longer heard either. I must not come out of my hiding place.

The sound of falling porcelain plates makes me jump and my head hits a hard surface, waking me up in pain. My mouth opens to scream, but I manage to control myself and the bursting cry freezes in my mouth as I hold my breath and my eyes are wide open, looking in the darkness as if trying to penetrate it through the wooden boards that close on me. Where am I?

It takes me a moment to remember where I am, and where all this darkness around me came from. My legs ache from prolonged sitting without movement and the inability to straighten them, and I need to go to the bathroom so badly. How long have I been here? How did I let myself fall asleep after they took Mom and Dad and Jacob out of the house?

"Where did she hide her jewelry?" I recognize the voice of our neighbor Yvette, whose apartment door is across the hall. "Don't mess around, the stinky Jews will not return." She keeps talking, maybe to her son.

How can I stop the tremors? My hands hold my legs tightly while I fold into an uncomfortable sitting position with my back against the rough wall.

"And look for food too. They must have left something behind. I know she has stock for hard times." Her voice moves away along with the footsteps on the hardwood floor, and I guess she's going to look through the rooms of the house. Why are Mom and Dad not coming home to expel her? Dad would stand in the hallway with his authoritative look, and straight away she would smile and apologize, saying she did not mean to, and that she just wanted to keep things safe for us and not take anything. The creaking sounds of moving furniture on the floor penetrate through the wooden board and I remember my private diary, where is my diary?

The diary I received as a gift for my fifteenth birthday, with a brown hardcover on which I gently wrote the initials of my name in rounded letters. Every evening I wrote my hidden thoughts in it. Page after page, I told it everything that happened and sometimes drew flowers from memory. We are no longer allowed to go to the Tuileries Gardens, the sign at the entrance forbids it.

What if she discovers the diary in her search? Reads my secret words? I need it now, close to me in all this darkness and all the noises around.

My hands cover my ears, trying to get me away from this whole horrible day that won't come to an end. The porcelain plates are wildly placed on the kitchen counter above my head. Suddenly I am surprised by a flash of light that dazzles my eyes as I open my mouth without saying anything.

My eyes blink from the bright light and I want to hide, to be part of the wall, a page in my diary, a small corner in the dark, but it is too late. The light penetrates my hiding place, leaving me no place to hide anymore. My gaze rises slowly, and my eyes notice Theo, the neighbor's son. He leans on his knees next to my hiding place, holds the wooden board in his hand and looks at me with a serious look, without a smile. My eyes try to get used to the daylight as I stare at him, still sitting folded in my breached hiding place.

A few seconds of silence as we examine each other. I wait for him to do something, depending on desires and what he chooses to do, like I'm the mouse we saw some time ago. We'd played together in the courtyard of the building, and stood and laughed over it, watching it run along the wall and try to escape the grey cat. Slowly the cat approached and caught it in the corner, waiting patiently to strike the deathblow.

"Did you find her jewelry?" Yvette's voice comes from the other room and her footsteps noisily approach on the parquet, and before I can ask him not to say anything or betray me, I feel his hand resting on my lap for a moment and think he is about to pull me out. But the door slams shut and I'm in the darkness again.

"What did you find? Did you find anything?"

"No, Mom, there's nothing in the kitchen here. They left nothing except the porcelain plates."

"Didn't you find anything they hid? I'm sure she hid her jewelry, it's so typical of her."

"No, nothing, some food, that's all."

My fingers gently feel the apple he left in my lap, wrapping it slowly as if it were a precious jewel, feeling the hunger as a pain in my stomach. All I want is one bite, but I hold off as long as I can hear Yvette's footsteps in the kitchen, settling for smelling the apple and sliding it over my cheek. For some reason, its smooth touch soothes me, reminding me of the touch of the wool blanket in my bedroom, the one that covers me every night. I'll hold back and keep the apple for later.

The front door slams shut, and the noise of footsteps and the dragging of property is no longer heard. The silence has returned to the small shelter I am in, but despite my sore legs, I have no courage to go outside or even change position. How did Theo discover me in this hiding place? I must not fall asleep again.

What time is it? Earlier, when I pressed my ears to the wooden wall, I could hear the sounds of the street, but now

I hear nothing, what does that mean? Is it night already? Maybe Mom and Dad and Jacob will be back? For a moment I think I hear footsteps in the staircase, and I press my ears tightly and listen hopefully, almost tempted to get out of this darkness I'm in. Maybe the police realized there was a mistake in the lists and sent them back home?

They would come through the door and forgive Yvette for robbing them and not guarding our apartment, as she promised, and Mom would fix the dishes in the kitchen and hug me like she used to, and she would not mind at all that we had no food left, until the next time we'd get ration coupons.

The apple? Where is the apple? It must have fallen out of my hand as I nodded off. My hands search the floor of the small space until I feel its smooth touch, and I pick it up again in my lap, promising myself to keep it for later. I'm so hungry.

Is it night already? Where are Mom and Dad? And what about Jacob? Is he still crying? If he was crowded here with me, I could sing him a lullaby and calm him down, as he liked when he was younger, before the Germans came. I used to hum to him quietly until he fell asleep.

> Go to sleep my little brother
> Go to sleep my little brother
> Mom is making you a cake
> Daddy will bring you chocolate

I want a cake so much right now; I have not eaten one in so long. Every Friday night we would sit around the table, lighting candles and singing Shabbat songs, and Mom would give us a slice of baked cake. The memory fills my mouth with saliva, and I swallow it in frustration. Since the Germans arrived, we were almost left without food, and on Fridays we no longer sang, fearing that by chance someone from the street would hear us. Only Dad would quietly bless the food we had, and Mom, after making sure the house curtains were closed, would light two small candles she had specially hidden. By that time, we no longer had candlesticks, Mom had sold the family's silver candlesticks on the black market in exchange for a pound of meat.

For my seventeenth birthday Mom brought me a chocolate bar, I have no idea how she managed to get it or how much she paid for it. She came to me and hugged me, even though we'd had a fight the night before. She told me that I was now seventeen and mature. I hugged her back even though I was still angry with her, and so happy about the chocolate. For days I would hold back and take small bites of it, making sure to keep it as long as possible, knowing I would have no more chocolate after I finished the tablet.

One small bite of the apple, just one.

I can repeat what I learned in school, so I won't forget anything. The capital of the United States is Washington, the longest river in Europe is the Danube. The student Monique Moreno will stand in the corner and give me the note she was trying to pass to her friend. Just one more bite of the apple and I'll stop. From today on, the student Monique Moreno must wear a yellow badge attached to her clothes, and she may not play with her friends during the school break. The student Monique Moreno will not join the class tour because Jews are not allowed to enter museums. A little more of the apple. The girl Monique Moreno will walk down the street with her head down, not looking at the posters pasted on the walls, showing the Jews as rats taking over the world.

German language, I can whisper and practice my German language. Where's your ID? Where are your food stamps? Go and stand last in the line, no butter allowance remains today for the last in line. Get up against the wall as a German soldier passes by, head down you filthy Jew.

How long should I stay? I cannot be here anymore. The creaking of the wooden board sounds like a thunderbolt to me and I change my mind and quickly close it up again, but after few minutes my fingers open it once more.

The house is dark and quiet, and I crawl out of my hiding place, sitting on the kitchen floor. For a moment I try to stand and look out a window, but my leg muscles that had been cramped all day betray me, and I have to kneel back on the wooden floor, stretching my legs slowly and trying to listen to the sounds of the street while sitting on the floor. But my attention is on the front door. If they try to catch me now, I won't be able to escape.

The darkness of the empty apartment threatens me, but I am afraid to turn on the light. What time is it? I use my hands and lean on the windowsill to carefully peek out. The street is empty and no one is passing by. Only a streetlight illuminates the deserted sidewalk in a dim light, painting it yellowish.

The diary! I rush to my room, feeling my way in the dark and almost tripping over a pile of thrown belongings in the hall. My bed moves and my hands grope in the dark through the space next to the wall, right on the floor, relaxing only when my fingers feel its hard cover, bringing it closer to my heart as if it could provide me some protection against this whole day.

I must not turn on a light, if they know I'm here they will come again, knock on the door with their fists and shout "Police!" What should I do? Where are Mom and Dad? When will they return?

"God," I pray quietly as I lie on the floor of my room and press the diary to my chest. "I promise to be a good girl and not quarrel with them anymore when they say we should cut back. I promise, just return them to me, please, I will never shout that I am tired of being Jewish and that I am not willing to sew a yellow badge on my dress."

I have to get dressed, to be ready. The candle I found in the kitchen drawer illuminates my messy room as I search for a dress. I find my shoes lying at the entrance to the kitchen, but apart from them, the cupboards are empty. Mom's silverware is gone and so is the food from the pantry. There are only a few breadcrumbs left that I manage to scrape off the shelves with my fingers, putting them in my mouth and licking ravenously, but that does not quench my hunger. I have to keep some of the apple.

The sound of footsteps on the staircase of the building makes me jump, and I blow out the candle, standing still. Did they hear that there was someone in the house? Please, make them be Mom and Dad and Jacob. God, I promise to behave well and never quarrel with them again.

But the door remains closed and there is no key rattling in the lock, or loud knocks on the door. The steps continue to climb up the stairs as I slowly catch my breath.

I must not stay home, they will look for me, the policeman said they would pick me up. Why did Mom tell him I would go to Aunt Evelyn's? I'll go to her, she'll probably know where the police took them.

I have to hurry before they come back and pick me up. The dark stairwell looks less threatening than the empty apartment, and I go out and slam the door behind me. My hands search for the banisters as I carefully go down the dark staircase that leads to the street, my gaze focused on the dim light emanating from the open door of Odette, the doorwoman, who lives at the entrance to the building.

Paris, at night.

"Monique, stop," Odette cries, but I do not listen to her. My feet run past the open door of her room, skipping over the strip of light that is cast into the darkness of the entrance hall, and I keep on running. The fear of her spurs me on as I forcefully pull the latch of the heavy front door, open it a crack and run out into the street with only my dress on and my diary pressed against my chest. I'm too afraid she will try to catch me, and I'm not looking back.

But as soon as I slow down in the street, careful not to stumble on the pavements slippery from the light summer rain, trying to catch my breath, I notice them and I want to scream.

I have no idea what time it is, but if it's after the middle of the night, it is curfew time, and no one is allowed to be on the street, especially not a Jewish girl.

They both stand at the end of the street, wearing policeman hats and looking like dark shadows in the light of the lantern, which shines with a faint light.

Are they looking for me? Waiting to arrest me? That was what the policeman had said in the morning. My hands quickly go through my dress pockets, searching for the key to our home, realizing I forgot to take it. I have no way back. I also forgot my ID.

"A Jewish girl caught during curfew is as good as dead," Mom would scold me when I'd come home late at night, trying to close the front door as quietly as I could, knowing she was lurking for my return and that I would not be able to get away from this.

"You must not forget who you are," Dad used to tell me with a tired face as he emerged from their bedroom late at night, slowly adjusting his robe. "The situation is difficult," he added when he got in the middle of the fight between us, and Mom called on him to impose discipline on me.

"I'm not Jewish, I'm an ordinary French girl," I answered

him with a stubborn face, but despite all the harsh words I said to him, refusing to look down, I was really frightened of the police. I used to get back at safe hours, sneaking through the front door of the building, passing Odette and her remarks, and sitting quietly in the staircase, waiting there for hours until it was late, and only then entering the apartment and quarrel with Mom. Dad once found me sitting in the dark on the staircase, shivering cold and waiting, and wasn't angry at me at all, he just stroked my head and said we are in a difficult time, and that Mom has enough worries besides where her daughter walks at night, and no matter what happens I must not forget who I am. I want him to stroke my head so much now, and tell me the same things, as I'm in the middle of the street in front of two cops during the curfew.

Please do not look in my direction, please do not notice me. For a moment my feet freeze in place and I almost stumble on the pavement, but manage to recover and walk a few steps towards the shadow of the building which hides me from them. Quietly I lower myself behind the entrance stairs, while my hand keeps looking in my dress pocket for my ID, but it's not there.

Where is it? Did the police take it with them in the morning? Did I forget it at home? I'm as good as dead without that beige cardboard. What would I do without my photo and my fingerprint and a blue stamp of taxes in the amount of 12 francs that Mom had paid to the clerk? I must have my ID, even though it has a large, humiliating red stamp on it: "Jew."

After the Germans arrived, we received warrants that ordered us to go to the police station. I was ashamed to go, shouting at Mom that we are proud French citizens and we have the right to refuse such humiliating instructions. What would I do now without my ID?

I have to get to Aunt Evelyn; she will find a solution. I walk against the walls of the buildings, slowly getting away from the two policemen, but there, around the corner, I hear more voices and I have no courage to keep going. All I can do is crawl between two trash cans, hide and wait for morning, exhausted, tired and hungry.

When the sun rises, I will reach Aunt Evelyn and she will help me.

"They're not here, the police took them," Mathilde, the doorwoman at the entrance to Aunt Evelyn's building, tells me, as she holds the heavy wooden door a crack open, preventing me from entering the building.

"Please, I'm alone, they took my parents, where did they take them?" I beg her. She's known me since I was a little girl, bouncing merrily on the street and knocking on the wooden door and shouting: "Mathilde, I've come to visit Aunt Evelyn." Too small to reach the bell.

"The police came yesterday morning and took everyone. I have no idea where, I'm sorry, I cannot help you." And she slams the big wooden door in my face.

I look to the sides, searching for a sign of French policemen or German soldiers. Maybe it's my time to be captured, I've run out of strength to keep running. At least they will take me to where Mom and Dad are, I have no place to hide.

I'd hidden among the bins until first light, shivering from every noise, and as soon as people started walking in the street I came out of hiding, careful not to run and not to arouse suspicion, constantly checking if I was being followed and looking for round helmets in the streets. But Aunt Evelyn is not here, and Mathilde doesn't let me in.

The passersby on the street ignore me, looking forward while walking, and I knock again on the brown wooden door. I have nothing to lose.

"Mathilde, please."

"Well, come in." She eventually opens the door and pulls me inside, immediately closing it with the big black latch.

"Help me, please, I have to find her, where did the police take them?"

"They were not home when the police officers came to pick them up," she surprises me as I follow her into the courtyard. She lowers her voice as she walks, looking around to make sure no one is around, not even a neighbor going down the stairs.

"I told the police they left Paris." And she walks over and moves a rickety wooden ladder that rests on a small door of a shed standing at the back corner of the yard, knocking three times on the wooden door.

"They're inside, waiting to be evacuated. Join them, and make sure to be quiet."

"We have no place for her."

"But Albert, she's my sister's daughter. I cannot leave her on the street."

"You heard the man from the resistance. He only has room for four people, not even one more. We have no choice, she must go."

"We have to get her in. They'll catch her."

"Do you want us all caught? Do you want us all sent to eastern Poland?"

"We will succeed in convincing him to add another person, he will agree."

"No, he will not agree, not without her having forged papers."

"I cannot leave her alone. She is my family."

"We are your family; do you want to endanger your whole family?"

"She will die here alone in the streets; she will be caught and she will die." I hear Evelyn's silent cry through the open door to a crack in the shed, but Albert does not answer her anymore, and closes the door in my face.

I stand still for a few moments, gazing at the closed door. What's the point of knocking again? They will not open up for me. Slowly I sit down on the ground, lean against the wall of the building and start crying.

It's not a loud cry, but small breaths of despair mixed with tears. If only I could be a little girl again, like I used to be. To take a walk down the streets of Paris without worries, knowing Mom is waiting for me in the warm house with the smell of cinnamon cake, lying down every night in my cozy bed. Smiling and filling up my new diary with words of imagination about what I will be when I grow up.

Sounds of footsteps are heard from the entrance of the building, but I do not raise my head, continuing to read my diary which rests on my crossed legs. I do not look, even when the sound of footsteps is already close to me, I don't care who comes to look for me and catch me. I will die soon anyway.

"Come on, hurry, what are you doing out here?" Mathilde's hand grabs my arm and she's dragging me into the interior of the building. Almost by force she puts me in her little room by the front door, quickly closes the door behind us and seats me on the wooden chair in the corner.

"What are you doing out there?"

"They are not willing to take me with them," I mumble

and look down, my hands holding the diary tightly.

"Well, well." She approaches and hugs me for a moment. My hands hold her gratefully, but she releases my hug and just puts her hands on my shoulders. She is not probably used to expressing feelings, or recognizing the class difference between us, which may now have been completely reversed, as I am a hunted Jew and she is safe in her little room.

"I cannot help you. I have nowhere to hide you, and if they catch me, they will kill us both," she says as she turns her back on me and walks over to the small kitchenette. She takes out a loaf of bread wrapped in brown paper, and begins to slice it, and I eagerly look at her fingers holding the bread.

"I do not know where your family is, but you cannot trust anyone, you must rely only on yourself." Her words barely reach me as she bends over and takes a jar of jam out of the cupboard, opens it, and spreads a thin layer of strawberry jam on the slices of bread.

"You must forget who you were." She repeats her words several times as she sits next to me and I hold the plate in my lap, taking small bites of the bread, savoring the sweet taste of the jam.

"Are you listening to me? You must forget who you were."

"Yes, I must forget who I am." I must change.

"What are you doing?"

I raise my gaze and notice him. He is about Jacob's age, but he looks more neglected as he stands and watches me curiously.

"I found this dress and I'm fixing it."

"Mother says all the Jews are dirty and it is lucky the Germans are taking them."

An hour earlier, Mathilde expelled me from her little room, forcing me to leave its safety, out into the streets and the city beyond the building's heavy wooden door. "You have to go," she told me, not before she gave me another hug and tucked an apple and two slices of jam-smeared bread, wrapped in brown paper, into my dress pocket.

"Keep the food for later, my dear child, may God be with you," she whispered as she pushed me out and made the sign of the cross in a quick motion. And I had no other choice but to start walking with my head down, among all the people returning from work on a summer afternoon.

I go down the street with no real direction, lifting my head from time to time, waiting for the policemen to pick me up. But no policeman attacks me or calls me to stop, nor do I see any German soldiers. Even when I climb several stairs at the entrance to one of the buildings and look down the street, I don't identify any blue hats of policemen blue hat or the grey-green uniform of soldiers.

The city remains the same, the people walk their same normal walk. The men in suits and hats, and the women in summer dresses. No one slows down, or breaks into a fast run, everyone gets on with their lives. Most of them don't even look at the yellow badge attached to my dress, even though it makes me feel so exposed.

It's like nothing has changed in the world since yesterday, and the police are not looking for me, and did not take Mom and Dad and Jacob to an unknown place.

I keep on moving from street to street, with no direction, until I notice them in the distance, further down Rivoli Street, and stand still. At first they look like a dark block slowly moving in my direction, approaching me step by step. But when they come close, and all the people in the street go to the sides to make room for them and the policemen guarding them, I can see their faces.

I must hide, and I bend down behind some empty wooden food boxes that lie atop each other next to a grocery store, making sure to hide the yellow badge with my palm. Despite lowering my gaze to the pavement, trying not to stand out, I can't help it, and from time to time I sneak looks at them. They walk quietly, dead-eyed, holding their coats in their hands. Some carry heavy suitcases or a bundle packed in a piece of cloth. And only one girl walks between her two parents, giving them both her hands and bouncing cheerfully, as if she were on an afternoon walk.

As they pass me, I look down again, so as not to arouse suspicion. I hear her ask her father where they are going on this trip, and I have to stop myself from running those few steps and joining them. Just to not being alone.

It's a matter of time until they catch me. The thought runs through my head as they walk down the street, and I escape into a neglected alley beside the main street. I have to do something; I have to forget who I am.

Some stones in the street have been taken out by city employees, and I decide this is the right place to let my diary go. I dig into the hard ground by using a small wooden stick and my fingers, working quickly before anyone notices the Jewish girl sitting in the corner of the unfamiliar alley.

My injured fingers hold my diary one last time, and I press it to my chest and bring it closer to my mouth, kissing it with my lips, feeling the smell of the hard cover, and then placing it in the little hole I made in the ground.

After my hands cover it with dirt and stones, I stand up and pack in the ground with my feet while looking around, trying to remember the exact location in my memory, promising myself to come back one day and get it back.

"Now it's time for the Jewish girl issue," I whisper to myself as I sit down and lean against the wall of a nearby building, trying to unravel the yellow badge from the dress with my fingernails and teeth.

"What are you doing?" the strange boy asks, surprising me, but it seems to me that my answer satisfies him. He just stays close to me, watching curiously as my fingers try to tear the sewing stitches.

"Hang on a second." He runs down the alley.

My eyes follow him, but I have to get back to my unraveling, I have to hurry before someone notices.

"Try this." He hands me a rusty nail and I thank him with a little smile.

"Are you afraid of the Jews?"

"No, why?"

"Mother says that the Jews bring diseases, like the rats, and that they want to take over the world, she saw it in an exhibition." I look up at him, trying to figure out his intentions, popping the stitches more quickly with the help of the rusty nail.

I must not think about the posters for this horrible exhibition. They have been pasted on billboards all over the city, inviting the public to come see how we have big noses and lots of money. Posters that made me hate myself and my family every time I passed them by.

"The Jews are just ordinary people," I answer him, and wonder what to do with the yellow badge resting in my palm. I despise it, but Mom had to pay for it with expensive clothing stamps instead of buying clothes last winter. I'd sat in our cold living room and watched her silently embroider them on our clothes, hating her for giving in to the Germans' rules. Where is she now?

"Mom says they're like rats, and the sign can be seen." He points with his hand, and I notice that a less-faded mark remains on the dress fabric where the yellow badge had been.

"Hang on a second," I hear him say as I try to rub the cloth and smudge the less-faded place, noticing that he is running down the alley again, dipping his hand in a bucket filled with water which lies at the entrance to one of the buildings.

"Here you go." His mud-smeared hand passes over the fabric of my dress and smears the area, painting it brown as he passes his hand over my chest, not noticing my cringe.

"Now you can't see." He steps away and carefully examines the covered stain, while I look at my dress. Now I'm just a normal, neglected girl.

"Are you hungry?"

"Yes."

"Hang on a second." He turns away from me and runs, entering the doorway of the next building. But after he disappears from sight and only the sound of his footsteps is heard, and although I am still hungry and know I must get more food, I get up and quickly walk out of the alley to the main street. I have to stay away from his mother, even though I am not a Jew girl anymore. I left my identity and a buried diary under the street stones behind me in the alley, but the yellow badge is still in my dress's pocket. I could not throw it away.

Les Halles, Paris center food market, four days later.

"She's hiding somewhere here, check between the horses." I hear the panting voices of the two policemen looking for me.

For three days now I have been hiding in the streets near the huge market building in the center of the city. Every time I hear voices coming close, I change my hiding place and try not to be noticed by anyone, silently praying while closing my eyes. For three days now I have been waiting for the dark hours, so I can go out and look for something to eat, moving carefully among the merchants who unfold woolen blankets and stay asleep on their goods stalls, guarding them from thieves like me. Every night I move slowly under the huge market construction, hiding and peeking behind the big wooden carts used to transport sacks and goods, waiting for an opportunity. A fallen vegetable, a few forgotten radishes, a slightly torn sack of potatoes that I can expand with my fingers, I will settle for anything I can lay my hand on.

After four days of running, I'm hungry and tired and dirty. Mathilde's slices of bread are a distant memory of a sweet taste, but I try not to think about them, it makes me hungrier.

For the first two days I was lucky and managed to find some cauliflower that fell from a broken wooden box and was forgotten, but that's all. Yesterday, I almost stole some carrots. I noticed a skinny merchant who'd left his cart abandoned for a few minutes. He went to greet his friends, joining them for drinks, and I tried to take the opportunity. Slowly I approached the cart while they talked, careful to stay shaded and not enter the light of the small lantern which hung over the stand.

"This Calvados is pure nectar; Pierre always has the best apples."

"For you, always the best."

"Finally, the Germans are cleaning the city."

"Yes, they show us how to lead herds in the streets, without a lot of dirt."

Under the cover of laughter, I took a few more steps towards a torn sack of carrots.

"Pour me some more Calvados."

"Now you are becoming like the Jews, wanting to rob all my property."

The sounds of laughter became stronger, allowing me to stretch my hand towards the cart, but as I pulled my hand out of the sack, holding a handful of sweet carrots, one of the sacks fell on the market floor, and Pierre's friend noticed me.

Since then, they and the police have been trying to lay their hands on me.

My dress is already torn from that time I slipped on the stones as I ran at night between the aisles, escaping from the policemen's whistle and the footsteps of their hobnail boots approaching me. I managed to escape that time, but my knees have been bleeding since then, painting my legs in burgundy stripes.

Only the cargo horses do not care. They don't chase after me, allowing me to hide among them in the haystack that lies in front of them. Their soft noses sniff me curiously as they leisurely chew the straw, indifferently waiting for the end of the day. Close to each other they hide me in their presence until evening time, when they are harnessed to the merchants' carts. Then they will say goodbye to me, not before letting me stroke their noses with gentle motions, assuring me they will return tomorrow before sunrise with new merchandise.

"Shhhhh... be quiet," I whisper to them. Soon the evening will come, and I will be safe. Maybe the policemen will give up and go hunt another girl, or return to their families and to the dinner table. I must not think about food, the hunger makes it difficult for me to hide motionless. Please go away, with a little luck I will live another day.

"There she is." I hear the shout followed by a whistle from the policeman, and footsteps pounding the pavement. I rise from my hiding place and start running through the haystacks, skipping over a metal fence and not looking back, ignoring my painful knee.

I must not stop running. My feet carry me into the narrow passages between the empty boxes, panting while passing among some sellers who follow my run, but the steps behind me do not give up. The pounding of their feet hits my ears like a speeding train moving after me and never stopping. No matter which aisle I choose, they keep following me, whistling and yelling at me to stop. I can't give up, I run with a hunched back, so as not to attract attention as I skip past a pile of sacks waiting to be thrown to the garbage, choosing a new path and trying to listen to the chasing voices, even though my breathing interferes. Have they lost me? Their voices are no longer heard, I have to look back while I keep on running, and then I get hit and fall.

He's a big man, really big, sweaty, wearing a grey tank top full of stains and smelling of sauerkraut, a filthy beret on his head, and his eyes looking at me with interest as I lie on the floor at his feet. He bends down to pick up the wooden crate that fell from his hands when we bumped into each other, and to my horror, I see a yellow badge on the pavement at his feet.

The big man's movement stops.

My gaze meets his as my fingers search the pocket of the dress, feeling the tear there. What can I say to him? I gasp and try to overcome the pain in my leg, ignoring the blood, but I've run out of energy to escape.

"Did you see a girl run down here?" I can hear the cops' voices on the other side of the pile of crates.

"I have not seen, ask him."

My eyes beg for mercy as I look at the big sweaty man in the grey tank top, not knowing exactly what to ask from him. Maybe he will protect me or help me, please do something. In a moment they will emerge around the corner and I will be part of a group of Jews gathered in the street, marching towards an unknown destination like a herd of cattle.

The man looks at my begging eyes and through the narrow aisle over my shoulder, seeking those who are chasing me. After a second, without saying a word, his huge arms, which until then had loaded empty wooden boxes into a grey pickup, grab me as if I'm a sack of potatoes. With one push he throws me into the van's trunk and I hit the hard metal floor, fighting not to scream from the intensity of the pain.

"Have you seen a girl running here?" I hear them panting while they speak to him, as I crouch in the trunk, hiding behind the wooden crates that he continues to load.

"Gypsy girl?"

"We suspect she's Jewish, we are catching them all."

"She was really stinking; she passed me and ran that way."

They do not even answer him, only the sounds of their shoes are heard moving away from me, mingling with the thumping of wooden crates which are loaded on the van at a steady pace, building me a growing protective wall, while I lie on the cold metal floor, letting my breath relax a little.

Finally, I hear the trunk door slam shut and the twilight which has penetrated through the opening is replaced by darkness, and after a few minutes the pickup engine makes a rumbling noise and we start driving. The bumps of the shaky vehicle on the pavement stones hurt me, and I try to sit so as not to get hit by the metal floor.

I have no idea where he's taking me, but I can't think about it right now.

Why has the car stopped? My ear presses against the metal side of the trunk, trying to listen to the sounds outside. The van door opens and closes, shaking the van slightly. I can hear footsteps nearby, talking and laughing, is he alone? Is there anyone else with him? Did anyone wait for him? What are they planning for me?

The creaking of the trunk door and the noise of the crates being moved makes me jump and I notice his silhouette in the dark.

"You can come out." But I'm afraid to, I feel safe here.

"You can come out now, it's safe," he repeats himself and gives me his hand.

My palm disappears in his big hand as he helps me

stand on the street, supporting me for a moment as I try to straighten my sore legs. Even though we are already out of the market, the smell of his body remains as strong and unpleasant as before. We are still in Paris, but in another neighborhood I do not know. The street is narrow and almost completely dark in the evening, and I cannot read its name from the small sign painted at the end of the nearest building. Where am I?

I try to look around, but he rushes me. A barrel thrown in the street, a wooden cart tied to a stand, several posters taped to the wall expressing appreciation for the government's achievements, and one streetlamp scattering a dim light. That's all I get to see. Where did the man he was talking to go? The one I'd heard while in the car?

"Follow me." The big man enters the nearest building.

My foot stumbles when I bump into the first step in the dark and I hit the wall, trying to stabilize myself with my hands, but he does not stop and I have to follow him into the dark stairwell. The creak of his shoes on the wooden boards is clearly heard, where is he taking me? My hand holds the simple railing firmly, leaning on it for support as I get ready to turn around and run away.

His place is small, much smaller than our apartment. Does he live here? Only one room without an entrance hall, and that's it. First he goes to the window and closes the curtain tightly, and only then does he turn on the light. I can still hear his breaths from the climb, as I watch him arrange the blankets on the metal bed, turning his back to me. In one corner there is a bathroom niche, a clothesline tied with several clothespins, a kitchen corner, two wooden shelves, a small table and three chairs, a tall, narrow wooden closet, and the iron bed next to the wall by the window. The big man turns around and faces me.

We inspect one another for the first time after those few seconds in the market. He is still big and sweating from the summer heat, in the same dirty tank top with the smell of sauerkraut, and the beret that had previously been on his head lies on the small table, but still he's not smiling at me.

"Sit." He hands me a chair, places it in the center of the room in a clumsy motion, and I sit down, watching the cream paint peeling off the walls. What shall I tell him if he starts asking me questions? But he stays silent, still checking me, shifting his gaze from my messed-up hair, down my filthy, torn dress, to my bare feet with clotted streaks of blood, and I look down.

"Your dress, take off your dress." I hear the words coming out of his mouth, and slowly grow terrified.

Can I escape? Can I get up from the chair and run to the door? Did he lock the door? Where's the key? Why didn't I notice? Why did I follow him up the stairwell and not escape into the street? Why is this happening to me? Where is Mom? What should I do?

I give him a questioning look.

"Take off your dress," he repeats and reaches out his hand. I freeze, so cold.

In a slow motion I get up from the chair, go to the corner of the room, turn my back to him and open the buttons one by one. A tear goes down my cheek, I cannot do it, why is he so big? I don't deserve this.

The dress is sliding from my hands to the floor and I imagine I hear the noise of the fabric hitting the wood like a gunshot. Sometimes, in the evening, I would hear shots from the window. I sit down on the floor and cringe. My stomach becomes a lump of pain.

In slow motion I turn to him in my bra and panties, covering as much of my body as I can, and give him a pleading look. I have no strength to fight him, nor to escape.

"The dress, bring me the dress." I kneel on the floor and carefully gather the cloth with my fingers, rolling it into a lump and placing it in the palm of his hand, protecting my body as much as I can with my other hand and looking at him. Why is he doing this to me?

When will he return? Will he return alone? I must be ready.

I have no idea how long it's been since he took the dirty dress from my trembling hands and left. He bundled it in his huge palm, smiled at me and walked out the door, leaving me kneeling on the dirty wooden floor with only a bra and panties covering my body. Before I could escape, I heard the sound of the lock imprisoning me.

What should I do? How should I prepare myself? I must get out of here. Carefully I move the curtain that covers the window and watch the dark street. The streetlight is too dim and I'm not sure if there are two people standing in the dark entrance of the next building or if it's just my imagination, but I step back, afraid they'll see me peeking out of the window.

The door, is there another key in the room? How can I get out onto the street like this? In just a bra and panties? I have to find something to wear, but the door is locked and my fingers searching the high shelf next to the door can't find a key. There are footsteps in the stairwell, run away! And I quickly get away from the door, sitting on the iron bed, not on the bed, I have to stand, or sit on the chair, the main thing is to be ready.

It's not him, it's someone else, the steps continue on. I must do something, there is a brown bag with bread on the kitchen counter, but despite my hunger, I don't have the courage to eat, I'm too nervous, I want to scream.

Will he do to me what my mother always scared me about? I'll die, it's better for me to die, or defend myself and die, a knife, in the kitchen drawer there is a knife, I'll use it. Again I hear steps up the stairs, be prepared, like this, when

I sit at the end of the bed, my back close to the wall, holding the knife tightly in my hand, hidden behind my back, I must stop shaking, there is a key turning in the lock.

"It's the best I've been able to get." He places a package wrapped in newspaper, tied with a simple rope, on the chair. But I do not move from my seat at the end edge of the bed, I must be ready. My palm holds the knife tightly behind my back until my muscles tremble from the tension.

"What is it?"

"I got you another dress, more or less the same size."

I slowly get off the bed. The noise of the metal springs rings in my ears as I carefully approach the package. My hand is still holding the knife behind my back, ready for any surprise, but he's not trying to catch me. With a shaking hand I place the knife on the floor and open the bag, keeping the knife close to me. In the package there is a simple grey women's dress, and I press it to my body in order to hide my nakedness.

"I hope it's good enough."

"Thanks."

"You need to clean up," he says, and turns to the small bathing corner, collecting ready-made soap and placing it in my hand. If he notices the knife lying on the floor, he ignores it and says nothing. He simply turns his back to me and goes to the kitchenette, starting to arrange groceries. I'm so hungry.

How can I clean up next to him? I can't go to the bathroom corner to wash myself, knowing his eyes will look at my body. I can't do it, it's too much for me.

As he turns from the kitchen corner, probably wondering

about the sound of breathing he heard, he finds me sitting on the wooden floor and crying. Without a word he walks to me, picks me up like I'm a rag doll and takes me to the bathroom. After placing me next to the bucket of water, he makes sure I am stable enough and puts the soap in my hand again, but I keep standing still with a begging look, smelling the strong scent of his body.

"We'll figure something out," he replies though I've said nothing, and after a few seconds of thinking, he loosens the clothesline that hangs on the wall, pulling it to the other side. Then he brings in a sheet from the small closet, and hangs it, giving me some privacy.

With my back to him and with closed eyes, as if I was a little girl hiding my eyes with my palms and not wanting to be seen, I start cleaning myself. The rough soap scratches my skin and hurts me, when will all this end? What will he do to me? I must not think about it now, I must hurry to clean up and get dressed, to be safe again.

My hands are still shaking from the cold bathwater, as my fingers struggle with the buttons of the grey dress. I hate this color. Since it all started two years ago, this color makes me shiver. Endless rows of German soldiers wearing grey-green uniforms, marching on the Champs Elysees, ignoring the shocked people watching them in fear. They looked like giants to me with their helmets and rifles, like this man. I'm afraid of him too, despite the smell of cooked food slipping through the sheet that hides me. Will he give me some of his food?

Two plates are waiting on the table, and we sit and eat the stew he has prepared in silence. I think he even put some meat inside, I have not eaten meat in so long. After I finish all my food, carefully cleaning it all with the spoon, as much as I can, he pours another heaping spoonful of stew into my plate and I finish it all too. Doesn't he want to ask me some questions? Where is my family? Why am I running away? What is it like to be a stinking Jew?

"Thanks." I stand in the corner of the room next to the wall as he arranges the bed, taking another thin blanket out of the closet and places it on the floor, straightening it gently with his big hands.

"You are welcome."

"They took my parents and I ran away."

"I know."

"I was a normal girl, and I have a little brother, Jacob, they also took him. The police just came to our house a few days ago, and I've been running ever since." I can't stop talking, even though he does not ask. In peaceful movements he arranges the bed and the blanket on the floor and goes to the bathroom corner, closing the sheet curtain behind his back as he cleans himself, and I look at the iron bed and the neat blanket on the wooden floor. Will he attack me? Can I trust him?

"I went to school and I speak German and some English, and I was the best in my class, but one day they said I couldn't go to school anymore, and I was sitting at home, thinking that I hated my mother, pretending I was already asleep when she would come into my room at night to talk to me, and now I miss her so much."

I keep on talking, not knowing if he is already asleep or lying in the dark, looking at the ceiling and listening to me. Maybe my words are keeping him up?

The feeling is strange to me and I can't sleep. My eyes are wide open in the dark as I lie in a foreign bed next to an unfamiliar man who lies on the floor next to me. Every now and then I move my body until I hear the creaking of the metal springs of the bed, can I trust him and close my eyes? I want to ask for his name, and why he saved me, and what happened to the yellow badge that was lying on the floor, and how the cops did not notice it, but I am embarrassed and instead keep on talking about myself in the dark. Maybe he is listening.

Latin Quarter.

My eyes slowly open to the morning sun, searching for the floral curtains of my room. In a moment, Mom will enter my room and get mad at me because it's late and I have to get up and go to the grocery store on Capone Street, to stand in the endless line for flour, or oil. In a moment I'll start arguing with her that because we are Jews I have to stand at the end of the line until nothing is left. These are not the curtains of my room.

The blanket is tossed aside, and my bare feet touch the floor, feeling the rough wood while my eyes search around, looking for escape routes.

The small room is quiet and has no one but me. The table in the kitchen is still in the same place and the three chairs have not been moved either. The sheet placed on the clothesline for privacy is rolled aside and there is no one behind it, but the blanket that was spread out last night at the foot of the bed is folded on the side of the room beside the wall.

It takes me a while to calm down. Where did he go? Why did I not wake up when he got up? I anxiously check the room, slowly walking around and looking for suspicious signs.

"I'll be back in the evening." That's all he left me in a sloppy note written on a piece of cardboard on the kitchen table, next to a plate with two slices of bread and a pear. Yesterday's knife was back in the drawer, but I pull it out again, placing it on the table within reach of my hand.

Is everything all right?

The daylight penetrates the small window through the

closed curtain, illuminating the apartment in a yellowish hue, and it looks slightly larger and more neglected. The peeling stains of the paint from the walls are noticeable, and the brown door also needs painting. The kitchen has dark marks, and the wooden floor is not as smooth as in our house, but I do not care about any of that. I have food here and I'm less scared than I've been in the last few days, that's enough.

One slice of bread for now, and the other slice of bread I'll eat at noon. I put the pear in my dress pocket, in case of emergency, and I allow myself to cut another thin slice of bread, convincing myself that he won't notice when he returns in the evening. What time is it?

When I pull back the curtain, I can see the street in daylight. A man is walking by and a boy plays in the street with a ball, throws it on the wall and manages to catch it. I could not keep Jacob.

Why didn't I insist as Mom told me to? Why didn't I pull him with me, ignoring his cries? We could be here together. With food and a place to sleep. I could look after him, show Mom that I'm helping. She always asked me to take care of him and I started arguing with her, and now they are gone.

My face is buried in a blanket while I cry and my body shakes and can't calm down, as much as I try to convince myself that they are OK. It's my fault Jacob is not here with me, in this small room, with food. If they return, I promise to myself that I will take care of him, wherever we go.

"We have to go," he tells me in the evening, after I waited for hours in the dark apartment. I leaned against the window for most of the day, pulling the curtain slightly aside and watching the street for signs of danger, searching for policemen in blue uniforms or German soldiers wearing round helmets. Every now and then I left my position by the window and went to the locked door, bringing my ear to the keyhole and trying to hear if there were any steps coming up the stairs, stopping by the door, but the stairs were quiet.

Finally I notice the lights of the pickup truck emerging into the alley, and the vehicle disappears from my sight as it is probably parking near the entrance, I take the knife and wait close to the door, ready for anything.

The big man walks in and prepares dinner for both of us. He keeps quiet while eating and says nothing, even if he notices that I took a slice from his bread. Once more he serves me an extra helping of the stew after I clean the plate with my spoon, but at the end of the meal, after placing the dishes in the sink, he turns around and stands in front of me.

"We have to go."

"Where?"

"To people I know, they will take care of you."

I must trust him, he is a good man, he will take care of me.

Like an obedient Jew I do not say a word. I get up and walk to the front door, giving one last look at the room that had been my shelter for a day. The knife lies on the counter, I wish I could hide it in my dress pocket, but it is too late now. At least I have a pear and a slice of bread.

He takes a look into the staircase, checks that no one is there, and before we go out of the building into the street, he places his hand on my arm and stops me at the dark entrance, checking that the street is empty of people. Inside the back of the van, behind the pile of boxes, he spreads an old blanket on the floor of the trunk, and I sit on it, but then he surprises me.

"Do not take it off during the ride." He pulls a dark blindfold from his pocket and ties it around my eyes before I crawl into my hiding place.

"Why?"

"That's the way it must be."

"Will they do something to me?" My fingernails scratch my palm.

"You are safe, everything is OK."

And the trunk door slams and locks, leaving me in double darkness. My fingers carefully feel the blindfold cover my eyes as I breathe heavily. Where am I being taken? What will he do with me?

He's not a bad man, he'll protect me. The jumps of the van and the noise of the engine do not let me relax, not even when I try to quietly sing a lullaby, and not even when the van stops and I hear voices in German. My body tenses and my mouth opens to scream, everything is not OK.

"Where to?" the German man asks him in bad French.

"I bring supply to the market."

"Why are you going at such a late hour?"

"I have to get a shipment of chickens."

"Do you have certificates?"

My ear is close to the metal side of the trunk, but I do not listen to him and the German stranger's conversation, but to the other voices around the vehicle, walking and speaking to each other in German.

"Do you think we'll go out this weekend?"

"Light up under the trunk. I don't think they'll let us out."

"I'm tired of checking all those cars."

"What is he carrying in the trunk?"

"Did you see how big he is? How did he get into this small van?"

"Maybe he's smuggling something?"

"This big one? He can smuggle all the Jews of France under his shirt."

"And there will be room left for some resistance fighters."

"I hate the resistance; they scared the hell out of me."

"Shall we check the trunk?"

For two years now I have been shaking in fear of the German soldiers. Every time I go out into the street, I look for the grey-green uniforms, afraid to meet them on my way. My eyes scan for round helmets, and if I notice one, I look for another way to go. For two years now, I've had nightmares, dreaming of them stopping me in the street and putting me against the wall. I don't dare walk by the Opera and Concord Square, where the German Headquarters is located. I try to listen to every word while my hands tremble.

Everything will be alright, the big man will save me, the people he's taking me to will save me, someone will save me. What are they saying?

"Let our stupid sergeant decide."

"Yes, he thinks he can speak French."

"Or detect French smugglers."

"I hope he lets us go out this weekend."

"You can go." I hear the sergeant in his bad French. Please don't change your mind.

"Have you ever dated a French girl?"

But my ears don't hear the rest of their conversation, while the van continues along the way until it stops again. This time, the big man gives me a hand to help me get out of the trunk, supporting me as I get down with shaky legs, searching for stable ground and walking slowly with my eyes covered. Only weak machine noises can be heard around me, where is he taking me?

"Be careful, there are stairs going down." My small hand is holding his big hand, can I trust him? Will I hear German words again?

Philip

"Sorry, we have no place for her."

My fingers grip the black blindfold I've just removed from my eyes, while trying to adjust to the light of the yellow ceiling lamp, examining the interior of the basement and the stranger who does not bother to look at me.

He's wearing brown pants and a white tank top; his dark hair is in a quiff and he's a little older and a little taller than me. He stands in front of us for a moment, looks at me for a split-second, and then turns his back and continues his business inside the dirty, machine-laden workshop. My eyes look at his back and the pistol in his belt.

"Please, you must help me." Even though he is not looking, my eyes beg him as I raise my voice, trying to overcome the noise of the rattling machines around.

He looks up to me, while holding a printed poster in his dirty hands, as if noticing my presence for the first time.

"I'm sorry, since the Gestapo started the big deportation operation, we have a lot of fugitives. The whole resistance is full of Jews trying to get out of Paris, to the south or to cross the border into neutral Spain. You are not the only one."

"They took my family."

"I'm sorry, really, but I have no hiding places left, and the roads are full of German army checkpoints. The escape routes to the south are closed." He turns his back to me again.

"I have nowhere to go." I raise my voice and talk to his back while he is busy with the printing machine, hitting hard on one of the handles.

"Maybe in a few months, things will change, but until then, I can't help you, I'm sorry." He tries to shake the handle by force.

"They will kill me." I approach him and place my hand on his back. He must hear me, but he does not answer. His brown eyes look at me sadly for a moment, but then he turns to the printing machine again, striking the metal handle once more and cursing it.

"I'm willing to do anything you ask." I have nothing left to lose, this basement with this man who carries a gun in his belt, and the noise of the machines in the background, are my last chance to live.

"I'm sorry, really, I can't get you out of Paris." And he turns his back to me for the last time, moving away from me, and I look at the back of his neck and at the printing machine that emits paper leaflets at a monotonous pace, another leaflet and another and another.

"I can give you some food I have," he turns to me.

"No thanks, I'll manage."

No one will help me, not this man nor anyone else. What will another meal do for me? The black blindfold in my hand suddenly seems like a pleasant place to sink into, to wrap myself in the darkness.

I turn to the big man who has been standing on the sidelines all this time, handing him the piece of black cloth, but he ignores my hand and walks to the young man. He puts his huge arm around his shoulder, and they whisper with their backs to me, turning and looking at me occasionally.

"Do you speak German?" The young man approaches me, asking in bad German.

"Yes, I speak German."

"How good?"

"As a native language."

"How do you know German so well?"

"My family had a business in Germany when I was a child, so we lived there for a few years, until 1933, when the situation became problematic and my father sold his factory, got us out of there and back to France." I answer him in German, not sure he understands me, while he stands close to me and his eyes check me out.

"Do you want me to sing you a song in German?"

"Do you read and write in German?"

"As I told you, it's a native language for me."

He gives me the poster, pulls a pencil out of his pocket and hands it to me.

"Write."

"What do you want me to write?"

"Whatever you want."

Stand up, damned of the Earth
Stand up, prisoners of starvation
Reason thunders in its volcano
This is the eruption of the end.
Of the past let us make a clean slate
Enslaved masses, stand up, stand up.
The world is about to change its foundation
We are nothing, let us be all.

My fingers write the words of the International, the socialist movement in France, on the back of the poster. Translated into German, in as round and beautiful handwriting as I can. My hand holds the paper on a metal plate of the printing machine, which keeps working and shaking as I'm writing, and I mumble the words as they are written.

"Here." I give him the piece of paper.

He glances at the written words for a second and stuffs it in his pocket, looking at me again.

"And are you Jewish?"

"Yes."

"You can call me Philip."

"My name is Monique." Maybe I've got a chance, is Philip his real name?

"Please sit here." He grabs my arm, not by force or violence, and leads me to a simple metal chair which stands against the wall, taking a pile of papers from it and ordering me to sit.

"Wait here."

My eyes follow him as he approaches another man in

the corner of the basement, whom I had not noticed until now. Tall and thin, hunched over a wooden table laden with papers, stamps, cutting tools and ink jars. The tall man sits with his back to me, concentrating on his work by the table, until Philip leans over his shoulder and talks to him. They both look at me. He thinks for a moment, takes something out of the desk drawer, gets up and leaves his cluttered desk, standing in front of me.

"Are you Jewish?"
"Yes."
"What is your name?"
"Monique."
"What's the last name?"
"Moreno."
"What are you praying for on Friday?"
"Blessed are You, Lord our God, King of the universe, who has sanctified us with His commandments, and commanded us to kindle the light of the holy Shabbat." And I remember Mom standing by the candles and blessing in her quiet voice while Dad stood next to her with a look of pride on his face.

"You bless before or after lighting the candles?" The stranger interrupts my thoughts.
"After."
"And what do you do with your hands?"
"I cover my face with them." I've got tears in my eyes thinking of Mom.
"Why are you crying? Are you stressed?"
"No."
"So why are you crying?"
"Just a memory." I must not show weakness, they will expel me.
"What do you prepare for Passover soup?"
"Kneidlach."
"How do you make them?"

And I explain how Mom would get matzah flour and eggs and oil, when it was still possible, and add a little salt, and how the whole kitchen would be filled with their smell when they were cooked in hot water. I used to taste some of them from the strainer basket, and Mom would pretend she was angry at me, but not really. Where had the police taken them?

He then lets me read prayers from a small prayer book he holds in his hand, examines whether I can read the Hebrew prayers, and I read every page he opens to him, until finally he turns his back to me and walks over to Philip, who stands aside, leaning on one of the machines, watching me all this time as I've been tested.

"I believe her, but she's too young."

"I'm nineteen years old." I turn my gaze to Philip, looking straight at him.

"She doesn't look nineteen to me."

"I just look younger."

"She will not succeed, it's too dangerous."

"I will succeed."

The tall man looks at me with anger for my interrupting his words, but Philip continues to look at me with interest.

My eyes are fixed on the wheels of the machine that keep turning, while Philip and the tall man turn their backs to me again and argue. What else can I say that will change their minds? I have run out of other options, I depend on their mercy.

"Maybe we can help you."

I want to hug him, or fall at his feet and kiss them, but I'm afraid that tomorrow he will change his mind and I'll find myself alone again, and I just look down and say nothing.

"In the coming days we will contact you and see how we can help you." He ends the conversation between us and returns to the printing machine.

"Come with me." The big man with the dirty shirt is waiting for me, but for a moment I stand still, looking at Philip's back and the gun in his belt, wondering if I can trust him, even a little bit.

On the way back to town, blindfolded in the trunk of the bouncing van, along with crates of chickens, I sing to myself the Shabbat songs we used to sing as we sat together around the table, letting the tears come and soak in the black blindfold, and when we lie down to sleep in the apartment, I whisper "Good night" to the big man, feeling a little more secure and a little more protected.

"Filthy Jew."

The scream that is heard in the room is mine, as I am thrown from the bed to the floor, and a hand grabs my hair tightly and drags me to the wall, forcibly pinning me to the peeling yellow cracks. I scream again, trying to wake up and figure out where I am.

"Where is he?" the man throwing me against the wall shouts in German, his hand resting on my neck and strangling me. I can barely breathe.

"Who are you looking for?" I answer him in tears.

"Where is the man who lives here?" And his hand tightens around my neck and I gargle words and try to breathe. My eyes search the room for the big man who will protect me, but to my horror, I notice a soldier in a green grey uniform and a round helmet standing by the closed door, holding a gun in his hand.

The hand that close on my throat releases me a bit and his evil face come close to me, stinking of tobacco.

"Where is he?" he yells at me.

"I do not know where he is," I bitterly weep. Where is the big man? What happened when I slept? Why is he not here to help me?

"You liar," he slaps me in the face, and I scream. "We saw

you together, you are a member of the resistance with him, where is he?" He slaps me again.

"I'm not in the resistance." I cry, feeling the pain of the slap. Who betrayed me? Did Philip with the gun in his belt betray me? Why did he do this to me? I can't take it anymore.

"You're lying, you are a filthy lying Jew, they saw you praying, where is he?"

"I do not know where he is." My words barely come out against his tight hand and the tears blur my vision, where is the man? I don't want to die.

"Last chance, where is he?" His awful hand grips my hair tightly and I scream again as he lowers me to the floor, my head almost hits the wooden floor.

"Please, I don't know." I look at his brown shoes and the hem of his coat, see my tears wetting the parquet in small circles and hold my breath for a kick to come.

"You don't know where he is?"

"I'm just a French girl, please."

"Last chance, where is he?"

"I do not know, please."

"Kill her." His whisper is heard to the soldier who is standing in the doorway and I breathe quickly, hear his footsteps approaching and see the tips of his black army boots. My eyes close as I feel the cold barrel touch my head and wait for the black to arrive. Maybe it's better that way, to stop this awful place I'm in, it hurts so much.

Silence,
And the silence goes on,
And the hand that grabbed my hair and nape slowly lets go and releases me,

And the gun barrel is no longer touching my head.

And I hear footsteps and a door opens, and slowly I open my eyes, still seeing the old parquet floor of the apartment, which the morning sun paints in a light shade of brown. The little circles of my tears are still visible, but the black soldier's shoes are gone and the brown shoes of the man who hit me are gone too. I do not dare to look up, knowing that they are still in the room and having fun, playing with the Jewish girl before the final execution.

"It's OK, drink now." A huge hand rests on the back of my head and even though I flinch in fear, he does not hurt me. And a simple glass of wine is served to my lips and I take small sips, doing what I am told, trying to get used to the bitter taste which is combined with the sour smell of cabbage.

"It's OK, it's over, you were OK." And I look up and see the soldier next to the horrible man in the coat, standing at the door and looking at me, but they no longer look at me in hatred. The big man's hand supports me, keeping me from collapsing on the floor, as he hugs me and hold the glass of wine to my mouth. "Drink, let the breath come back."

Later on he walks over and confides in them, as they look at me placing the glass of wine on the floor, looking down and staring at the rays of the sun that penetrate the wine and create small waves of cheerful burgundy on the floor, as if it does not care what happened here minutes before. And when I raise my head and look at the door, the terrible people have gone, and the door is closed. I haven't even heard the sound of it slamming shut.

The big man gets me up from the floor and supports me, lifts the kitchen chair that was turned upside down when they dragged me by my hair from the bed and slammed my body against the wall. He arranges it in place and sits me down.

After he makes sure I'm fine and I'm not going to fall on the floor again, he gently touches my shoulders for encouragement and turns his back on me. His hands take the loaf of bread out of the paper bag in the kitchen and start slicing it.

Two slices of bread on a plate, smeared with butter and a bit of strawberry-flavored jam, bitter in my mouth with the taste of my tears, a slice of yellow cheese, a glass of sweetened milk, and two cubes of chocolate substitute.

"Why did you let them?" The pain is clear in my voice, I feel unsafe in this place.

"We had to."

"Who is 'we'?"

"They will explain it to you in the evening."

"What will happen to me in the evening?" Will they play at killing me again? The lump of cheese sticks in my throat.

"In the evening we go again."

"To the same place?" The place where they don't want me? To the man who told me he was sorry? To the same road? With the checkpoint of the German soldiers, who didn't open the trunk of the van just because you are so big? What if this time there will be other soldiers? Will I die in the evening instead of dying in the morning? And if I tell you what I heard; will you cancel the ride? And then I'll walk the streets until they catch me? It's hard for me to swallow the sweet slice of bread.

"You'll know in the evening where you are going, it does not matter." Maybe it really does not matter, it's just a matter of time before someone catches me and kills me.

"Do not open for anyone and wait for me in the evening," he tells me after the meal ends in silence, and he clears the dishes and gets ready to go. I do not want to be left alone.

After I hear the door slam, I go to clean up and scrub myself. Will anyone come in and surprise me?

The knife is within reach of my hand as I clean myself, even as I peek into the street through the open curtain, jealous of the young girl walking without fear, even when I hear footsteps in the stairwell. I come close to the door and try to listen. All day the knife is in my hand and I'm ready for anything, with the pear and the two slices of bread in my dress pocket. I'm ready all the time.

"We have to go."

Since this morning I have been afraid of these words, knowing they will come at the end of the day. My thoughts are constantly on the German soldiers that will stop us on the way, and the questions I will hear through the thin wall of the trunk. Will they believe him?

"Go inside and sit." The trunk door closes behind me, imprisoning me again, blindfolded. My hands stabilize myself for sitting. It's too late for second thoughts.

The pungent smell of gasoline of the engine carries in the air, as the van goes down the stone road, shaking me inside the cramped trunk. I must think of something nice, like pre-war summer and vanilla ice cream. I must not think about ice cream, I just need to relax and breathe quietly, stop listening to all the noise outside, breathe and count for myself. Why did the van stop?

His big hand leads me slowly down the stairs, and the smell of print rises in my nose, even though I cannot hear the sounds of yesterday's machines.

"You're back."

His fingers gently remove the blindfold, placing it in my hand. The gun is still stuck in his belt and he is close to me, looking into my eyes which are again trying to adapt to the burst of light of the yellow ceiling lamp.

"Yes, I'm back."

"Are you fine?"

"Yes, I'm fine." Your people have done terrible things to me.

"Do you want to know why we did it?"

"No, it's OK." Because you, like them, want to see if you can trust the Jewish girl or accuse her in treason. We are always suspicious of something.

"How old are you?"

"Nineteen years old."

"You are not nineteen, how old are you?"

"Seventeen years old."

"Why did you lie to me?"

"Because I want to reach the age of nineteen."

Philip silently looks at me, as if thinking what to do with the Jewish girl standing in front of him, and I stare back.

"We had to make sure you were not a Gestapo agent, one who would betray us all."

"I had a father and mother and Jacob that the Germans took. Do you still think I'm a Gestapo agent?"

"You'll have to learn to be more polite, and don't lie to me anymore." He turns and walks to the table at the end of the room. "Come here."

I sit down in front of him on the wooden chair. My hands are under my thighs, feeling the roughness of the wood, but close to the knife hidden in the dress pocket, along with the pear and the two slices of bread.

"You have two options," Philip leans towards me and looks into my eyes, putting his hands on the table as if he wants to show me that his intentions are good. I stare at the color print stains on his fingers.

"First option, we can take you back to Paris, you will go

55

your own way, you'll probably try to get to the south on your own and maybe you'll succeed in crossing the border into Spain. With all my heart I'd wish you good luck. I will also give you some food."

"And the other option?"

"You will join us."

"Which means?"

"Everything we need."

"And who are you?"

"We are the fighters for free France."

"Will I die?"

"Maybe, maybe I will die too, life is given to those who are willing to fight for it."

"I want to live."

"I cannot guarantee you that."

I can feel the metal touch of the knife in my pocket. I am tired of running by myself, living from minute to minute in such fear.

"What would I do for you?"

"You will bring us information about the Germans."

"I'm scared of them; they will kill me."

"They'll probably kill us all."

"I'm Jewish."

"You'll have to forget who you are, you'll become someone else."

"I hate who I am."

"Good."

Philip smiles a little at me, for the first time since noticing me last night, and turns around and calls out to the tall man, who is leaning over his stamping table, busy with his work and ignoring us. The stamp man delays for a moment while concentrating on some document, then he takes a cardboard box off the shelf above him and takes out a camera.

"Come over here, stand by the white wall. I need to photograph you for a fake ID."

As I get up from the chair and try to digest what I have

chosen, I turn to look at the front door of the basement, searching for the big man who brought me here, wanting to thank him for saving my life. But he is not here anymore.

A New Life

May 1943

Secret

5/3/1943

From: Western Front Wehrmacht Command

To: 34 Corps Paris

Reorganization, Regulation 53

Purpose: Paris Area is Declared a recovery home base for German army troops.

General: The remaining divisions of Rommel's African Corps are retreating from North Africa, under pressure from American and British forces.

The number of casualties in battles against the Russian army on the Eastern Front is steadily rising.

Therefore, Paris will be declared a recovery home base for German army troops.

Method: Regulation 53 will replace Regulation 15.

German soldiers throughout the Paris area will be allowed to purchase goods at local stores. Local Army Headquarters will select and approve stores according to their needs.

Food rations: Issuance of food ration certificates for the selected stores is the responsibility of Logistics Division 221.

SS. Telegram 821

Paris, May 1943

"ID, please."

My fingers pull the ID out of my leather bag, and I hand it to him, watching as he examines it carefully. He is taking his time, checking all the details and stamps, reviewing the picture and comparing it to my face while looking at me.

"Name?"

"Monique." Philip insisted I not change my name, so I would not be confused when I got nervous.

"Last name?"

"Otin."

"Date of birth?"

"December 14, 1925."

"How do you know German so well?"

"I grew up in Strasbourg."

"That's German territory today, why are you in Paris and not with us in Germany?"

"Dad had a lumber business, and Mom was a teacher, and I grew up there, but in 1937 Dad wanted to grow the business, and we moved to Dunkirk."

"Why Dunkirk?"

"It will not work. They will never believe me." My eyes look at Philip, sitting on the other side of the wooden table, examining me with a serious look.

"Don't stop; keep answering me."

"They will check and find that I'm lying, and kill me."

"They cannot check; thanks to the American bombers, they have nowhere to check. Strasbourg City Hall was bombed during an American raid a year ago. They tried to hit the railways and missed, destroying City Hall. What did you do in Dunkirk?"

"We were in Dunkirk until May 1940 when the Germans invaded."

"You can't recite your story; you must fill it with emotion. There will be a German investigator sitting in front of you, not me, you must speak emotionally. You must imagine that I am that German soldier who hates you."

"We lived in Dunkirk until three years ago, May 1940, when you invaded France and Belgium." Most of the time, I think he hates me.

"And what happened then?"

"They will not believe Dunkirk, why not somewhere else?"

"Because the German guns destroyed Dunkirk, not a single piece of paper was left there. Go on talking, how did you get to Paris? Do you want the German to believe you? Where are your emotions?"

"When the German army broke through the lines of defense, Dad decided we had to escape, they woke me early in the morning. When I got out of the house, the car was already fully loaded, everything Mom and Dad could pack in a hurry. We tried to escape to the south, but on the way, they were killed."

"What happened?"

"A plane. On May 23, one of your airplanes killed them."

"Watch your tone here; you are speaking about the German army."

"Sorry, I apologize."

"How did it happen?"

"A German Stuka passed by and fired at the convoy of refugees we were in, just like that." And I close my eyes and imagine the story, getting the words out slowly and emotionally.

"We'd been on the roads for two days by then, strolling down a narrow road full of cars and people and horses with carriages. The cars' roofs were loaded with mattresses and suitcases tied with ropes. The horses walked so slowly, and the air was constantly filled with the smell of fear."

"Keep on talking."

"An endless convoy headed south; I can remember the sun; it was so hot that day. Every now and then, we had to move to the side of the road, to allow a group of dirty soldiers sitting in an old truck to pass our way; they were heading north, trying to join the battle and stop you. Even though they already knew it was a losing battle."

"Stopping us?"

"Stopping the German tanks marching towards Paris." I have to imagine them, feel the story.

"We abandoned Dad's car that morning after it ran out of gas, and Mom allowed me to take only one suitcase, which I was already having a hard time carrying while sweating from the heat of the sun. We'd been walking for a few hours by the time they appeared above us."

"I'm listening."

"At first, they seemed like insignificant tiny dots in the sky to me; I looked up at the disturbing hum that overcame the noise of the cicadas in the fields, and saw them. Have you ever heard the sound of cicadas in the wheat fields in May and June?"

"No, never."

"There were four planes. Suddenly they changed course and dived on us, getting bigger by the second. We all ran away, screaming into the fields on the side of the road and scattering everywhere. The buzzing noise changed to a painful squealing of engines whirring, with the hammer's pounding of machine gun fire along the ruined road. Maybe they thought we were military men, maybe they were just coming back from a mission and were left with some ammunition, and didn't want to return it to base."

Philip is silent, sitting and watching me, and I go on talking.

"I never thought planes made such terrible noise." I must think about them, even though I'm trying not to.

"Yes, they make terrible noise."

"Then there was silence; only the noise of the bombs resounded in my ears while I rose from the ground, scratched by the weeds I had flattened upon in the field. I searched for Mom and Dad with my eyes, among all the people who stood up between the trampled oats, but they didn't stand like all the others. They just lay quietly on the side of the road, in an embrace. Dad had tried to protect her with his body, wearing a white shirt that now had a growing bloodstain on his back, and Mom lay with her face to the sky, smiling at him, as if indifferent to the red puddle coming out of her back, painting the grey asphalt." I see them in my imagination while speaking slowly; what really happened to them?

"I'm listening."

"But the people didn't care, they just got up and checked themselves, seeing if they were all right, returning to the road, keeping on strolling heading south. I still remember the pitying looks they gave me. Do you know what's the stupidest thing?"

"What?"

"All that time, what bothered me was that Mom would be mad at me for losing my suitcase when I ran from the planes into the field."

"And did you find the suitcase?"

"No, I just stood on the side of the road staring at them, not knowing what to do, while the whole convoy passed me in silence. Until one woman took pity on me and picked me up with her, bringing me to Paris to my aunt, with whom I live to this day."

"Now that was good enough, you've convinced me of your story. I hope you will persuade the German who might sit in front of you. It's important that you talk about your arrival in Paris and where you live. By the way, the tear you shed when you talked about your parents, it was good."

"See you next time." I get up from the wooden chair and head out, waiting to climb the stairs and exit the damp basement where we are meeting.

"See you next time. And try to get more information."

I have known him for almost a year now, meeting with him about once a month. And for almost a year now, he has been examining me, making sure I do not fail, and for almost a year now, he is not happy with me.

At least I'm not Jewish anymore. I'm Monique Otin, who lives in the 8th arrondissement, working in a boulangerie on the boulevard next to the opera.

"You're late." Simone, the boulangerie owner, scolds me as I quietly enter the next morning, closing the glass door behind me.

"I apologize, Mrs. Simone."

"Hurry up; your kingdom is waiting for you."

"Good morning." I hang my bag on the hanger and smile at Claudine, the second employee, who stands behind the counter.

"Good morning, how are you?"

"Monique, the tools in the back are waiting just for you."

"I'm going there, Mrs. Simone."

I quickly tie the white apron around my waist and rush into my kingdom in the back room, near Chef Martin. Here I spend my time washing dishes and cleaning the floor, sometimes I help Martin knead the dough, but usually I devoutly scrub the large baking pans.

From time to time, I have to go out among the customers, move a cloth around on the floor and wipe baguette and croissant crumbs off the seating tables. While working quietly, I listen to the buyers' conversation, keeping my head down.

"If you're done washing the baking pans, help Martin arrange the stock in the pantry, and then help Claudine clean the tables."

"Yes, Mrs. Simone." I wipe the sweat off my forehead and get up from the little wooden chair in the corner, going to the pantry to help Martin.

There is fine butter on our shelves, and there is no shortage of flour, cinnamon, or any other ingredient that would prevent Martin from baking. Even real chocolate arrives once a week, unloaded from a special truck approved by the authorities. We have everything needed to please the

German soldiers during their stay in Paris, or as Simone calls them, 'our happy German customers.' A crispy morning baguette on the way to the Headquarters at Rue Rivoli, fragrant croissants to bring to a commander's meeting, and in the evenings, a slice of chocolate cake to the mistress waiting in her apartment.

Porcelain trays display Martin's masterpieces, protected by showcase glass and sold by Claudine's smile, all for German Reichsmarks or Vichy government francs. Every coin is welcomed in Simone's outstretched hand, quickly entering the cash register with a cheerful ring. We can be happy; after all, we are a favorite Nazi boulangerie in the heart of the Headquarters area.

"Take a break; I'll manage on my own." Martin expels me from his kingdom, but I stay, handing him the sack of flour. Even though it's my job to go out among them, it's hard for me to listen to the German soldiers in the boulangerie.

"Go, Claudine needs you."

The boulangerie is full of soldiers in green-grey uniforms; they stand patiently in line, laughing with each other and filling the small space with cigarette smoke and the odor of male sweat.

"Shall we go for a walk at the end of the day?" Claudine asks me as she takes an order from a German officer, flirting with him with her eyes.

"Yes, of course."

"Three and a half Reichsmarks." She reaches out her hand to him, and he puts the money in her palm, holding her fingers for a moment as if inviting her to a prom dance.

"Thank you very much. Come again." Her smile is dedicated especially to him.

She always looks perfect with her wavy black hair, just

like the latest fashion. Sometimes she even puts on lipstick, ignoring Simone's remarks about it being inappropriate.

"Who's next? Monique, help me."

"And what's the name of the young frau?" A fair-haired soldier turns to me, and I look down, having a hard time looking at his uniform and staying calm.

"He is waiting for you," Claudine whispers to me as she lowers her voice and turns to serve a handsome pilot wearing dark grey uniforms.

"I saw you were excited about him." Claudine teases me after we say goodbye to Simone and Martin, starting our walk down the boulevard towards the Opera metro station.

"I saw you were excited about the pilot."

"He was flirty. I think he is a fighter pilot."

"How do you know he's a fighter pilot?"

"All fighter pilots are sure of themselves, and he also has a lot of medals of honor, probably for shooting down enemy aircraft. Not many like him arrive at the boulangerie."

"And what did he say to you?"

"He said that I have beautiful eyes and that I should go out with him."

"And will you?"

The exit of the metro, at Place de l'Étoile, is packed with German soldiers who have come to see the world-famous boulevard, and I cringe in the aisle, careful not to rub against them.

"Monique, you are not listening to me."

"Sorry, what did you answer?"

"I told him I don't know him at all and that I can't go out with him."

"And that's it? Did he give up?"

"No, not at all, I told you he is sure of himself."

"So how did it end?"

"He said he would return to Le Bourget, they have a Messerschmitt squadron there, but he will come again tomorrow."

"And will you go out with him?"

"I don't know."

"Doesn't it bother you, going out with a German officer?"

"At least he will treat me politely and take me out, not like all the French men, talking all the time about how difficult life in Paris is these days."

"I wouldn't be able to go out with a German soldier."

"Maybe we should go out together, me with my pilot, and you with the one who wanted to talk to you."

"He didn't like me at all."

"He does, you'll see he will come tomorrow, he's interested in your beauty, you just have to start wearing makeup."

"How do you know he is interested?"

"Because I have experience with that sort of thing."

"But I'm not pretty."

"Believe me; you are, I know about this." And she folds her arm in mine as we walk down the Champs Elysees, watching the café full of German soldiers and their girls.

I never thought I was beautiful. How beautiful could I feel if, from the day my breasts started to grow, everyone looked at the yellow badge stuck on my chest? How attractive could I feel in the simple dress Mom bought me? Or in that old coat I was wearing, trying to become as invisible as I could?

"The worst thing is getting noticed," Mom had explained to me, firmly refusing to have my hair permed as I'd seen in the glittering posters of movie stars hanging on the billboards in the street. "Worst of all is drawing the attention of a policeman or a soldier." She yelled at me when she discovered the magazine with the pictures I had tried to hide.

"You will never dress like those whores." She ripped it apart and threw the pages into the fireplace, replacement for the heating logs we were so desperate for.

"I'm sorry I was born into this family," I yelled at her in tears and ran to the dark stairwell, unable to see the torn magazine on fire.

But Claudine thinks I'm beautiful as we walk around the cafés, even though I do not have perfect wavy hair like hers.

"This soldier is also interested in going out with you." She squeezes my arm and laughs, pointing to a handsome armored soldier standing in his black uniform, watching us pass the boulevard, and I'm trying to smile. She must never know why I hold back from the German soldiers.

"Good night, see you tomorrow." Claudine is walking to her home, and I'm heading to the apartment which has been my home for almost a year.

How would my life look if I was in her place instead of mine? I think as I pass the large billboard on the street. Would I be excited about hanging out with German soldiers? Or would I continue to worry every morning on my way to work?

"ID, please."

Just a few minutes' walk separates the quiet boulevard and the billboard with the worker's poster looking to the horizon and the guards' post in Concorde Square, the checkpoint for the Headquarters area.

"Guten morgen." I hand the cardboard card to the guard, looking around as he examines it carefully. The barbed wire fences and wooden barriers are spread along the road, destroying the square's beauty. Why are they looking at my ID for so long? They should already know me by now. Did they notice my trembling fingers?

"Name?"

"Monique Otin, I passed here yesterday and the day before and the day before."

"Where are you going?"

"I work near the opera."

For almost a year now, I have been passing by the guard post every morning, and for almost a year now, I have to calm myself down as I approach the German soldiers standing near the barbed wire.

The sergeant looks at the ID for another moment, examining my face in front of the photograph as I look back at him until he relents, returning it to me.

"Have a nice day, Frau Otin." He taps his heels tightly and makes me cringe for a second as I return the ID to the leather bag resting on my shoulder.

"Have a nice day, Sergeant." I try to smile at him and

continue walking down the street, looking at the senior officer's cars, parked in a straight line in front of the building, under the huge red Nazi flag that flies in the morning breeze.

Keep going ahead, look down, memorize the vehicle numbers, count the guards at the Headquarters entrance, and smile at the bored drivers polishing their officer's cars. I hope they engage me in conversation and provide me with some information along the way, like last week when I learned about the new division arriving in France.

The quiet sound of the red flag above my head makes me quicken my steps, though I need to calm down, must not arouse suspicion. It moves calmly and serenely, looking down at me, and I lower my gaze, trying to avoid the black swastika sewn in the center of the white circle, just a few more minutes of tension.

The edge of the building is already approaching, my eyes examining several military trucks that pass through the street in slow motion, memorizing the unit symbol painted on their sides. In a few steps I'll turn to the avenue leading to the opera.

"Mademoiselle." I'm looking back to the soldier running towards me, and I stand still.

Breathe quietly, do not tremble, and do not run away; keep calm.

"Mademoiselle, the scarf, it fell from your bag." He catches up with me, all sweaty, handing it to me with a smile.

"Danke schön." I smile at him and turn onto Opera Avenue, taking a deep breath and holding the leather bag tightly until my fingers turn white from the effort. In a few more minutes, Simone will ask me why I'm late again, and Claudine will ask if we will go for a walk together after work among the cafés on the boulevard.

"Not today," I will have to answer, "Today I cannot."

At the end of the day, the boy will probably be waiting for me next to the newsstand.

"I apologize, I have to go visit her mother today. I promised I'd do it after work."

"I thought we could take a walk down the boulevard." Claudine fails to hide her disappointment as we leave the boulangerie at the end of the day, walking arm in arm down the avenue. "She's always asking you for favors."

"I owe her, she let me sleep in her home, I cannot refuse her when she asks me to help her."

"Do you want me to join you?" She stops next to me at the newsstand.

"No thanks, you'll be bored."

My fingers search among the newspapers hanging on the walls of the stand. I pretend to look for a particular newspaper from the poor selection of wartime magazines, but my attention is on the boy with the grey casquette, the one standing with his back to me.

"Metro Opera," he whispers to me as he loads a pack of newspapers into a large leather bag, continuing on his way, and I do not answer him, hoping Claudine did not hear his whisper.

"Why are you looking for a newspaper? They're just full of war stories anyway."

"She likes me to read to her. It's already hard for her to read."

Claudine takes a magazine with a red title and a photograph of a pilot on the cover, handing it to me.

"Buy her the German Army newspaper in Paris, the Signal; she probably won't notice."

"Put it back; they'll think we intend to buy it." I laugh at her.

"No one cares what we do." She waves the magazine in front of my face, but finally relents and returns it to the stand.

"Goodbye, I have to go, she's waiting for me, we'll meet tomorrow." I hug her quickly and walk away, holding one of the government newspapers in my hand. It announces a further reduction in meat rations. The man near the Metro Opera is waiting for me already.

Next to the billboard, I stop and look at a poster showing a new movie star in a red dress, taking the time to look over my shoulder. Is anyone following me? The soldier by the stairs is waiting for me, or has he made an appointment with another girl? And what about the café across the street? It's full of German soldiers, are they looking in my direction?

At a slow pace, I cross the avenue and approach the marble railing of the entrance to the metro, looking around and pretending I'm looking at the opera house which overlooks the boulevard, ignoring the red flags with swastikas hanging in front of it.

"Come with me," a stranger whispers as he hands me a bicycle, and we start pedaling down the streets. I do not know where, but I must trust him to lead me to the meeting point with Philip.

He waits for me at the entrance to a basement in the Latin Quarter, standing at the bottom of the stairs, looking up as I descend towards him, and finally climbing a few steps in my direction. He's still wearing a simple white shirt with his sleeves rolled up below his elbows, his quiff still wild, and he still has a gun sticking out of his belt as he looks at me with his brown eyes, examining me.

"How are you?"

"I'm fine. How are you?"

A small table and two chairs stand in the corner, but he does not offer me to sit, and we remain standing, facing each other as I look up at him.

"How is the underground? How is the revolution progressing?"

"We will win, but revolutions do not happen in a single day. What did you bring with you?"

"Not much."

He walks away from me, taking a few steps into the small basement as I follow him with my gaze.

"I can't get much information, the guards near the headquarters examine me all the time, and in the boulangerie I hardly walk around among the soldiers. Simone wants me to wash dishes all day."

For almost a year now, I have had the feeling that he is disappointed in me, sorry he had not found a more effective German speaker instead. One that would not be afraid of the German soldiers entering the boulangerie, or would be willing to go out with them. They are walking like tourists all over the city, holding city maps supplied by the German army, looking for French girls to guide them through the wonders of the city of lights. But I'm not effective as he expected; in the end, he will get rid of me, leave me to my fate.

"There are some new senior officers' cars outside the headquarters, and I have new gossip from Claudine."

"Do you have the vehicle descriptions or numbers?" He approaches me again, takes a piece of paper and a pencil out of his pocket, but still does not ask me to sit down.

"Let me write the numbers for you."

"I'll write. If they catch me and get to the paper, they must not recognize your handwriting."

"You were wrong here," I point out and correct him, touching his fingers by mistake and looking away in embarrassment, but continuing to tell him the numbers, ignoring the warmth of his touch.

He has the pleasant smell of a man mixed with the scent of a printing house, but I have to concentrate, trying to remember every piece of information, even the smallest ones, like what I heard from Claudine.

"She is now excited about a pilot stationed in Le Bourget."

"That's good. Maybe it will bring us more information." Why am I not like her?

"Don't you want to check my story, like last time?"

"Not today, I have to hurry. We'll continue to build your story next time."

"Will we meet next month?"

"Yes, we'll meet next month." He walks away from me again, turning around in the damp basement as if he already wants to get out of here, into the air outside. He is disappointed in me.

"Goodbye." I turn and head up the stairs.

"Monique," he takes my arm, stopping me.

"Yes?" I look up at him.

"Be careful."

"You too, take care." I release my hand and turn my back

to him, climbing back onto the street. The man with the bike is waiting for me outside. He will escort me back to the city's east bank; from there, I will continue home by myself. Like always, at the end of the boulevard I will make a detour, avoiding the billboard with the huge poster.

For months now, "Come Work in Germany" has been glued to the giant billboard on the boulevard. The words are written in black square letters, and above them is a painting of a sturdy worker. In his hands, he holds a sledgehammer while his eyes look beyond the horizon. Maybe he knows something?

***

My footsteps in my simple shoes hit the avenue's pavement stones. It is too late, and I have to hurry home; it was a mistake to stop again in front of the billboard. My name is Monique Otin and not Monique who could not hug her parents goodbye. I have a new life, and I must not think about them, but maybe the painting on the billboard can give me some clue? The sledgehammer in his hand? The green fields behind him? The blue sky?

I raise my eyes as I approach the billboard and examine every detail closely. Who are the French men going to work in Germany? Why are they willing to work in factories and farms instead of all those recruited German soldiers? Could it be that the Germans took them too? Why haven't I heard from them for almost a year? Maybe the man painted in the poster knows? Perhaps he knows what happened to Mom and Dad and Jacob?

But the poster doesn't have a drawing of a barbed wire fence. Why did I let the train worker stop me a few months ago when I ran towards the fences? Why did I let him knock me down on the railway?

My hand wipes away the tears as I continue my way home. I shouldn't go near the billboard, and Lizette is probably waiting at home. At least I have someone taking care of me.

Lizette

My footsteps are barely heard on the marble stairs as I quickly ascend to the fifth floor, pull the key out of the brown leather bag Lizette bought me as a gift for my eighteenth birthday, and quietly open the white door.

"Shall I make us some coffee?" She always asks me that when I walk into her house and put the bag in the entrance hall, even though it's my job to serve her and not the other way around.

"I will make some, you can continue reading your book." But she is already getting up and walking to the kitchen with her high-stepping walk.

"You worked all day; it's good for me to do something."

As we wait for the water to boil, I look at her hair, which

has started to turn silver, and at her hands, gently holding the porcelain cups while placing them on the silver tray.

"You were late. I'd already started worrying about you."

"Simone delayed me at work, sometimes she asks me to stay, and I have to."

"Did you cry?"

"I have to learn not to take the things she says to heart."

"Shall we sit in the living room?" She holds the kettle in her manicured hands and pours the boiling water carefully. "I got some sugar, one teaspoon can make life much sweeter, and also improve the taste of this disgusting coffee." She smiles at me as she places the glasses on the tray while the silver bracelets on her wrists rattle, making me remember the first time we met, almost a year ago.

"Lizette, this is Monique Otin, she's going to help you with the apartment, just like you asked." The woman who'd brought me introduced me to the impressive woman standing at the door of the fancy apartment. She examined me, and I lowered my eyes and looked at my torn shoes. Lizette looked a little older than Mom, and her hair was starting to turn white at the edges, which added charm and splendor to her appearance. Her dress was a lovely mustard color, and she wore new leather shoes, not a cheap wartime imitation like I had. I was ashamed to stand in front of her like that, with my old grey dress, and all my belongings packed under my arm in a paper bag, one more used dress and a pair of underwear given to me by the woman who accompanied me, whose name I did not even know.

"Nice to meet you," Lizette shook my hand cordially, inviting me in. "I'll show you to your room."

With her hand on my waist, she soothed my fears, accompanying me up the stairs to the attic, my new home, not before saying goodbye to my companion who then disappeared into the darkness.

And just like that, my new life started. Every morning I assist this impressive lady with the management and cleaning of her apartment, and in return, she gives me a place to stay. Soon after finishing the housework, I will hurry to my second job in the boulangerie as a dishwasher, beneath Simone's comments. But Lizette always treats me right. "Your help is important to me," she tells me every time she buys me a new dress or jacket, and most of the time I think that it's not the need for help that caused her to let me into her house, but her loneliness.

She places the silver tray on the table in the living room as I sit down in front of her and wait patiently; her peaceful movements relax me.

"So what happened that you got back so late?"

"Simone is disappointed in me."

She must not know about my double life; I will never be able to tell her.

"Why do you think she is disappointed in you?"

"She expects me to be more efficient, and I am not."

"Maybe you misinterpret her behavior?"

"It does not seem so; she always asks me questions and hurries away from me at the end of the day."

"What we feel is not always what they think; it takes time to get to know people."

I lean back and look around the elegant room, staring at the picture in the silver frame, the one standing on the mantle in the living room, as I sip my bitter coffee.

"It also took a long time for you before you knew?"

"No, I knew from the first moment, but I'm just an old woman, you do not have to listen to me," she smiles at me.

"At my age, you don't want to change the world anymore, you just think about the small things in life, like adding a teaspoon of sugar to terrible coffee."

Lizette is right; I have a place to sleep, food in my stomach, and Claudine as a friend to walk with after work, that should be more than enough for my new life.

"Let's go to sleep; tomorrow is a new day." She smiles at me, and I head up the stairs to the attic. Tomorrow is a new day.

The Champs Elysees is quiet in the early morning hours as I walk down the boulevard on my way to work. The car traffic is sparse due to the lack of fuel, and the wide road seems too big for the few vehicles that pass through it from time to time. A military truck full of soldiers passes by, its tires making noise on the rough road, and it leaves behind a sharp smell of burnt fuel and a greyish cloud as it heads to the Concorde Square barricaded by barbed wire fences.

The gazes of the soldiers in the truck make me back away from the road to the safety of the cafés, walking between the empty chairs.

"Coffee, mademoiselle?" asks a bored waiter standing at the entrance, looking at me as if trying to remember whether we'd already met.

"No, thanks." I continue walking. I was delayed this morning in arranging the house, and I must hurry. At such hours they do not serve real coffee to the French people on their way to work. The espresso machines pour a leaky liquid made from ground beans, which were browned and called "coffee substitute" by the waiters even though it doesn't taste like coffee at all. The fragrant coffee bags that come by special delivery will only be opened in the afternoon, especially for the customers who wear grey-green uniforms and those willing to get acquainted with them.

"Mademoiselle, can you take a photo of us?" I am asked by two German soldiers standing on the boulevard and holding a camera. I pretend not to hear them and speed up my steps, Claudine would've known what to answer them.

"Did you see how he looked at you?" Claudine whispers to me, pointing towards a young man who passes us and smiles at her while we walk hand in hand, enjoying the afternoon sun.

"He looked at you, not me."

"Of course not, he wants to invite you for a walk with him."

We both walk up the Champs Elysees, looking at the cafés full of German soldiers and their French girls. Claudine critiques their dresses, and I examine the men's uniforms, memorizing their rank insignia.

"You need to smile more often; you're so serious."

"But it's embarrassing to smile."

"You are wrong, it's fun, and besides that, you have a nice smile. Do you see the guy standing by the café? Smile at him and lower your gaze, signal to him that you like him, but he has to make the first move."

"But he's looking at you."

"He is looking at us, and he is interested in you, in you and your beauty."

"How do you know?"

"I already told you, I have experience in men's gazes."

"How's your flirty pilot?"

"He came in today and invited me out. Even Simone smiled at him after she saw how many cookies he bought."

"And will you go out with him?"

"Look at her." Claudine stops, pointing with her head at one of the fancy cafés on the boulevard, my eyes following her.

"Who is she?"

"She's a famous movie star."

The famous movie star is wearing a fashionable long red dress, sitting in the café, laughing gracefully. She holds a white cigarette with a perfect hand covered in a black glove, surrounded by several high-ranking German officers, shining in their neat uniforms and medals.

"Who is she?"

"Her name is Arletty, but you don't go to the movies anyway, so you will not know her."

More passersby stop and look out the café windows, but some look away and spit on the pavement while walking on.

"Let's go on; it's unpleasant here."

"It seems to me that everyone is in love with her."

"How can that be?"

"Because she's so special."

"And how do you know you're in love?"

"You feel it, all over your body, you're hot, and you get

excited when you know you'll meet him soon."

"And it's nice?"

"It's a little stressful, but it's also pleasant, like when you walk together, and you let him hold your hand, feeling the warmth of his palm, or when he hugs you, and sometimes even more."

"And what's that 'even more'?"

"Monique, Monique Moreno?" I hear a call and turn my head.

"I'm Monique, but Monique Otin, not Moreno," I answer the young man who approaches us, feeling a cold wave pass through my whole body.

"Monique Moreno? Don't you remember me? Jean, Jean Bosse, I studied with you in school."

"Sorry, I do not remember you, we're in a hurry."

"Monique, how are you? How are you surviving the war with all the restrictions?"

"I'm sorry, we have to go." I grab Claudine's arm and pull her towards the road, wanting to cross the avenue to the other side.

"Who is he? What happened to you? You're hurting me."

"Sorry, I did not mean to."

"Who is he? Why did he call you Moreno?"

"He was confused by the name. I hated him at school. He used to hit me."

"Isn't Moreno a Jewish name?" Claudine lowers her voice, getting closer to my ear.

"I have no idea. I hated him. What about your pilot? You didn't tell me the end of the story."

"Are you Jewish?" She stops and looks at me, releasing our hands.

"No, I'm not Jewish, I hate Jews, I told you he had me confused for some other Monique."

Is he following us? I must not look; I must act as if nothing has happened. I am not a Jew; I have never been a Jew.

"Will you go out with your handsome pilot?"

"What about the woman you are living with? Does Lizette know?"

"I already told you, I'm not Jewish; he was confused." I must keep going as if nothing had happened.

"Monique, wait," Claudine catches up with me and grabs my arm again. "It's okay, I promise not to tell, it's a secret between us."

"There is no secret, I am not Jewish, and you should continue telling me about the pilot." I grab her arm and look at the German soldiers in the cafés; they look more threatening.

"Obviously you're not Jewish, just stay away from my wallet." She laughs and continues to hold my arm as we stroll down the avenue. I keep on smiling and behave as if nothing has happened, but my heart is racing now. Why is this happening to me? Why did he suddenly appear? Will she tell anyone else?

"You promised to tell me about the pilot."

"The pilot? The pilot wants to go out with me; most of all, I like that he has no big nose and that he is not stinky." She continues to walk with a cheerful look while holding my arm.

I must keep ignoring her, let her forget, it did not happen.

Philip is waiting for me at the bottom of the stairs, and I can already smell the damp basement; what shall I tell him about Claudine? For days I've been trying to decide what to say to him, especially since Simone started looking at me differently. But when I asked Claudine, she swore to me that she had told her nothing.

How will he react if I tell him? How angry will he be? I have to go down the stairs.

"How are you?"

"I'm fine." He smiles, keeps standing too close.

"Shall we sit down?" I offer, and he pulls away.

But even when he sits at the other side of the small table, his eyes make me nervous.

"What happened?"

"Everything is fine."

"Are you sure?"

"There are a lot more German soldiers in the boulangerie, and Claudine wants to go out with the pilot. She keeps talking about him."

"What is she saying?"

"That he is a fighter pilot in the Messerschmitt squadron, located at Le Bourget airfield. He was previously stationed in North Africa. A lot of new units are coming from North Africa these days, and she may suspect that I am Jewish."

"What does that mean?"

"His entire squadron was transferred to Le Bourget after the German withdrawal from North Africa."

"I did not mean that."

"So what did you mean?"

"What did you said about Claudine?"

"She may suspect me of being Jewish."

"How did that happen?" The creaking of the chair on the

basement's stone floor is jarring to my ears as Philip gets up from his chair and stands up, his hands leaning on the table.

"We walked down the boulevard, and she said something against the Jews, adding that I look like a Jew, and I didn't deny it fast enough."

"Is that all?"

"It seems to me she thinks I'm a Jew, even though I denied it."

"Was that all?" He walks away from the table and turns his back to me, but after a moment he returns and watches me, as if I'd disappointed him again.

"Yeah, that's all it was." I also stand up and put my hands on the table. "She probably realized I'm a Jew and she's gossipy, that's Claudine. She's also my friend."

"She's not your friend; she's Monique Otin's friend." He puts his hands on my palms and brings his face closer. "And she likes to talk." His scent is strong to me.

"I know she likes to talk. All the information you get from me comes from her mouth because she likes to talk." I release my hands and stand still, looking up at him. The main thing is not to look down, so he doesn't notice I am afraid of him.

"Okay," he calms down and sits, looking at me with a look of disappointment, "we'll see what to do with her."

"Okay." I also sit down and continue to report everything I know to him, lowering my eyes and concentrating on his fingers on the table, thinking how it felt to touch them the last time we'd met.

"Take care of yourself," he tells me as we say goodbye.

"Do not worry about Claudine," I say goodbye to him, and touch his palm for a moment. "She will not speak."

But in the days to come, she never stops laughing at my big nose, even though my nose is small.

Claudine 1922-1943

"Monique, I need you," Claudine calls out through the hustle and bustle of noon, and I leave the baking pan I'm cleaning in the back room, wiping my hands and walking over to her.

"Yes?"

"Please take care of these two gentlemen." And I freeze in my place.

The Boulangerie space is full as usual, with German soldiers filling up the room with German jokes mixed with cigarette smoke, but my attention is on the two men standing in front of me. They do not wear uniforms, but long leather coats as they stand by the counter, waiting just for me.

"Yes, please?"

"Are you Monique?" The shorter of the two asks me, in good French.

"Yes." For a moment, I get confused while the tall one looks at me.

"Can you help us?" My fingers start shaking.

"Yes, please?"

"May we have two butter croissants and two chocolate croissants, please?"

"How did you know my name?"

"From your friend, she called you and told us." The tall one smiles at me, causing me to shiver.

After they leave and the glass door slams behind them, I escape to the back room, unable to stop scrubbing the baking pans forcefully, even though the boulangerie is still full of soldiers and Simone asks me several times to go out and help. What will I tell Philip the next time we meet?

"What happened to your fingers?" A few days later, I sit down in front of him in the basement, placing my hands on the old wooden table.

His hand tries to grab my scratched fingers and examine them, but I hurry to remove my hands from the table, placing them in my lap.

"What happened to your hand?" I look at his hand on the table.

"It's nothing." His palm is wrapped with a dirty bandage, and I notice the bloodstain.

"How did it happen?"

"It's not serious, how are you? What happened to your fingers?"

"It's just scratches. Does your hand hurt?"

"It's a pain, but it looks a lot worse than it is. What information did you bring with you?"

"Not much."

On my way back to the east bank, I wonder if I did right by not telling him about the two strangers in the long leather coats, or that every night, when Claudine and I part, she calls me Monique Moreno with a smile. Should I have told him?

It's probably just my imagination which makes me so tense.

"Let's go to a different place, let's go to Husman Avenue." Claudine tries to persuade me to join her on an evening walk, while we both wait for Martin to lock the bakery's iron back door.

"I don't know." I'm afraid to deviate from our routine.

"Come on, let's do something different; the evenings are warmer, and maybe there are new clothes in the storefronts." She goes on, and I don't want to tell her that I have no clothing ration tickets, nor money to buy what the shops on the boulevard have to offer.

"I don't like the spring fashion; it's boring."

"This whole war is boring. I wish it were all over." But she gives up, and we are heading on our way down the avenue, walking side by side.

"Maybe you should think again about going with a German officer?" she asks me as several soldiers pass by and stare at us.

"I don't think I could do that."

"The pilot won't give up; he keeps inviting me, and not just him. They are so impressive in their medal-decorated uniforms."

But my attention is given to the newsstand and the boy leaning in the corner. He is hanging the newspapers in his usual way, even though only a few days have passed since my last meeting with Philip.

"What did you say?"

"That they are very polite when they invite me out, even when I refuse."

"But they are our occupiers; they can decide when to be polite and when to behave less politely."

"You don't have to be afraid of them; no one can guess about you, even though your nose might cause a big problem." She takes my hand and laughs.

I know she doesn't mean to hurt me, but I don't know how to make her stop; anyway, I have to go now, the kid at the newsstand is waiting for me.

"I'm sorry, I completely forgot, I promised Lizette that I would help her."

"Don't you get tired of her asking things from you? You should stand on your own," she complains when we kiss goodbye.

"I have no choice; I owe her." I kiss Claudine on both cheeks and turn around, heading to the newsstand.

My eyes search for the boy at the back of the newsstand, but he is not there. The newspapers hanging outside are lined up perfectly, the man inside the stand is sitting sleepily, and as much as I look around and down the street, I can't see him.

"Two newspapers, please." It's a sign of danger, my hands are shaking while I'm paying the man.

"Mademoiselle, you took one or two newspapers?"

"Two." Why is there a dark vehicle standing in the corner?

"You paid me only for one."

"Sorry, I apologize," I hand him more money. "Where is the boy?"

"Which boy?"

"The kid who's always in the back here, arranging the newspapers."

"Theirs is no kid here; I'm here alone."

"Never mind."

"Are you okay?"

Stay calm, stroll down the avenue. How come the vendor at the newsstand doesn't know the kid? Carefully examine all the passersby. Why are they looking in my direction? Do not stop walking, has there been something unusual lately?

Where's Claudine? I must find her; we'll keep on walking together as if nothing happened. I'll tell her I got confused and that we can continue strolling down the avenue.

The man with the long coat, have I seen him before? What does he have in the suitcase he is carrying in his left hand? And the young man in the corner standing next to his bike, why is he looking in my direction? Who are the two people running towards the crowd gathered at the end of the street? What is going on there?

I must keep walking as if nothing has happened, cross the street to the other side. All the people are crowded around something, a few of them are kneeling on the sidewalk. A woman is lying in the road, wearing low-heeled cream-colored shoes; Claudine has low-heeled cream-colored shoes.

"A vehicle passed at high speed and hit her," a woman in a greenish scarf speaks excitedly as she describes what happened to the policeman while he writes down her words in his notepad. "He did not stop at all, luckily I noticed he was approaching, he almost hit and killed me too."

As I get closer to her, I must use my hands to push myself through all the people surrounding her, moving them by force. Carefully I lean over the hard asphalt, ignoring the policeman's request not to gather and not listening to all the talking above my head.

Someone put a coat under her head, and someone tried to arrange her hand, which is lying at an unnatural angle, but it does not seem to bother her anymore. Her eyes remain open to the sky with a look of misunderstanding, and through my tears I see a man's hand reaching to her eyes, slowly lowering her eyelids.

The painted figures from the New Testament watch me from the church ceiling with an inquisitive gaze, as I raise my head and study them. While trying to identify their names, I wonder if they will start shouting that I do not belong here, nor does the simple coffin painted with dark varnish and placed in front of me.

I have no idea how I got home that day, whether on the metro or by foot, crying and stumbling on the pavements shaking under my feet. I do not even remember if it started to rain or if there was a chilly evening breeze. The only thing I couldn't forget were the sirens of the approaching ambulance, and the policeman cried out: "Do not gather, anyone who has seen how this happened will approach me, all the rest, please leave."

Churches scares me; at least this one doesn't have threatening demons like in the Notre Dame Cathedral. Demons screaming at me from above that it's my fault she's dead.

Because of me, we did not go around the shops as she wanted, because of me we delayed those few seconds when we parted on the sidewalk, and I went to look for the child near the newsstand. If I had only accepted her offer, none of this would have happened. We would have left the boulangerie by now, waiting for Martin to lock the back door and strolling hand in hand, like every day.

"You are to blame," the nightmares had shouted at me last night, waking me up with screams of black bats biting me and hurting my body.

Few people came to the ceremony, and the church is almost empty, befitting days of war and scarcity. Some women in black, some hunchbacked old men holding walking sticks made of decorated wood, Simone who smiles at me even though everything happened because of me, Martin the chef, dignified without his white apron, and that's it. Not a single man that loved her, not a single man she loved. Not even the pilot arrived, nor any of those soldiers in grey-green uniforms, the ones who would chat with her in a very polite way. They must be wondering why the glass door is locked today, and they cannot enjoy the pleasures of the French capital, crispy croissants, and a woman behind the counter to flirt with.

"They don't know who the driver was," Simone is whispering to me. "A policeman came this morning and informed me that they don't have the car number." She is trying to hug me. "It's such a pity; she was a lovely girl."

"I am so sorry," I say voicelessly to the simple coffin in front of me, looking up at the ceiling paintings of Jesus and the Virgin. Maybe they will forgive me for not walking with her down the avenue, as she'd asked.

"Monique, come and help me for a moment." I hear Simone's call in the back room.

"I'll be right there." My fingers place the baking pan in the sink, and I'm wiping my hands, hurrying to help her serve the German soldiers.

"Go, I'll wash it," Martin offers to help. Since Claudine died, everyone has tried to treat me more nicely, even Simone. But her expressions of affection seem to me like a wolf dog's attempts to restrain herself from a passing rabbit, making me wonder when she will not be able to hold back and return to scolding me.

Where is the boy? Why did he disappear that day?

Although I'm not supposed to stop at the newsstand, I can't resist myself. My fingers run across the line of German army magazines, showing a picture of a new airplane on the cover, while I'm pretending to concentrate on the photography and looking around for the boy. Why has he not been there since? I can't ask the seller.

"May I help you?" he asks, waking up from his sleepy gaze.

"Do you have cigarettes?"

"Do you know that according to government regulations, women are not allowed to smoke?"

"Yes, it's not for me."

"Counterfeit?" He lowers his voice.

"No."

"The real ones are very expensive."

"How much?"

"25 francs."

I take the imaginary sum out of my wallet and put it in his palm. With a swift motion, he puts a blue pack in my hand, taken out of some hiding place, returning to his indifferent stance at the stand.

I have nothing to do with those cigarettes, and I hold the box in my hand, intending to throw it into the nearest bin. But I change my mind at the last second and push it deep into my bag, maybe one day I will use them. The people who pass me look curiously at the young woman standing in the street, wiping her face with her hand.

"Can I offer you a handkerchief?" I hear a man's voice and look up.

"No thanks." I continue on my way, walking around the street corner where I last saw her, I can't return to that place.

The cafés on the Champs Elysees are still full of soldiers and their girlfriends, and I stand as far away as I can, trying not to hear the talking and the laughing around the tables. If some stranger calls my name, I will ignore him this time. Those two women walking ahead laughing remind me of the both of us. I cannot stand the avenue anymore; I have to get out of here.

Finally, I find the entrance to the metro, stepping down into the tunnel. The metro's darkness will embrace me, an escape from the cafés and the street.

Standing in the corner of the dim platform, I can examine the coming train, searching for the right car to get into, but a gang of running German soldiers arrives and push their way in just before the doors close.

"Mademoiselle, will you show me the city?"

"Mademoiselle, choose me. I am much more handsome. Nice to meet you, Max." He reaches out a hand.

"Don't choose him; Max replaces his girls all the time. You should choose me." Another soldier is reaching out.

But I lower my eyes, staring at my leather shoes, the ones that Lizette bought me, trying to avoid looking at their leather hobnail boots.

"She's a spoiled impolite Frenchwoman who doesn't like talking to handsome German soldiers," I hear one of them say to his friends in German. "She should thank us for saving her from Stalin's clutches. If we weren't here, she'd be speaking Russian by now." He keeps on talking, while my head is down and I say nothing, watching their hobnail boots getting closer. But finally they get away from the spoiled impolite French girl, walking to the other side of the metro car.

The creaking sound of the metro on the railway breaks the silence, while the rest of the people in the carriage watch me and say nothing, a dark grey mass of people who stood back and watched the German soldiers harass me and did nothing. My hand holds the metal rod tightly for support, and my fingers are becoming white from the effort. "Trocadéro," the white sign at the station appears, I have to get off.

At the platform, I stop for a moment, letting all the German soldiers get out of the metro car and go on their way outside, trying to avoid being crowded among them. I can still smell their tobacco on my way out, and hear them in the distance. The breeze in the corridor allows me to breathe, but when I go up the stairs into the square, they are all over me again.

The surface is crowded with soldiers, walking as tourists of victory, talking loudly and waving. Some of them are holding a camera or a Parisian girl, taking pride in their new purchase during a short stay in the city of pleasure.

I turn my gaze away from them, unable to watch their uniforms and the swastika flag stuck at the top of the Eiffel Tower, and I approach the older woman standing at the corner of the square. She is wearing a dirty coat and stands hunched, selling flowers to the soldiers and their girlfriends.

"How much will a flower cost me?"

"For you, it's free, my girl." But I insist on paying her.

"May a loving man give you a flower," the older woman whispers to me as she hands me the flower and receives the coin, holding it carefully in her wrinkled fingers.

"Don't cry, my girl, he will arrive one day." And I'm fighting the urge to hug her, turning my back and walking away.

The small cemetery is hidden behind the high wall overlooking the square, and it takes time for me to find the narrow entrance gate. I walk along the break in the wall until my eyes notice the small metal gate that creaks open under my hand. But I remember how to find the fresh grave. My steps slow down as I approach, placing the flower on the marble headstone.

"This is for you, my girl, may a loving man give a flower to you," my lips whisper to her when I sit down next to her.

"You know, Simone treats me much nicer, even though it's clear she prefers you to me." I smile at the letters engraved in the stone.

"And your pilot doesn't come anymore, at least I haven't seen him, but the boulangerie is always full of new soldiers, surely you could find someone else to invite you for a walk on the boulevard, buying you mint ice cream." I dry my tears slowly.

"There are many new armored and engineering soldiers in town. I have to memorize their unit numbers; it's for Philip. You do not know him yet; I promise to tell you about him the next time we meet." But the boy from the newsstand, I don't have the courage to tell her about him.

Before I say goodbye, I promise to visit again as soon as I can, heading to the small cemetery gate and on my way home, to Lizette.

But even the night talks with Lizette don't help. Time

after time, I almost slip when I try to explain to her why I left Claudine in the street, looking for reasons and finally going silent. She must never know what happened that day, but the thoughts do not stop, making me feel so guilty. It did not happen because of me. It happened because of the boy who'd disappeared. It happened because the driver ran her over; it happened because Simone delayed us for a few minutes in the boulangerie before we left.

"Good morning."

"Good morning, Monique, this is Marie; she's going to replace you at the dishes. From now on, you'll work with me behind the counter." And I stop for a moment at the entrance, leaning on the glass door and watching the very excited new girl who is standing still.

"Nice to meet you." I shake her hand and take her to the back room, guiding her through the list of chores that have been my responsibility until now, and finally handing her the old apron used for washing the baking pans, taking the clean white one from the hanger. The one that has been hanging around for days, waiting for Claudine.

"Do you need help?" Marie asks.

"No thanks, I'm fine." My fingers get mixed up tying the apron as I turn my back to her, I don't want her to ask about my eyes.

The soldiers keep coming, running from the rainy street

into the warm space, filling it with German language and the strong cigarette smoke of poor-quality tobacco. They laugh at each other while the doorbell rings again and again as it opens and closes, making me tense. Many of them pay in silence and walk away, just glancing at me, but there are the more daring ones who try to start a conversation, practicing their poor French while I keep quiet and lower my head, not answering them.

Ranks, I need to look at their ranks, memorize them. Also unit tags, I should learn to recognize their tags. What about the red stripes sewn on some of the soldiers' pants? What does it mean? Should I start up a conversation with them? That's what Phillip expects me to do.

Occasionally, when there are fewer soldiers in the boulangerie, I go to the back room, looking for excuses to watch Marie, but mostly looking for a quiet moment to myself away from the doorbell noises and the German words in my ears.

Soon the end of the day will come, and I'll visit her and buy her a flower instead of a loving man. But on my way to the metro, when I pass the newsstand, I see the boy standing with his back to me.

"Metro Palais Royal." I hear his whisper before he disappears, not stopping to provide me some explanation about what happened last time, and I'm standing and watching him walk away. I must hurry, Philip will tell me what happened, he will calm me down.

Philip's silhouette looks to me like a dark shadow waiting for me in the dim light of the basement lamp, but I know he is just protecting the entrance, making it safe for me.

"How are you?" He is still leaning against the damp wall,

and I go down one more step, getting closer.

"I'm good. How are you? How is your hand?" My fingers caress his hand, examining the wound in his palm, refusing to let go.

"I'll be fine, shall we sit down?" He gets away from me.

"Let's sit down."

"Everything is okay?"

My hands grip his body as my head searches for a place to rest for a moment under his enfolding arms, and tears begin to flow from my eyes. I know he is disappointed with me, but I can't hold back anymore; I need to tell him all about her.

"What happened?" I feel the warmth of his arms around me.

"It's Claudine." I start sobbing and hug his body more tightly. His fingers gently caress my hair, smelling of gun oil mixed with printing colors and his pleasant scent.

"She is dead." The tears flow with all the words that have been waiting for so long. Without stopping I tell him about the accident and all the people gathering around; I even tell him about the coat under her head and her shoe, which remained on the street after the ambulance left.

"I wanted to pick up the shoe, out of some illogical thought that she might need it, but I just couldn't and kept going. And the next morning, as I passed and looked from a distance at the street corner, the shoe was gone." I can't stop crying under his caressing fingers.

"The rain washed the blood off the street, and passersby kept walking down the street, not stopping and thinking about the woman who lay there yesterday." I'm sobbing.

"Shhh…" He gently strokes my hair.

"And I was in church, and I apologized to all the angels

who are guarding her from now on, and they forgave me, and Simone brought Marie to replace me with the dishwashing, and now I'm behind the counter instead of Claudine, having a hard time with all the German soldiers."

"Shhh... everything's fine." He continues to caress my hair while I hug him, trying to relax in the warmth of his pleasant body and hands that encircle me.

"And now you'll be happier with me." The tears do not stop.

"Shhh... it doesn't matter... what about the driver, did they catch him?"

"No, a policeman came to the boulangerie, saying they don't know who it was. What happened to the boy? Why did he disappear that day?"

"He had to get away, so he disappeared."

And I keep telling him about the soldiers coming in, entering the boulangerie and ordering their pastries, asking for his guidance on ranks and tags, because now I'm exposed to a lot more.

But suddenly, while I'm talking about my new place behind the counter, I have a terrible thought about that day, and even though I keep reporting everything I heard to him, that thought doesn't leave me. Like an ambulance siren, it rings in my mind, and slowly my speech slows until I fall silent.

"Shhhh... everything's fine." He continues stroking me, but I push his body away and look into his eyes, examining him through my tears.

"Why wasn't the boy there?"

"Because he had to go."

"The boy's disappearance is related to Claudine?"

"The boy's appearance is related to you; the boy is not

related to Claudine."

"But I left her, and someone ran her over."

"It has nothing to do with you."

"How did you know the police haven't found the driver? I did not tell you about that." I try to get up off the floor and stand.

"It's not your business how I knew." He also gets up and walks away from me, watching me with his brown eyes.

"Did you run Claudine over?" I raise my voice.

"No, we did not run Claudine over."

"Did you kill Claudine because she exposed me? Please tell me you didn't kill her." I shout as I grab the wooden chair, supporting myself.

"No, we didn't." It takes him a while to answer me.

"What do you mean, you didn't? Who killed her?" The noise of the chair falling to the floor sounded like it was shattering on the concrete.

"Answer me, please, who ran her over?"

"It's not us."

"Please tell me, who did this to her?" My hands are holding the table, keeping me from falling on the floor again.

"Someone else did it."

"Who is the someone else? Please, you must tell me."

"The Communist underground did it."

"But why? Why did they do that to her?" My tears flow down my cheeks as I look at the wall, examining the dark moss stains. I cannot look at him.

"Because we asked them for help." I hear his tired voice, as though coming from a distant place.

"But why?" I ask, again and again, knowing the answer in my heart but unable to stop, wanting to hear it in his own words.

"Because that's how it works, they are fighting the Germans, and we are fighting the Germans, and because we have a common enemy, we have common goals."

"But why kill her?"

"Because she endangered you and us with her big mouth." He tries to stay calm and get closer to me again, but I walk away, looking at the dirty wall.

"She wouldn't have spoken." My fingers scratch the wall, peeling off the plaster.

"If she hadn't said something yet, it was only a matter of time before she started to talk, and the Germans would find out all about you. Do you want to find yourself in the basement of the house on 84 Avenue Foch?" He tries to control his voice, but he sounds so distant to me.

"And what about me? Will you kill me too? If I'm not good enough?" I'm having a hard time breathing.

"You are one of us, and there is a reason why we accepted you." He tries to lower his voice and bring his hands close to me again for a hug, but I stop him with my hands, feeling the rough wall at my back.

"Just as long as I bring you what you want?"

"You are one of us; she wasn't. She was the one who wanted to go out with German soldiers, to lick their boots, do you remember that?" He talks about her with such disdain.

"She was my friend, my only friend." I must get out of this suffocating place, but Philip holds my arm, puts his hands around me, not letting me leave. His lips whisper soothing words to me, but all I want is to curl up in a teeny-tiny ball and hide at the same time.

"I'm so sorry, but we are at war; the Germans want to kill us all."

"She died because of me, if not for me she wouldn't be

dead now, how will I go on?" My hands try to push him away, but he holds me firmly against his body.

"She did not die because of you; she died because of the Germans. You must listen to me; she did not die because of you." He whispers to me again and again, his lips close to mine.

But I know he's lying. He's lying to me that she didn't die because of me, and he's lying to me that they wouldn't throw me to the German dogs if I'm not efficient enough. Or maybe they will ask their Communist friends to do the dirty work for them, when it's time to kill me, and he's lying to me with his hands hugging my body.

"I'm not angry at you. I'll be the best soldier you've got, I promise."

"I'm so sorry, but you must never forget who you are."

"I'm a French warrior." And my hands push his hug away as I turn from the wall and run up the stairs. I must get out of this dim basement. For a moment, I stop in the alley and wipe away my tears, noticing that I haven't said goodbye to him, but I can't go back into that dark place. Anyway, it doesn't matter at all; he doesn't care about me. To them, I'm just a replaceable girl in an occupied city.

I head to Lizette's house as fast as I can, quietly climbing the stairs into the attic where I live, closing the door behind me without turning on the light. Let the black night surround me.

I wonder what it's like to fly and hit the sidewalk. The first rays of the sun paint the grey roof panels in yellow, while my feet slowly approach the edge of the building, and I'm carefully looking down at the street, examining the hard-paved stones.

For almost a year, I have been living here on the sixth floor, and in all that time, my attic window stayed closed. Even the spectacular view of the city rooftops, and the Eiffel Tower in the distance, did not convince me to open the window and step carefully onto the grey zinc boards.

It's too frightening for me, sitting on the edge and looking at the city, in what could be considered a nest of privacy for a reclusive girl or an escape route when needed. But not for me, I'm too scared of the height and the street below.

What is it like to fly in the air? How did she feel? Did she know it was the end? Was landing on the pavement painful to her? I straighten up to stand on the grey roof panel, feeling it shake under my body weight, while I spread my arms to the sides and lift my chin, breathing the cool morning breeze and closing my eyes. Just one more small step.

I can't feel so guilty anymore, I'm just one girl who wanted to live, and I can't turn the clock back.

Why did I manage to escape from the police a year ago? Where are Dad and Mom and Jacob? Why did the railway worker knock me down that day, stopping me from running to the barbed wire fences?

"There's no one there anymore. They took everyone," he'd shouted at me and pushed me onto the railway, making me scream in pain. Why didn't I return to that place and try again?

My eyes look at the street below, the man walking on his way to work, looking like a small drop of paint on the grey street, the Eiffel Tower in the distance painted a reddish hue in the first rays of the sun. I can even see the Nazi flag shining in the morning rays.

"I must live." My legs bend as if on their own, and I sit on the edge, holding the metal plates tightly, and writing Mathilde's words with my fingers on the morning dew which covers the grey roof panel.

The morning rays will soon erase the words, and the street downstairs is waiting for me; it's time to decide. What should I do?

What would Mom do?

Carefully I close the small window to the roof, making sure to lock the latch as hard as I can. Claudine did not die because of me; she died because of the Germans.

"You're late," Simone tells me as I close the glass door behind me, gasping from the fast walk, but she hands me the clean apron from the hanger and even smiles at me as I wear it, taking my position behind the counter. Soon the first customer will walk through the door. I am a French warrior, and I am willing to do whatever it takes to live.

The Daughter of Kronos

June 1943

Secret

6/18/1943

From: Western Front Wehrmacht Command

To: Army Group France

Subject: Preparations for opening a new western front

Background: Due to the Allied invasion of Sicily, we estimate that the Italian army will surrender to the enemy.

General: By the orders of the Führer Hitler, offensive operations on the eastern front in Russia will cease immediately. We estimate that in the coming year, a naval landing will be executed from the direction of England through the La Manche canal.

Tasks:

Construction of a protective barrier along the western beaches.

Construction of protective bunkers to protect the Führer s secret weapon of revenge against London.

Method: Army Group France will be reinforced with engineering divisions that will be mobilized from the Eastern Front and the South Italy Front.

The headquarters of the engineering division for the canal section will be located in Paris.

Finding houses for the division's headquarters officers will be the responsibility of maintenance battalion 4II.

SS. Telegram 445

Violette and Anaïs

'Arletty & Arletty', I usually call them in my mind when I see them every few days. Usually, I notice them through the boulangerie window. They tend to stand patiently outside the shop, waiting for their spouses to finish buying the morning patisseries for them. Their dresses are glamorous, in the best fashion the summer of 1943 allows women, especially those who tend to enjoy German money. I watch their wavy hairstyles with envy, and they remind me of the famous movie star known for her warm attitude towards high-ranking German officers. With a hug, they greet their spouses as they walk out of the store, biting off the crispy croissants that were baked in robbed French butter.

"Monique, stop staring at the street outside, have you served the gentleman in the black uniform?"

"Yeah, he's waiting for the fresh pastry tray that will be out in a minute."

Their spouses are wearing neatly-ironed grey-green officers' uniforms, and with their cropped blonde hair and perfect smile, they could appear on any German Army recruitment poster.

"Danke." They thank me as I put the fresh pastries in the paper bag, and my eyes follow them as they rush to serve the fine butter to the girls my age who are waiting for them outside the boulangerie.

"They have money," says Simone after they disappear down the street.

"They have German army officers," I answer, and Simone smiles a bit.

'Arletty & Arletty' always wait outside for their gentlemen

to arrive, but today the pouring rain has driven them in, and they gently close the door behind them. As I examine them, they shake their wavy hair from the raindrops and approach me, the short one with a shy smile and the tall one with a defiant look.

"Good morning, we did not want to wait for them in the rain," the tall one with the lush brown hair tells me, and I notice that she has a small gap between her front teeth.

"Good morning, is it okay if we order? Can we?" the short one joins in; she's my height and has a delicate face and big eyes, the kind I always dreamed I would have when I still dared to dream of being a movie star.

"Good morning, what would you like?"

"Can I have a baguette?" the tall one asks; she has thick, beautiful lips.

"Can I have a baguette too?" the little one asks with an embarrassed smile, and I watch her delicate lips.

"Anaïs." The brown-haired woman reaches her hand beyond the counter.

"Violette." The other joins and reaches her hand too.

"Nice to meet you, Monique." I give them my hand, and for the first time I touch hands that have caressed a German soldier.

What would Mom think of me if she knew? Why couldn't I have found them a year ago, even though I tried?

"Luckily, the Germans are cleaning the streets of them; there is no food left in France, because of their greediness." I heard those two women in a grocery store, about a year ago. They were complaining about the butter ration, and my eyes remained lowered to the floor, carefully examining my old shoes.

"It's time for the Germans to put things in order on this issue," the other one agreed with her. "My sister told me there were even policemen who warned them to run and hide before the raid." Why did no policeman come to warn Dad?

For a moment, I looked at them, but I lowered my eyes again; no one else intervened in their conversation, and a few other women standing in line nodded their approval.

"At least they crammed all of them in camp Drancy; from there, they will no longer be able to rule the world." Another woman joined the conversation.

"Are you giving up your turn?" The older one between them asked me.

"Yes, I forgot my ration stamps at home." I answered her, and ran out of the grocery store.

My feet carried me towards the massive building and the barbed wire fences surrounding it. As I kept getting closer, passing the metal sign 'Drancy', I started to get scared. "They are waiting for me," I tried to encourage myself, to keep walking on the rails leading to the camp, but a railway worker wearing dirty clothes stood in my way.

"Hey, you, where are you going?"

"I have to find something."

"This is not a place for a girl like you, get out of here."

"I need to know something."

"It will cost you." He looked at me lustfully.

"I can give you that," I handed him my monthly butter ration stamps, my hand shaking, not knowing how I would explain the loss of our butter ration to Lizette.

"What do you want to know?" His black fingers collected the stamps, quickly shoving them into his pocket.

"My family, I need to meet them. I have to; please help me." My gaze focused on the grey building and the little figures walking between the barbed wire fences. I had to meet them.

"Are you Jewish?"

"No."

"They were taken east by train, to Auschwitz camp."

"Please, I must find them." My fingers quickly dug into the bag, handing him our meat ration stamps. "That's all I have."

"You cannot find them; they are in Poland now, go away from here, it is dangerous for you, they will take you too." He turned and walked away from me, refusing to take the meat stamps from my hand.

"What are you doing?" the train worker shouted at me as I started running towards the fences.

"I have to say goodbye to them," I shouted as I gasped and stepped up, not thinking whether he heard or understood my words.

"They will catch you and send you there too." He dropped me on the rails, made me scream from the pain of the fall.

"I did not have time to say goodbye to them," I whimpered into his shoulder as it pressed me to the ground, feeling the rails hurt my body and smelling the diesel and grease from his dirty clothes. "I have to, I have to say goodbye to them." I cried and tried to fight him off, wanting to keep running toward the fences and the people behind them.

"You must not; there is no point, they are no longer there, it is not them, they have been taken, now they hold POWs and American pilots whose planes have been shot down." He kept pinning me to the ground, not releasing me until he was sure I'd calmed down and stopped crying, and would not keep running.

"I'm sorry, they're not there anymore." I felt his grip loosen as he stood up, stabilizing himself and looking at me for a moment, moving away from me but staying close in case I got up and started running towards the fences again. When I finally got up off the rails and looked at him walking away, I noticed my butter ration stamps thrown on the rails beside my old shoes.

"What do you think of my new shoes?" Violette asks me a few days after we first met, as she blushes and raises her leg so I can see them.

"They are very beautiful." I bend over the counter; they are gorgeous.

"I told you she's nice." Violette laughs at Anaïs.

"She received them as a special gift," Anaïs adds a piece of information as she leans back against the wall, and Violette blushes even more, smiling awkwardly.

"Come walk with us down the avenue after work, please, the weather is nice," she asks.

"I do not know; I need to get home."

"The days are much warmer now; please join us." She looks at me with her big, round, dark eyes, as if begging for my company.

"Yes, that would be nice," Anaïs adds from the side as she sizes me up, and the apron I am wearing.

And I let them convince me, promising myself I'll be distant when we walk together, but meanwhile I say goodbye to them until the end of the day. I have no choice but to meet them; Philip expects me to bring him more information.

I arrange the croissants left on the trays in straight lines, placing the baguettes in the basket in order; what kind of smiles shall I show them? Cleaning the tables until they are shiny, checking and making sure there is no dirt on my dress, and washing the shop window facing the street, thinking what I will say. Slowly I return the change to the customer in the grey-green uniform, trying to avoid looking at the clock hanging above the door. Too soon, the end of the day arrives. They are not my friends; they'll never be, my stomach hurts.

"We need to hurry. They are already waiting for us." Violette rushes me as we walk to the metro, and I think I have not walked the boulevard since what happened to Claudine.

"Who is waiting for us?" I stop walking, surprised.

"Our guys." Anaïs smiles at me as if to confess a secret. "They've wanted to meet you for a long time."

"You did not tell me they were coming too."

"We told you, but you were too busy arranging all your baguettes and didn't listen to us." Violette laughs at me. "Don't be afraid; they don't bite, after you know them, you'll change your mind about German soldiers."

"They can teach you a lot of new things, ask Violette," Anaïs adds while Violette looks down, blushing.

"We must hurry, you can't change your mind now, I promised them you were coming." Violette takes my hand, and I walk with them, knowing they had not told me before. They must have been afraid I would refuse to join them, but now it's too late.

"I can stand it," I whisper to myself as we reach the stairs leading down to the Metro Opera station, passing a man in a long coat, his eyes staring at me.

"She's with us." Anaïs glares at him indifferently as she grabs my hand and pulls me after her down the stairs.

I'll never be one of them; I think to myself as we ride in the cramped metro car, I'll never go out with a German soldier.

"Monique, meet Fritz and Fritz." And for the first time in my life, I'm shaking hands with a German soldier, and I want to scream.

They smile at me very politely when I lower my eyes from their blue ones, introducing themselves formally. Their names are not Fritz and Fritz, but in all the storm blowing through my head, I cannot hear anything else as I try to smile back and raise my head. They reach their hands out to me, and I touch them for a split-second and pull my hand back quickly, feeling my palm burning. If only I had thought to bring gloves with me.

"We already know you," they say together. "From the boulangerie. You're the nice saleswoman."

"There was another girl, but we don't see her anymore, she was nice too, what happened to her?"

"She doesn't work there anymore." I rub my palm, pressing it firmly with my fingers.

"What about us?" Violette asks, and gets a warm hug from her fair-haired Fritz.

"We are here just for decoration," says Anaïs while she places her arm on the back of her private Fritz, bringing him closer to a long kiss while turning her back to me. "Shall we go?"

Had they notice that I held back when they touched my hand? I must learn to control myself, to make Philip proud of me. Their attention is on their girls as we walk down the avenue. They are watching all the people enjoying the summer afternoon, and my eyes are focused on Violette's fingers playing with Fritz's grey-green jacket.

The cafés are full of German soldiers and their accompanying young girls; the group is trying to locate a place to sit while I walk a little behind them; maybe the passersby will think I'm just looking in the shop windows and I'm not one of them.

"What do you think?" Everyone stops and looks at me.

"Sorry, I didn't hear you."

"What do you think of the new movie that came out?"

"What movie?"

"The movie we were talking about, with the French actress Arletty."

"I haven't seen it yet."

"Will you join us to see it? They say she plays wonderfully." Violette looks at me questioningly.

"I don't know; my evenings are usually busy."

What do the people on the street think of me? Do they spit or curse at us when they pass on the sidewalk? I feel as if strangers' eyes are staring at my back, penetrating me with hateful looks. I must learn to fit in with them.

"I would be happy to go if I had a day off."

"Great, you'll enjoy spending time with us." Anaïs looks at me and smiles. What does she think of me?

"Maybe next time we'll take care of Monique? So you won't have to hang out with us so lonely?" she adds as she turns to her Fritz and hugs him, making me look down.

"It's okay; I'm having a good time on my own."

"It's a great idea." Violette holds my arm with enthusiasm. "It's a lot more fun to walk down the avenue together."

After I say goodbye to them and start walking home, I hurry away from the Champs Élysées and the noisy cafés. But even on the quiet street, I can imagine the stares at my back, as if they remained and hurt my skin. Even my palm is still hot, burning from the touch of their hands.

"Are you okay, my dear? How was your day?" Lizette asks me when I enter her warm living room, and I shake my head and say nothing. I cannot tell her who I hang out with and why. What would Lizette think of me if she knew? Would she stab my back with her glare too? Or throw me out of the attic she'd given me as a place to sleep?

At night, before bed, I try to comfort myself; the first time is always the hardest, like when I was a girl and Dad took me to the Tuileries Gardens playground.

"Roll over, it's okay, the first time is always the scariest," he assured me in his calm voice, as I sat crying at the end of the ladder, afraid to go down. "After the first time, you will get used to and enjoy the feeling."

'Are you also getting used to Auschwitz camp?' I ask him in my imagination, but he does not answer me.

I haven't met him since that time he hurt me so much, after Claudine was killed, and I go downstairs in fear. How should I behave in front of him? How will he react?

He is waiting for me as always, at the bottom of the stairs, and we approach each other slowly, step by step.

"You are quiet." He is standing close to me.

"I have nothing to say."

"Say something,"

"I'm trying to learn and get better." Even though I haven't forgiven him, I stay close to him.

"How are you?" Philip doesn't walk away either.

"Working at the boulangerie as usual."

"And how is your new place? Is it comfortable?" He does not mention the name of the one I killed.

"I feel great." Nor do I.

"Does Simone treat you nicely?"

"Yes, she treats me well, and I've already met two new girlfriends."

"That's good." Philip leans back, that's probably what he thinks of me, that I hurried to replace dead Claudine with the living Anaïs and Violette.

"And how are they, those two new girlfriends of yours?"

"They are very nice, they usually hang out with German soldiers, so I am joining them." I also lean back, thinking of Claudine and her Messerschmitt pilot, the one who courted her for days, but disappeared when she lay in a simple wooden coffin.

"And is it good for you? To go out with them?"

"What's good for France is good for me."

"I'm happy." He walks away from me, and I can no longer smell his body odor.

"They want to bring someone else with them, their officer. They suggested I go out with him."

"And will you do it?" He turns his back to me; doesn't want to look at me at all.

"Yes, I'm willing to do it." After I killed Claudine, it's my turn to take her place. At least, that's what he expects me to do; the only reason he's kept me alive.

"Thanks." I hear his voice, though he is standing with his back to me. He will not stop me from hanging out with a German officer; he will keep his distance from me, waiting for my reports, sending me back to him, without asking me how scared I am. He won't hug me like last time; I do not want him to hug me anymore.

"I have a lot of new information to report."

"So sit down and report." Philip slowly turns to me and leads me to the small wooden table, touching my arm for a moment.

"What new information do you have?"

Now that Claudine is dead, I have a lot to tell him. All day I listen and remember, concentrating on all those soldiers who think I'm a stupid Frenchwoman who does not understand the German language, opening their big mouths and gossiping to their friends while waiting to see my smile.

"The Germans are starting to fortify the beaches against possible invasion. They have moved new engineering divisions from the East, and I will be much more efficient after I go out with my new friends and their acquaintances." But Philip does not place his fingers on mine, even though they are waiting on the table. I don't want him to touch me.

"Do not forget that they are not your friends."

"No one is my friend." I pull my hands away from the simple wooden board and say goodbye to him. He could have been nicer to me after he made sure I would be left without a friend.

"He's really nice," Violette whispers to me excitedly a few days later, when they enter the boulangerie.

"And he's high-ranking, they call his rank 'Oberst' in German, he has a lot of privileges as an officer. A lot of privileges are good for Monique," adds Anaïs with a secret smile, while taking a bite from the croissant I gave her.

"And he's lonely here in Paris." Violette continues, not understanding I have been waiting for their trap, knowing I would have to step inside and fall.

For days I've been hoping that maybe their German officer would change his mind, or be moved with his unit from Paris. Whenever the glass door opened and the bell rung, I looked up apprehensively and let out a sigh of relief when the entrants were German soldiers, not Violette and Anaïs. But now both of them stand in front of me, waiting for my acceptance.

"I'm not sure I'll be an interesting companion to him."

"You are beautiful, believe me, he will be interested in you," Anaïs looks at me and takes a box of cigarettes out of the fashionable handbag, but after she notices Simone's look, she chooses to return the package inside her bag.

"Will you come with us on Saturday?" Violette smiles at me.

"Monique, there are customers."

I want to ask Anaïs what she means, that he will be interested in me, but Simone calls me again.

"What's his name?" I have to go back to work.

"His name is Ernest, Oberst Ernest."

Oberst Ernest

"You should put lipstick on." Lizette hands me the red tube as I stand in front of the mirror, getting ready for the meeting.

My fingers tremble as I slide the soft burgundy tip over my lips, feeling its softness and weird taste for the first time.

"Let me help you." Lizette takes the lipstick from my hand and gently holds my chin while I concentrate on her brown eyes.

"There you go, look in the mirror." She smiles at me with

satisfaction, and I stare at the woman I become, trying to get used to my new me.

"Where are you going?" she'd asked me earlier when I was on my way to the door, hurrying to get outside and trying to avoid her.

"I've met someone." I immediately regretted telling her, afraid she would ask more.

"You can't go out like that."

"This is my nicest dress." I looked embarrassed in my simple beige dress, not knowing what to answer her, but she took me by my hand to her bedroom, ignoring me telling her that I was already late.

I was detained all morning, opening and closing the attic window, looking at the grey zinc tiles and the street below.

"You're a woman; you need to be at your best." She sits me in the chair in front of the dresser and starts combing my hair, turning it into the smooth waves of a movie star.

"What do you think?" she asks after helping with the lipstick.

"It's lovely; thank you."

I'd always dreamed of looking like that, but Mom never agreed to it. The only time she ever slapped me was when she caught me putting on pink lipstick I'd bought with a shaking hand, in those days before the warrants. We were still allowed to go into cosmetics stores, at least the ones far from the German headquarters. "Only prostitutes wear makeup like that!" she shouted, and tossed the lipstick in the trash as I ran from her, locking myself in my room and stroking my aching cheeks, hating her, and wishing she would be gone.

"Are you excited about the date?"

"A little bit, but I'm okay." I dab the tip of my eye. Where is she now?

"Something's missing," Lizette pulls a light pink scarf from the brown closet in her bedroom and ties it around my neck, looking at me with a satisfied look and hugging me warmly. "Take care of yourself."

"Thank you; I won't be late." My legs carry me down the stairs, wanting to get away from Lizette's warm hugs and all the lies I'm telling her. Maybe it's better Mom can't see me like this, not knowing who I'm going to meet.

I have to hurry; they are probably waiting for me.

Even though I've never met him before, I can recognize him from a distance and slow down, stopping and breathing deeply. They are all standing and chatting near the café where we'd arranged to meet. Fritz and Fritz stand tall, not moving, next to them are Violette and Anaïs dressed in cheerful cream-colored dresses, and they all give him respect.

He stands alone in a relaxed position and is a little taller than Phillip; he has short light hair rather than a dark quiff, and his uniforms are clean grey-green, decorated with many medals and ranks, not dirty with black printing stains. But as I stand at a distance, looking at him, I notice that he also has a pistol stuck in his belt. However, his firearm is hidden in a shiny new leather case.

Breathe slowly; I need to get close to them; he is waiting for me.

"Ernest, nice to meet you." He notices me, extends his hand, and I force myself to take the small steps left between us.

"Monique, nice to meet you." He looks at me with his green eyes, and I'm shiver

"Shall we sit down?"

And as we step between the tables outside, waiting for the waiter to accompany us to our reserved table, I feel his hand gently touch my waist, taking ownership of me. At any time, I can change my mind and back off.

"I understand you work in a boulangerie shop," he asks me politely as we sit down, after holding the chair for me; no one has ever done that before.

"Yes."

"And what do you do there?"

"I'm just selling croissants and baguettes."

"You should try them, their croissants are amazing." Violette joins the conversation.

"Maybe I'll do that one day," he smiles at her, returning his attention to me. "Do you like your job?"

"Very much," I try to be cordial as I can. "What do you do in the army?"

"Engineering matters, not something that would interest young women like you. We shouldn't talk about the army; we should talk about art and the superb culinary heritage that brings such splendid food to our mouths." I look down and feel the taste of the lipstick on my lips.

"Danke." He thanks the waiter who places the wine glasses on the table, not noticing the slight reluctance in the waiter's face. From a nearby table, I can smell real coffee. I missed that smell so much. How do I start a conversation with a German officer who frightens me?

"What do you like in our splendid Paris?"

"Well, Paris is still new to me; we were stationed here not long ago; it will take me some time to learn everything the city has to offer. Zum wohl, ladies." He raises his glass of wine in the air, and as commanded, everyone reaches out and holds their drinks. "To our lovely hostess in our splendid Paris, may we stay here forever."

"Zum wohl." Everyone smiles and clinks glasses, sipping

the wine, and I choke. I must get used to the taste.

"Are you okay?" He turns his attention to me.

"Yes, I'm okay, I'm not used to red wine."

"Shall I order you a different wine?" He raised his hand in command, calling the waiter.

"No, no, that's okay." But he is already giving instructions to the waiter, and within a moment a cold bottle of champagne appears on the table, with new glasses.

"And again, cheers," Ernest raises his glass, "to a new German-French friendship." I take a small sip of the sweet liquid, avoiding telling him I'm not used to drinking at all.

We only had some wine on Friday evenings. Dad would pass the Kiddush glass of wine carefully from one to another, letting us taste the sweet red flavor, but that too had gone two and a half years ago, in that terrible winter, when we almost ran out of food.

"The food here is delicious, so delicate, many flavors, for that I must admit, French cuisine surpasses German." And everyone agrees.

"At least they know how to do one thing properly, unlike fighting." says Violette's Fritz, and everyone laughs, except Oberst Ernest, who looks at me.

"And what about the beautiful women they manage to bring into our hands?" Fritz of Anaïs donates his part, and everyone rejoices, laughing when she kisses him on the lips. Oberst Ernest continues to smile at me, his polite smile; I don't want him to.

"It is so nice here on the boulevard." Violette contributes to the conversation.

"To a lasting partnership for a thousand years." Anaïs raises the glass of wine, and everyone joins.

Later, after eating a pie with real cherry, flour and sugar, we march on the Champs Élysées, and even though I try, I can no longer separate myself. What do passersby think of me?

"Do you enjoy our company?" Ernest asks me, navigating the two of us so we can walk a few steps ahead of the rest.

"Yeah, everything's fine. I'm just not used to going out like that."

"How come?"

"I'm not like Violette and Anaïs; I'm less Parisian than they are."

"Where is the place you call home?"

"I grew up in Strasbourg and also in Dunkirk." I'm thinking of my real home, the one I left running. Is he waiting for me? I never went back, too afraid to be recognized; what if someone calls my name again while I'm walking beside a German officer?

"Monique?"

"Sorry, I was thinking about my childhood home."

"In Strasbourg?"

"Yes, I apologize for not listening."

"If you grew up in Strasbourg, do you speak German?" He moves to his language.

"Like a native," I answer him in German.

"And all this time, you let me struggle with my French?"

Had I annoyed him? I stop walking and look into his green eyes, trying to read the expression on his face, but I can't. What should I answer?

"We're in Paris, I was taught that a man should strive for a woman." And he laughs out loud.

"You have courage. I love that in a woman." And I think that if he knew me, he would have known how cowardly I am, but I keep on looking in his eyes and say nothing for a moment before lowering my eyes, not wanting to cross the line.

"And when did you move to Paris?" he continues.

"It's hard for me to talk about it," I allow myself to answer him. "And when did you get to Paris?"

"A month ago."

"And where had you been before?"

"It's hard for me to talk about it." He smiles at me as if we have found a shared secret that brings us closer, and I try to smile back, wondering if I have any more lipstick left on my lips. Maybe I should have gone to the restrooms earlier and get organized? Like Anaïs?

"What are you talking about?" Violette interjects between us, as per an agreed-upon sign which ended the allotted time of a young couple's privacy on their first date.

"Museums and art," Ernest answers her as he watches me.

"I do not like museums; they bore me," she answers him.

"And you?" He turns the question to me.

"I like them." I think that's what he wants to hear.

I never liked museums. Ever since I was a child, walking with the whole class, looking up in fear at the enormous threatening paintings of people fighting, injuring each other, cutting off their heads, while the teacher spoke passionately about the duty of sacrifice for the homeland. But three years ago, I really started hating them. It was on that class trip to the Louvre when we came to a sign at the entrance: "Jews are not allowed." And the teacher took Sylvie and I out of the line, sending us home, while everyone grinned or looked at us sadly. I hated their pitying looks.

"Would you like to go with me to the Louvre? I always wanted to see the huge paintings of Napoleon with my own eyes, to watch all his battles and victories."

"I would be happy to join you if it interests you."

"Like you, I'm the quiet type and find it difficult to connect with the Parisian bustle. I prefer to watch the art of the great painters." And I manage to smile at him again as if we have found another thing that connects us, the desire for silence.

The street is quiet in the evening, and even though I enjoy the silence, I rise from the bench in the garden and start walking to the place I call home. It is already late, and the small attic is waiting for me.

After we said goodbye, I could not return to Lizette; I had to relax for a few minutes. We all stood under the Arc de Triomphe, looking at the figures engraved in marble, while Fritz and Fritz talked about Napoleon's victories, and Ernest gently held my waist, leading me apart from the others.

"Monique, I've enjoyed getting to know you. You were a perfect companion."

"Danke," I answer him in German.

"I would be happy to invite you to see me again."

"I'd like that too." I know this is the only answer he expects to hear.

He bowed formally and came a little closer, kissing my hand, and I can smell his body scent mixed with quality male perfume.

"Good night, Mademoiselle Monique, we'll meet again in a quiet place." He smiles at me, talking in French.

"Good night, Herr Oberst Ernest," I answer him in

German and slowly start walking away, turning my back to him.

"How is he?" Violette catches me before I walk away. "He's very nice, isn't he?"

"So what do you think of him?" Anaïs joins her, arriving in a peaceful walk. "You'd better get him for yourself."

"How did it feel to me?" I ask myself later, as I sit alone on the bench in the street, rubbing my palm where his lips kissed it and holding my aching belly.

"How is he?" Lizette asks me when I enter her apartment.

"He's nice and polite."

"Will you join me for coffee?" And even though I'm afraid of her questions, I accompany her to the kitchen.

"He was very polite, and he was clean," I try to describe Oberst Ernest to her.

"It is important."

"It's not easy to make a decision."

"It usually isn't."

"How did you get to know your husband?" I dare to ask as we relax on the couch, sipping the bitter and disgusting sugarless coffee of war.

"I wasn't polite, but it was a long time ago," she smiles at me. "We met at a demonstration for women's suffrage, before the previous war."

"Please tell me."

"I was a rebellious girl from a rich family, and he was a young bank clerk who volunteered to help us carry our protest signs when we escaped from the police."

"And what happened next?" I'm happy to divert the conversation away from me.

"He was killed, and we still don't have voting rights like men do, so it probably wasn't that successful."

"That's sad."

"Yes, life is sad sometimes, but the look in his eyes was worth it all." She smiles for a moment, and I lower my eyes from his picture above the fireplace, concentrating on the bitter black cup between my hand.

Later, before going to bed, I stand in front of the mirror in my attic, scrutinizing myself.

The face has remained the same; the lipstick is long gone, the hair has also returned to its original shape, the waist and breasts remain the same, nothing has changed.

Dad was right; the second time is much easier, even the stabs in my back from the looks of passersby are almost unnoticed.

"Good night to you, licking German boots, Frenchie," I whisper to myself before turning off the light. What shall I say to Philip next time I meet him?

The afternoon sunlight paints the city roofs in shades of gold, but the rays do not penetrate the dirty alley of the Latin Quarter, leaving the street grey as I walk to meet him.

What does it matter what I say to him? All that he cares about is the information I bring with me. He doesn't care about me. My legs almost trip over a broken wooden crate that was thrown into the street, and a woman in the opposite store examines me while her little daughter is holding her feet firmly, curiously peeking at me and my new dress.

The stairs to the basement are waiting for me; I have to learn how to stay alive, to give him what he expects from me.

Philip is waiting for me at the bottom of the stairs, in the same alert position; I mustn't get excited by him, he will not protect me if he has to choose.

"Good afternoon, how are you?" He tries to get closer, but I pass him and go inside, smelling him for a split-second.

"I'm fine. How are you?"

"Did you meet him?"

"I met him."

Philip says nothing, just walking around the small basement, examining me with his dark eyes.

"We all went out together, walking down the avenue, and we also sat in a café. He ordered me champagne."

For a moment, he approaches, still silent, as if to grab me by force and shake my body, but he stops himself. Why don't you say something?

"And we talked a lot about museums and art. He would like to take me on a visit to the Louvre. I can't wait to walk to the Louvre."

Can anything hurt you? Like you hurt me?

"And he asked to meet me again, and I accepted his invitation, isn't that what you wanted in the first place? That I get more German information?"

"What German information did you get?" he asks in a distant voice.

"They are starting to mobilize forces for the fortifications of the coasts, and they call the project 'The Atlantic Wall,' they assume the invasion will take place in the coming year through Pas-de-Calais. They employ forced laborers to build the fortifications, and he admires Napoleon, especially his journey to Moscow." I pause for a moment to breathe, but Philip still says nothing, just listening to me as he grips the back of the old wooden chair.

"And your officer told you all that information?"

"His name is Ernest, and his rank is Oberst."

"And your Oberst Ernest told you all that information?"

"No, I understood all this from conversations between them, when they thought we women were only interested in wine and cherry pies. But Oberst Ernest also talked to me about art."

"Yes, I understood you like to talk about art."

"Do you like art?" Why does he never tell me anything about himself?

"And is there any more information you received from your Oberst Ernest?"

"Why do I know nothing about you? What did you do before the war?"

"What does it matter what I did before the war? The war is the general who decides what we have to do and who we are; we are only the pawns." He looks at me, still distant.

"Oberst Ernest likes art." Has he always worked in a printing house? Will he ever tell me anything about himself?

"And did you get more information from Oberst Ernest who likes art?" He is not interested in me.

"No, but if you want, I will meet him again."

"Do it."

He does not touch me as we part, and on the way to Lizette's apartment I see the Arc de Triomphe in the distance, and feel a pinch of envy for a moment, remembering the last time he hugged me before he hurt me so much. If only things could be different. Why can't I be happy like Anaïs or Violette?

Violette

"Where's Anaïs?" I ask a few days later when she enters the boulangerie before I go home, gently closing the door behind her.

"Today I've arrived alone." She smiles at me.

"Would you like to have something sweet?"

"Is there anything left?" Since becoming my friends, they stop by from time to time without their Fritzes, asking if I have anything for them at closing time. Some baguettes, perhaps sweet chocolate or butter croissants. With grateful fingers, they pick up the leftovers of the German soldiers at the end of the day.

"Yes, there are some pastries left. I'll pack them for you."

"I'll wait for you outside, is that okay?" she whispers to me when she notices Simone's look.

"It's fine. I'll join you in a moment." I gather the leftovers into a paper bag, wondering where Anaïs is.

"Young women need to have values," Simone quietly says while she counts the money in the cash register, looking at me as I'm rushing out.

"Is it okay for me to wait for you outside until you finish work?" she asks when I hand her the paper bag with the pastries, turning to go inside. I have to clean and close the place up.

"Is everything okay? Did something happen?"

"Everything's fine. I just wanted to walk with you a little bit. Can you?"

"Where is Anaïs?"

"Anaïs is with her Fritz, showing him Paris the way she knows how."

"Wait a minute," I go inside, hurry to clean the tables, and wonder what she wants to talk to me about.

"I would not choose such company," Simone keeps talking to herself, making sure I hear, but I ignore her; I have no other girlfriends to choose from; the last one died because of me.

"I'd be happy if we could be friends," she tells me as we walk in silence, passing the Lafayette Gallery store, which showcases the summer fashion for German officers' spouses.

"What do you mean?" I pretend I don't understand.

"The two of us never meet alone, walking together, telling each other our thoughts."

"I thought you and Anaïs were friends like that. I always see you together."

"Yeah, but Anaïs only does what is good for Anaïs, especially in relation to the entertainment side of life."

"I thought you liked spending time with her." I hold her arm. It seems like she needs it, but after a few steps, the contact between us feels fake to me, and I release my hand, continuing to walk beside her in silence.

"What do you think of these?" She stops by a lingerie store window, pointing to a white bra and garter belt.

"For whom?" I ask hesitantly; this is an expensive store for rich women. I have never worn such underwear; even Mom never dressed like that, telling me more than once that only prostitutes walk with garters.

"It's for me. Fritz wants us to do it." She finally speaks the frightening words, as if she has been preparing for this moment for a long time.

"Is he insisting on it?"

I have no experience with such things. Everything I know I learned from Claudine's stories, I have not even kissed anyone on the mouth, only read about it in the magazine, the one Mom ripped after she found it.

"Yeah, he says that if we're a couple, we should do it."

"And what does Anaïs say about that?"

"She does not know."

"And it does not bother you that he..." And it is difficult for me to say the words.

"He says he loves me and that they are winning the war."

What shall I tell her? Shall I tell her all the jokes I hear in the boulangerie, listening to the German soldiers that don't know I speak their language? Shall I tell her about the Panzer tank man in the black uniform who laughed a few days ago?

"Shut up; I have an announcement," he'd raised his voice, and all the other soldiers got quiet. "Himmler announced that anyone who did not return from Russia in a coffin is entitled to receive a Sexual Disease Medal from a French prostitute." Shall I tell her how they all laughed about it?

And what about the soldier who added to the cheers of laughter: "We can receive it for free, the French girls ask for it." How much shall I tell her?

"Are you sure he loves you?"

"He told me that after the war is over and they win, he will marry me."

"And do you believe him?"

"I don't want to be hungry. Two years ago, in the winter, I was standing in line at the grocery store, shivering and holding the food ration tickets. I'd prayed for a sturdy man to come save me, and he came. So he is not French, but he is nice to me; I want to be on the winning side, not the hungry side." She doesn't stop talking, spilling her guts while we look out at the shop window, at a satin corset with a price tag that ensures the store has a stock of real tights.

"Wouldn't you act like me?" She looks at me.

What can I tell her? That in the winter, two years ago, we almost starved? I was standing last in the endless lines, only to find at the end of the day that there was no food left for the Jews? If Dad had not kept a few pounds of flour and oil hidden in the kitchen, I wouldn't be standing here beside her. Or maybe I can tell her that I know how to hide? Or that I'm learning about myself that I know how to lie much better than I thought I could?

"He's nice, but I'm afraid he just wants to get into your panties." I choose especially rude words, surprised at myself that I can say them.

But Violette laughs at my rude words, and she gives me her hand, and we keep walking down the boulevard like a couple of friends; why is she not Claudine? And why did no one tell me what a man does when he gets in your panties, and how does it feel?

"We have to tell you something."

Violette and Anaïs enter the boulangerie the next day while folding their arms and approaching the counter.

"We have an invitation to a picnic this weekend." Violette is excited.

"How are you today?" I try to whisper to her.

"Come with us? Please come." There is a pleading look in her eyes.

"Please come," Anaïs adds, "It's less interesting without the new girl."

"Sit down; I'll give you something." I have to serve a German soldier waiting in line. I want to ask Violette how she is, but she makes sure to stick to Anaïs.

"Here you go, two croissants, how are you?" I place the metal tray in front of them on the table in the corner. "Everything okay?" I whisper to her again, but she ignores my question.

"Yes, everything's okay." Anaïs bends down and pulls a box of cigarettes out of her leather bag, puts a white cigarette in her mouth, and waits for one of the German soldiers to approach her with a lit lighter.

"Danke." She thankfully smiles at him while he proudly returns to his place in line. As she leans back and blows the bluish smoke toward the ceiling, her gaze wanders between Violette and me, as if trying to find a hidden connection.

"You should come," Anaïs looks at me. "Ernest will come too."

"Does he wants to meet me?"

"He said he would be happy if you could join us; he is not used to hearing the word 'no.'"

I walk back to my place behind the counter, serving the other soldiers. I can do it, I can be nice to everyone, give them what they want, Violette, Oberst Ernest, Philip, even Simone.

"Monique, the customer is waiting," I hear Simone's impatient voice. Probably after Violette and Anaïs leave, she will mention that she does not like them and that only immoral, promiscuous women smoke, especially in public. I'm not like them.

"Monique, you have your chores to do."

"Sorry, I apologize." I have chores to do; Phillip also said I should do what is needed, even though he is not really interested in me. I smile and apologize to the soldier who is waiting, handing him the pastries and the change. Despite Simone's examining look, I approach Violette and Anaïs for a moment.

"Where is the picnic going to take place?"

"They are taking us to the Marne river, do you like water?"

I have never been to the Marne river.

Marne River, Northeast of Paris

"Come on, Monique, Anaïs, don't give up, we are beating them!" Violette's screams are heard over the quiet river, frightening some ducks, and they flee from the serenity of the riverbank, spreading their wings and passing over us in a peaceful flock.

"Come on, don't give up; they are getting tired." She continues to cheer us with loud shouts, and even though the three of us are panting heavily while holding the paddles, hitting the water in an attempt to maintain a steady pace, we have no chance against them. The officers' walnut-colored boat is far ahead of us, their paddles hitting the water uniformly as they listen to the sound of Oberst Ernest, giving them a rhythm in his quiet voice.

Earlier, with the first rays of sunshine, we three girls met at the foot of the Arc de Triomphe, waiting for them and examining each other. They had more beautiful dresses than mine, why didn't I put lipstick on my lips like them?

The two bored cops guarding the gate barely addressed us, but I walked away from them, making sure to be closer to

Violette, even though since that time we talked she has told me nothing, avoiding me when I ask.

"Guten morgen," the officers greet us warmly as the open-roof army vehicle stops next to us with a squeak of the brakes, causing me to freeze for a moment, watching the cops near the Arc step back and look down.

"Guten morgen, how are we all going to get in here?" Violette asks and laughs.

"They'll tie one of us on the car hood like a hunted deer," Anaïs offers.

"If anything, then a rabbit or a fox," Ernest answers her and smiles at me. "Good morning, Mademoiselle Monique."

"Good morning, Herr Oberst Ernest."

"You girls will sit in the back with us," Fritz answers her. And they seat me respectfully next to Ernest, who is in the driver's seat, while everyone else huddles in the back, Fritz next to Fritz and Violette sitting on the knees of the giggling Anaïs, close to Fritz's knees.

"I'm glad you chose to join us," Ernest quietly whispers as he exchanges a hidden smile with me.

"I'm happy too," I answer him quietly, returning a small smile while my fingernails scratch my palms, fearing he's noticed.

"And now, everyone pay attention, we'll teach you a German song," Fritz announces from the back seat, trying to overcome the whistling wind on the ride and Violette's laugh.

And we all follow him, line by line, shouting the chorus as I translate the words into French for the two girls. Even Ernest allows himself to sing quietly while he concentrates on driving, his hands clad in black gloves gripping the steering wheel tightly, and occasionally he glances at me.

"Ihhhh... this is a dirty song," Violette announces in a protest of laughter as I translate the last line, hoping Ernest does not notice that it is difficult for me to say these words.

"That's how it is; we are rude people," Fritz informs us with a laugh and chooses a new song to study, while the morning sun lights our way.

Near a small town, we turn onto a dirt road and park the car on the riverbank near an empty dock, where two walnut-colored wooden rowboats are waiting for us, painted with shiny varnish.

"Just for us," Fritz announces while I wait for Ernest to come out and open the door for me, learning to be a woman.

"You thought of everything," Violette expresses admiringly.

"That's who we are, singing dirty songs and planning everything," Fritz lifts her in the air while she laughs and blushes.

"Shall we share equally?" Fritz suggests.

"I think it's time for France against Germany," Anaïs offers.

"The girls against the boys." Violette joins her. I have a feeling Ernest is interested in a different division, but he says nothing and gives me a little smile as I join them, waiting for Fritz to stabilize our boat, gripping it to the dock to make it easier for us to get into it.

"France is winning," Violette announces as we start rowing, not waiting for the men to get into their boat.

Still, they easily close the gap, leaving us far behind despite Violette's shouts of encouragement.

"We were defeated, we are yours," Violette dramatically announces as we get out of the boat and climb to the bank, spreading her arms to the sides and lying down on the green grass.

"Did you enjoy it?" Ernest asks as he serves me a meat sandwich, and I nod my head, wondering if they ever miss anything.

"Come and join us; it's not good to sit alone with a German officer." Anaïs takes me by my arm, leading us behind one of the trees while Ernest follows me with a smiling look.

"What are you doing?"

"Changing into a swimsuit."

"A swimsuit?"

"Yes, the river is nice and cool."

Shall I tell her I don't have a swimsuit at all? That my last swimsuit was from childhood, before my breasts had even grown? At home, no one thought of sewing a yellow badge onto a bathing suit; we never thought of going for a swim in the river, too frightened by the German soldiers. In the warm summer, I used to walk through alternate streets, not wanting to see all the people sunbathing along the banks of the Seine.

"I did not bring a swimsuit with me. I did not think of it."

"Too bad," Violette looks at me sadly. "It can be enjoyable."

"You can jump in with your underwear. Ernest will love what he sees," giggles Anaïs as she arranges the straps of her blue swimsuit, checking that they are in place.

"Do you want me to give you my swimsuit?" Violette suggests, "I don't mind going in with underwear." But I thank her and refuse, preferring to stay on the riverbank, I cannot expose myself like that to the eyes of men.

"Don't you want to swim in the river?" Ernest asks me as we emerge from behind the tree. They jump towards the dock and the water, and I turn to sit on the picnic blanket the men have spread out for us.

"I apologize. I forgot to bring my bathing suit."

"I've given up swimming. I do not want to get wet." He informs the Fritzes who have taken off their uniforms and placed them in an orderly manner as if in a parade, and he sits down next to me on the blanket. The Fritzes express only a minor protest before turning to throw the girls into the river and jumping into the cold water after them.

"Don't you like to swim?"

"I'm more a kind of land animal."

"I noticed that you also didn't put on lipstick, like the other girls."

What should I answer him?

"I wanted to be different from them. Do you like a woman to put lipstick on her lips?"

"I think a woman is more feminine if she behaves like an elegant woman." My lips feel naked all of a sudden.

"I'll try." I look down at the grass, feeling so simple compared to Anaïs' and Violette's dresses.

"What about poetry? After we talked last time, I was wondering whether you like poetry."

"Yes, I enjoy listening to poetry." When I was a young girl, before it all started, I would lie in bed, unable to sleep. The news reports at the cinema frightened me, showing Hitler's declarations of war and the vast endless army marching in rows towards the border.

They are just being threatening, Dad explained to me, the Germans are a cultured people, a nation that has brought poets and philosophers to the world like Heine, Ghetto, and Schiller will not kill just like that. With his hand caressing my hair, he suggested reading me their poems.

And I would sit in bed, patiently waiting for him to return with a book in his hand. He would then sit next to me on the little chair, and start reading me poems. Dad, where are you now?

"Do you want me to read poetry to you?" He wakes me from my thoughts.

"I'd love that." And he gets up and goes to the car, returning after a moment holding a book and sitting next to me on the blanket.

"Shell I start to read?"

"Yes, please."

"Whoever has succeeded in the great attempt,

To be a friend's friend,

Whoever has won a lovely woman,

Add his to the jubilation!"

He reads Schiller's "Ode to Joy" to me in his quiet voice, and I close my eyes and hum the notes from memory as tears begin to flow from my eyes.

Tears for Dad's voice that I already have a hard time remembering, tears for not having time to say goodbye to him when the cops knocked on the door. Tears for the man that stopped my running at Drancey camp, and for what I became. Tears for not being hungry anymore, and for this hot, sunny day and the sounds of laughter coming from the river.

"I'm sorry if something I read hurt you, I apologize."

"No, it's okay. Thank you for reading to me."

He continues to read in his quiet voice, and I find myself listening to him, but I am no longer able to contain the words, letting my thoughts fly to the east, looking at the water sparkling in the midday sun.

"You missed all the fun," Violette laughs as she comes running in all wet, looking for a towel and dripping on the blanket, causing Ernest to put the book away.

"What were you doing while we weren't watching?" Anaïs joins and lays herself on the spread blanket, panting and dripping as well.

"We read poetry." I smile at her as she grimaces.

"Do you know that great battles took place here in the previous war? That time, we lost to you, the French." Fritz joins us.

"I told them we would have beaten you if only we'd pushed harder," Violette answers while hugging his shoulders.

"Last time you won, and you managed to stop our attack on the riverbank, but not this time. This time no one will stop us." Ernest looks at Fritz appreciatively.

"You men are so boring with all your war talk," Violette gets up from the blanket and snatches Fritz's officer's hat, which lies on top of the pile of clothes, putting it on her head and standing in front of us with her hands on her hips.

"Achtung!" She straightens up and salutes, wearing the German officer's hat and a bathing suit, while everyone laughs. "Wait a minute," she gets excited by the theatrical moment and also picks up her Fritz's shirt from the pile, putting it on her body while everyone grins.

"You're too small for his size," Anaïs remarks.

"Shut up, Heil Hitler." She salutes with her hand to the sounds of laughter.

"Raus, all the Jews out, we will kill all the Jews!" She continues to shout in a German accent to the cheers of the small crowd on the blanket. Everyone looks at her and enjoys the sight of her breasts moving from side to side in the open shirt, barely held by the swimsuit fabric as she waves her hands.

"Juden raus, Juden raus!" She continues to salute with her hand up.

My hand is stretched outside the car, feeling the pleasantness of the wind in my fingers as we make our way back to Paris.

"What do you think about Jews?" Ernest asks me, calming his voice while his eyes look ahead to the narrow road.

Is he examining me? Does he suspect me? What should I answer him?

My head turns back for a moment. Everyone is sleeping in the back of the car. Fritz and Fritz with their heads back on the seat, and their mouths open to the afternoon wind. Violette and Anaïs are hugging, each curled up on her Fritz.

"I do not like the Jews, but I don't think they are so dangerous."

"I saw you didn't laugh before when Violette gave her show."

"I used to have a Jewish girlfriend, her name was Sylvie; you couldn't tell she was Jewish."

"What happened to her?"

"We are no longer friends, and I am no longer in Strasbourg."

"I'm not happy about what they're doing to Jews either,

but there's no other way to treat them," he continues to speak to me quietly as only the noise of the wind bothers us. "If you understood the economy, you would know how they try to take over the world; they are like a wise fox who wants to break into a vineyard and plunder the grapes that don't belong to them."

Oberst Ernest is silent for a moment, as if trying to figure out how to explain the Jewish problem to me more appropriately.

"You see, I do not hate them either, it's like the hunter does not hate the fox, he appreciates its wisdom, but must hunt it; otherwise, it will harm the crop, destroy the economy. We must stop them; we have no choice." He looks at me, and all I can hear is the tire's noise on the road, jarring my ears.

"Do you understand what I mean?" The wind is drying my lips.

"I think I do." I smile at him, the smile of a good woman who appreciates an intelligent explanation but wants to jump out of the car into the hard asphalt, escape this metal box that takes me forward. Even Dad, who understood economics, did not understand enough about the Germans.

"Goodbye, German hero soldiers," Anaïs salutes in a sleepy voice. She tries to grab Fritz's officers' cap, but he pulls her hand away and does not allow it, while Ernest parks the car at the foot of the Arc de Triomphe, hurries out, and approaches to open the door for me.

"I enjoyed your company; you were a perfect companion," he compliments me.

"I enjoyed it too, thank you, thank you for reading me poetry."

"Have we arrived?" Violette asks in a sleepy voice and rises from her Fritz.

"Yes, we are at the Arc de Triomphe," Ernest answers her.

"To our triomphe," says Anaïs.

"Did you forget we won?" Fritz answers her, but she fills his mouth with a passionate farewell kiss.

"This is where we part." Ernest stands politely next to the vehicle, ignoring the rest. I think he expects me to kiss him. What should I do?

"Thanks again for a pleasant day." My hand is outstretched towards him, but I can't get any closer. I'm a Frenchwoman licking German boots, unable to kiss a German officer. I've never kissed a man.

As I start to move away from him, he grabs my hand for a moment, stopping me.

"Mademoiselle Monique."

"Yes, Herr Oberst Ernest?" Will he force me to kiss him?

"Next week, I have to go on a day trip to the North Shore area. Would you like to join me? Just the two of us." And I nod to him in the affirmative, releasing my hand and walking down the boulevard. What else could I answer him?

I'm a French prostitute who will have to kiss a German officer who wants to politely hunt down the Jews.

"How was your polite guy?" Lizette asks me when I walk in.

"He invited me on a day trip."

"And will you go with him?" What to tell her?

"I think I'll go, though sometimes I feel like I have to sacrifice part of myself."

"Will you drink coffee with me? Keep me company?"

"Have you ever sacrificed anything?" I ask Lizette as we sit down, and I hold the warm cup in my hands.

"I don't feel it was a sacrifice because I believed in what I was doing."

"And after that, weren't you disappointed in yourself?"

"Why should I be disappointed in myself if I tried my best?"

"I keep on trying, but afterwards I feel disappointed in myself, I so want to succeed."

"Life does not work this way; sometimes life can't even provide us a normal cup of coffee." She smiles at me and places the cup of bitter coffee substitute on the table.

"Thank you for listening to me."

"Thank you, my child, for keeping an old lady company; I think you've sacrificed enough for one evening. It's time for you to go up to your room to sleep." I get up and look at her husband's picture, which is in the silver frame on the fireplace. He stands in his army uniform, looking at me with pride, not knowing that a few days later he will run to his death in front of German machine guns on the Marne front, in that previous great war.

The First Kiss

"Are you waiting for someone?" Simone asks me a few days after the picnic.

"No, why?"

"Because you've been looking at the front door all day."

For several days now, I have been restless, waiting for Herr Ernest to enter through the glass door, feeling tense whenever the doorbell rings. How would I travel with him for a whole day? What does he want from me?

"Sorry, can I have two croissants?" a soldier asks me in bad French, and I hurry to serve him.

"Mademoiselle Monique?" Another soldier in a grey-green uniform approaches Marie, who is cleaning the tables with a damp cloth.

"No, she's there." She points at me over the counter.

"Mademoiselle Monique?"

"Yes, that's me."

"I have a letter for you." And he reaches his hand in a straight motion across the counter, while I move uncomfortably under Simone's scrutiny.

"The commander asked me to wait here for an answer." He speaks French with a German accent, cuts the words sharply before walking to the corner of the store, standing still, waiting for my answer.

"What's in the letter?" asks Simone, leaving the cash drawer for a moment.

"I don't know," I answer her, blushing and heading to the back room, tearing open the envelope and reading the words written in perfect handwriting, arranged in straight lines.

Dear Mademoiselle Monique,

You are kindly invited to join me for a day tour of northern France, two days from now.

My assistant is waiting for your reply.

Best Regards,

Oberst Ernest

Commander of the 566 Engineering Brigade

"Monique, there are customers." I hear Simone's voice, and I have to stop looking at Ernest's curly signature; I hurry back to the counter while holding the white paper in my hand.

"Tell him I will join him," I mumble to his assistant soldier, who has to get close to hear me.

"I miss the days when French women had dignity," Simone says to Marie a few minutes later, as they chat in the back room. My fingers arrange the remaining pastries on the tray, even though I already finished doing so before Ernest's assistant came in.

What is he expecting of me? I need to talk to someone. Marie passes by, and I think of Claudine. Why did I notice the boy that day?

"Monique, come here please," Simone calls me at the end of the day as I say goodbye to her.

"This is for you, your salary." She puts the green bills in my hands.

"You gave me too much." I return some of the bills to her.

"No, it's yours, you replaced Claudine, and I decided to give you a raise; you deserve it." And I hurry out into the street, forgetting to thank her. Why didn't I ignore the boy that day?

The boy near the newsstand does not hand me an official letter written on white paper, signed with a curled signature; he doesn't even wait for my answer, he just whispers to me: "Metro Opera." And right after that, he shoves a bundle of newspapers into a big leather bag, and starts running down the street while waving at the newspaper, shouting the news headlines everywhere. "The Americans are invading Italy; the German army has repulsed them in a heroic battle, read about it now in the Paris Soir newspaper."

As I walk towards the Opera, I can still see the boy running down the street and the people approaching him, paying in coins and taking newspapers from his hand, but my lips are dry and my thoughts are elsewhere; how will Philip react?

"What was it like going out with a German officer?" Philip walks around the basement like a panther looking for an exit in the damp walls that close in on us, hardly looking at me. My hands are placed on the wood table, waiting for his, but he keeps on standing, refusing to sit across from me.

"I did not go out with him alone. We all went out for a picnic day at the Marne." He didn't say anything to me when

I entered the basement, moving away and not asking how I felt.

"Is it nice to have a picnic on the banks of the Marne? I'll bet the river is quiet and cold in the summer heat; the wind is pleasant; you can lie on the grass in the shade of the trees and laugh." He continues his ugly speech.

"Yes, it is pleasant there."

"And can you still hear the machine guns' nonstop noise, or the cries of the wounded from the previous war against the green-eyed Germans?"

"We did not talk about it."

"Did you enjoy swimming in the river? Cooling your body off from all the heat and sweat?"

"No, I did not enjoy bathing in the cool water."

"Why didn't you enjoy swimming in the river? The German language didn't suit you?"

"Why are you asking me such questions?"

"Because I'm interested and want to know about you, isn't that what we do in our meetings? I ask questions, and you answer them?"

"No, I did not enjoy the water."

"So what did you do? Did you wear a swimsuit, especially for him to see?"

"I did not go into the water."

"Why didn't you go into the water? I heard the German officers enjoyed that their French dates wore swimsuits for them."

"Why are you talking to me like this?"

"Because I want to know who I'm talking to right now."

"I did not bring a swimsuit with me, because I do not have a swimsuit, because I have not worn a swimsuit in years." I get up and push the table away from me.

"Do you think I was interested in going for a bath in

the Seine when a day earlier I'd been searching for leftover food in garbage cans? Do you think it matters to me how do I look in a swimsuit? Do you think it's fun to sit in a car with a German officer? To talk with him about the Jews, not knowing if he doesn't like them, or maybe if he raised the subject because he suspects that I am Jewish? Do you think it's such a pleasure to be with someone who scares me and invites me to travel with him alone for a whole day, to try to think what I will do if he tries to kiss me?" I shout the last words and breathe quickly.

"I'm sorry; I did not mean that."

"You meant everything," I sit down in the chair again and cover my face. "Time after time, you send me from this basement to get you more pieces of information."

"I apologize." His arm wraps around me as he leans on the floor next to me, and I feel the smell of his body, with the same aroma of a printing press in his fingers. "Don't cry; I didn't mean to hurt you."

"I don't cry." My hands cover my face; I don't want him to see me like that. "He read me poetry; he asked me if I'd like him to read me poetry."

"I apologize; I love poetry." He lifts me from the concrete floor and hugs my body, his hands pleasant and warm.

"Do you really like poetry?" I look up at him, wanting to believe, feeling his hand stroking my back and not wanting him to stop.

"Yes, once, at the Sorbonne, in another life that will never return." His lips are so close to mine.

"Were you a student at the Sorbonne?" I did not expect his lips to touch mine, but they do.

"A poor student at the Sorbonne." I cling to him tighter and close my eyes.

What are all these sensations? I can feel the touch of his

fingers through the fabric of the dress as I breathe heavily. My hands cling to his shoulders tightly as our lips tighten and keep touching more and more, unable to stop.

"I have to go." My hands push him away, and I move backward, trying to catch my breath as I look into his dark eyes, feeling the rough wall scratching my back.

"I apologize." He's trying to get close to me again.

"Goodbye." I move away from his warm hands and lips, panting up the stairs. I know that if I stay, I won't be able to cross the bridge again to the German Headquarters area and walk as if nothing has changed under the red flags of swastikas fluttering in the evening breeze.

I have to stop for a few moments; I'm too excited. I need to talk to someone, someone who will listen to me without me having to lie.

"This is for you, my girl, may a loving man give you a flower." I place the bouquet on the cold stone and sit down next to her. The old saleswoman at Trocadero Square tried kissing my hand when I bought a huge bouquet, paying her in a pile of bills above the price she asked. Again and again, she thanked me, blessing me with love while I walked away from her, feeling cleaner without all those green-grey bills in my pocket.

The sun will soon set, and I have to hurry and tell her, before the cemetery gate closes.

"His lips were pleasant to me, but I was stressed. Suddenly

I began to breathe heavily." I'm trying to explain it to her.

"I still feel the touch of his hands as they passed over my breasts through my dress." The words come out of my mouth. But I'm too ashamed to tell her about the strange feeling in the bottom of my stomach. I don't want her to think that I am a prostitute who cannot control herself.

"I ran away from him. He said nothing about Oberst Ernest. I should go with him. I did not tell you about Herr Oberst Ernest. I'm so scared."

As I walk out of the cemetery, smiling at the older guard getting ready to lock the gate, I imagine Claudine whispering that I have nothing to fear from Oberst Ernest and that everything will be okay.

Everything will be okay.

"Do you feel comfortable?" Herr Oberst Ernest asks as I sit next to him in his army command car's back seat. I can smell the eau de cologne from his shaved face when he leans towards me and helps me arrange my small bag.

This time I waited alone at the foot of the Arc de Triomphe, my body slightly shivering from the autumn's early morning breeze, but precisely at the time we set, I heard an engine roaring from the empty boulevard.

"Guten morgen." Oberst Ernest got out of the bluish-grey car, holding his hand out and helping me get into the back seat while I hold his black glove-wrapped hand. His personal driver sat behind the wheel, ignoring my existence and looking straight ahead like he was welded into place.

"Now you'll be more comfortable." He takes his field binoculars out of side storage, hands it to the driver, and places my bag there instead. "Shall we go?"

The Champs Élysées is empty of cars at this hour, and even on the sidewalk only a few people are walking on their way to work. I look at them and imagine myself walking on the empty boulevard now. Would I look at the passing German vehicle, giving a look of contempt at the woman sitting next to the German officer?

"Should I ask the driver to close the roof?" Oberst Ernest asks me when he notices a shiver gripping me for a moment.

"No, it's okay, I'm not cold." I lie and stare forward at the driver's back, feeling that I deserve contemptuous glances.

"What are you thinking about?"

"The city waking up."

"This city is so special, look at the magnificent building facades, we Germans definitely have something to learn from you." He speaks to me while saluting the guards at the checkpoint in Concord Square. The car slows down as it passes the concrete block and barbed wire barrier, and I look down, wondering if these are the regular guards and whether they recognize me.

"We will make Berlin more beautiful than Paris. The Führer has already approved the plans, a combination of French art and triumphant Prussian spirit." He salutes the Headquarters guards as we pass under the huge swastika flag hanging from the Army Headquarters building, and my fingernails scratch my knees.

"Where are we going?"

"To La Coupole, near the border with Belgium, close to Dunkirk where you grew up. It's a small, unimportant village; you probably know the place." And I try to smile; my eyes are fixed on his black gloves while the driver speeds the vehicle through the quiet streets, turning on Opera Avenue towards the exit north of the city.

"Why are we going there?"

"Military matters that wouldn't interest a beautiful companion like you, you will surely enjoy the open nature and the lovely places we will encounter on our way."

"I haven't been there in such a long time."

"I'm sure you'll be happy to return to your childhood places; I have made you a small surprise." He smiles at me.

"Surprise?"

"Don't all women like surprises? But in the meantime, you can sit back and relax; we have a long way to go." He approaches me, and again I feel the smell of eau de cologne from his neck as he takes my hand and places it in his leather-gloved palm.

"Halt!" Ernest's hand quickly touches the driver's shoulder, and my body tilts forward as the vehicle stops, tires screeching.

"Wait here," he tells me and gets out of the vehicle, pulling his firearm out of the leather case, and I start shaking.

What happened? Is it about me? I look back at the road, watching him walking slowly, holding the gun in his hand. Is that the surprise for me? Shall I go out of the car and run away? I have to stop shaking.

A pair of grey ears move between the bushes, and a rabbit begins to run across the road while Oberst Ernest raises his hand holding the gun. I look down and close my eyes.

There is no gunshot, but I can't open my eyes, waiting.

"It managed to escape," he tells the driver as he opens the vehicle door, returning the firearm to the leather case.

"It was close." I hear him speak for the first time.

"I'll catch it next time," he smiles at him, signaling with his hand to start driving.

"We will not give up." The driver turns his head for a moment before pressing the accelerator.

"Did you see how it managed to escape?" He takes my hand again. I have to smile.

"I barely got to see it. I did not know you were hunting."

"The military is a profession; hunting is a hobby that every military man with sharp senses adopts for himself." He looks at me. "Are you cold?"

"No, I'm fine."

"You're cold; you're shaking." And he asks the driver to stop and close the roof before we continue down the narrow road. Occasionally we pass a horse pulling the cart of a local farmer or a military truck, but there are no civilian cars on the road, probably because of the lack of fuel.

"You're silent today."

"Sorry, I apologize."

"I thought you'd enjoy visiting the places of your childhood."

Why does he mention it? Why did I agree to travel with him for a day trip?

"I'm sorry, I'm a little hungry."

"Sorry, what a lack of consideration, we've been traveling for so long and I have not asked you if you had already eaten breakfast." Herr Ernest gives one short command to the driver, and within minutes the vehicle stops at the side of the narrow road, a blanket is pulled out of the trunk, and a picnic basket is placed beside a plowed field.

"The surprise, please join me." Oberst Ernest approaches the vehicle, inviting me to step out, and I watch on all the food arranged just for me on the picnic blanket.

"Is it good for you?"

"The food is delicious, thank you." I watch the fields around us, the ground is waiting for autumn plowing, some trees stand in the distance, and I can feel a pleasant morning breeze. Even though his intentions are good, his gaze makes me nervous, and the meat sandwich gets stuck in my throat, suffocating me.

"Tell me how you got to Paris," he asks, and I finally understand his intention by inviting me to join him. He promised me surprises.

"I thought we would not talk about it." I'm trying to smile at him, but too nervously.

"I thought I would like to know more about a lovely companion joining me on a one-day trip."

"You will not want to hear what happened; it has to do with you, the Germans." But I know I'll have to tell him what happened, this is why he invited me in the first place.

"I would like to hear your story, to know what happened to you."

"It's going to bother you."

"I promise it won't."

"It was three years ago, in the summer, only the wheat had not yet been harvested. The whole field was full of crops." And he looks at me with his green eyes, concentrating on my lips.

"We were running from you." I'm trying to think of the story.

"It was a hot day, the sun was burning my skin, and the road was full of people," I cannot remember the details, his gaze presses me.

"Is that all you remember of your mom and dad?" he asks, and hits his neck, killing a mosquito. What to tell him?

"We were in a neverending convoy," I try to think of Mom and Dad and Jacob, the real ones, not the ones from the story. My eyes close as I concentrate on all the horrible rumors recently coming out about Auschwitz, imagining them walking in front of me in the field, and I start to cry; I miss them so much.

"The road was full of people, and planes came and shot at us, and my father and mother." How did I get to sit for breakfast with a German officer instead of being with my family?

"I'm sorry that happened to you. It shouldn't have happened." He hands me a handkerchief. "I did not know that was what had happened to them."

"You couldn't know." I take the handkerchief from him and wipe my eyes; what happened to them?

"It is terrible what happened to the French people in this war; you shouldn't have declared war on us, forcing us to conquer you. You are such a culture-loving nation; there could be great friendship between us."

"I haven't left Paris since." I return the handkerchief to him. Herr Ernest takes it in silence and continues to look at me.

"And why did you agree to go out with a German officer after all that happened to you?" A feeling of cold surrounds me as the ground drops beneath my feet, what can I tell him?

My fingers tap the picnic blanket nervously.

"I cried for two years. I don't want to cry anymore; I want to live. I want to be on the side that talks about art, the side that has a purpose, I know the Germans are good people and that my parents died by mistake. Mistakes happen in war." Why couldn't I remember the story as I practiced it so many times?

"Yes, mistakes happen in war." Ernest relaxes back and sips the sweet drink, looking at me while nodding.

"Shall we continue on our way?" he suggests, and I relax, getting up and straightening my dress as he signals the driver to approach. "Will you take a picture of us?"

"A little souvenir from a day of fun," he tells me in his quiet voice as we both stand in front of the driver, and I think I've passed his test.

"Smile, he is pointing the camera at us." His hand hugs my waist as he gets me closer, and I feel the softness of the leather glove, which he put on his hand again, ready for the drive to continue.

"Magnificent." He smiles at the driver after he took our photo. "We've almost arrived."

"La Coupole" is written in German on the white road sign, and it is already the third military checkpoint we have passed in the last minutes, each more strict than its predecessors. The soldiers carefully examine us, saluting as they see Oberst Ernest.

"I need you to wait for me here. I have to see something, feel free to walk around," he tells me as the driver parks the vehicle on the side of the road so as not to disturb the concrete trucks that pass us.

"When will you return?"

"It's going to take me about an hour." He smiles at me before disappearing with the driver behind the hill, leaving me by myself in the vehicle.

It's nice to be alone for some time, breathing the free air, lying in the back seat and looking at the clouds in the sky or standing and looking around, searching for something to do with myself; I have an hour.

"TOP SECRET." It is written on the brown cardboard folder placed on the vehicle's front seat, in elegant black writing in the German language, with the stamp of an eagle spreading its wings, holding a swastika in its claws. They must have left it here by mistake as they organized the documents. For a few minutes now, I've been watching it apprehensively.

Although Philip warned me not to risk myself, this is my chance. I can bring him the real material he is so looking for, not just gossip from soldiers in their free time in Paris. My feet carry me around the car, checking that there is no other person or soldier nearby, only the trucks and tiny soldiers are visible in the distance, but they are far away. The trees hide the massive building under construction, and there is no German soldier nearby.

It's now or never. I must take advantage of their mistake, making Philip proud of me at least once; it's no time to be afraid now; all I need is a few minutes. My hand searches for paper and a pencil from my bag.

"What are you doing, what are you writing?"

"Nothing." I quickly get up behind the vehicle and straighten my dress, hiding the papers behind my back; the pencil is left tossed among the weeds.

"Show me that." Oberst Ernest stands in front of me, speaking quietly, the German language coming out of his mouth like a snake's hiss. His driver is standing next to him, holding the brown leather briefcase and binoculars.

"I'm not doing anything, just sitting outside the car."

"What do you have in hand? Show me your hands, both of them."

"It's nothing, just something I was writing."

"I thought we had a great friendship," his mouth whispers the words with a bitter smile as his black hand waits to receive what I'm holding.

My hands reach out to him slowly, handing him the wrinkled papers I hold in my fist.

"What is this?" he asks as he carefully examines the crumpled papers.

"Flowers."

"What are these flower drawings? Nothing is written here."

"Drawings of flowers."

"Why are you drawing flowers?"

"I was bored and delayed, so I got out of the car and sat down in the grass, drawing flowers, I like to draw flowers." Oberst Ernest looks for another moment at the papers gripped in his black leather gloves, and silently returns them to me. While I debate whether to say something, he walks away with the driver following him and turns to him, but I cannot hear their talking. My hand is on my stomach.

On the way back to Paris, everything returns to the way it used to be. Herr Ernest politely gives me a hand to help me get in the car and asks if I'm comfortable. As we turn onto the road towards Paris, he continues to talk about art and the Louvre Palace, and how special it would be to visit it. Still, I have a hard time listening to him and paying attention to the conversation. Most of the time my eyes are on the back of the driver who is driving in silence. What would have happened to me if I had not noticed the open binocular case left under the glove compartment? What would have happened if I had not thought of the grey rabbit that crossed the road?

My stomach hurts, and I try to close my eyes and breathe slowly, imagining what it is like to run through the wood, escaping from the hunter.

"We have arrived." I open my eyes in the darkness to the touch of a leather glove on my cheek, looking at the silhouette of a German officer leaning over me, and I want to scream.

"Mademoiselle Monique, we have arrived, wake up." The German officer whispers to me. It's Oberst Ernest, and I'm inside his military car. From the window, I can notice the Arc de Triomphe standing in the dark above us.

"Give me your hand." I grab his palm and stand in the street, getting used to the streetlights' dim lights, only a few of them shining due to war regulations, and the square deserted in the late hour.

"You were cold, so I covered you with my coat." I slowly look down and examine the heavy coat that covers my body, making me warm, realizing I'm wearing a Nazi German officer's uniform. My fingers slide slowly over the black metal cross close to my chest, feeling the tip of the blades.

"Thank you for taking care of me."

"Thank you so much for a fascinating day." He does not mention a word of what happened at the construction site.

"Thank you." I do not mention it either.

"I would be glad to meet you again."

"I would be glad to be your companion."

His hands grip my neck as he brings my face closer to his lips, pinning them to his. Despite the day's travel, I can still smell the eau de cologne from his cheeks as he pulls me closer while his tongue penetrates my lips.

My hands rest on the sides of my body while his tongue touches mine until he stops, and in the gloom of the evening, I can see him smiling.

"I'm glad we kissed," he says. What does it matter what I answer? He would have done it anyway. He's used to getting what he wants.

"I'm glad we kissed too."

"May I? Please." He raises his hand.

"What?" I ask him, not understanding.

"My military coat, can I have it?"

"Sorry." I take off the coat and hand him the grey-green cloth, feeling the evening's cold.

"Good night, Mademoiselle Monique."

"Good night, Herr Oberst Ernest."

My eyes follow the military vehicle moving down the almost-deserted boulevard, smelling the burnt petrol it's left behind and starting to walk home. The sleepy French policeman who guards the Arc de Triomphe monster follows me with his gaze, but I ignore him, directing my steps towards the single lit streetlight at the alley's end.

I need someone to hug me very much.

I count the stairs down the dirty basement in the Latin Quarter, waiting to hug him. So much has happened since the last time we met, when we kissed, and I'm so ashamed of myself. I kissed a German officer.

Philip stands waiting for me at the bottom of the stairs, as always, but when I approach him and try to hold his hands, he steps back.

"Monique, I apologize for what happened last time; it should not have happened."

I get closer and look at his dark eyes, examining them closely. Are they brown or black?

"I shouldn't have kissed you," he continues to strike me. "It is too dangerous for us; we have a mission to do."

"Yes, we have a mission to do." I turn my back on him and

go to the wooden table, sitting down in the chair, wanting him to stay away from me. I will survive, even without his hug. Philip approaches me and looks for more to say, but I no longer look into his eyes, instead carefully examining the grooves in the old table's wooden surface.

"They're building something big in the north. I don't know what it is."

"Did you hear what I said? We are at war, I'm sorry." He grabs my arm and tries to pull me towards him.

"There are a lot of army checkpoints, a lot of soldiers." I pull my hand away from him and sit down again, not wanting him to touch me.

"It's just not the right time. We're at war." He sits in front of me and places his hands on the table, and I look closely at the black color spots on his fingers, but I don't put my fingers on his.

"A lot of concrete trucks, maybe a big bunker."

"I am not allowed to do what I did. It endangers us and our judgment. Last time never happened."

"And he kept talking to me about art; did your Sorbonne never happen either?"

"You have to forget about the Sorbonne; my Sorbonne belongs to another life, it's not me anymore, now it's me and you here in a shabby basement in the Latin Quarter in an occupied and hungry city."

"He took an interest and asked me about my past." You don't really know what it is to be hungry.

"Did he suspect you? I do not want you to risk yourself." He puts his hands on mine.

"I didn't risk myself, and he doesn't suspect me at all. He treated me very nicely. He is not a poor student." I take my hands off the table.

"Did you see some documents? You need to be careful not to get close to the documents; it might be a trap."

"No, nothing, just the trucks, and one rabbit running across the road."

"I do not want you to get hurt."

"I will not get hurt, I know how to take care of myself, we even took pictures together, he has a picture of both of us. I think you should get me a camera next time we go, so I can take pictures too." At least someone will have a souvenir from me.

"Did you take a picture with him? Why do you need a camera? It's dangerous."

"Because if I had a camera, I could take pictures of the bunker they are building." And also get caught and be executed, maybe that's what happens to one like me who kissed two men. You regret it and say it never happened, and the other is a German officer.

"I'm not bringing you a camera, it's too dangerous. Why did he photograph you?"

"Because he wanted to have a souvenir from our trip, of the one he kissed." Or the one he is trying to hunt.

"Did you kiss him back?" His hand is no longer on the table, he gets up and walks around the room, and I look again at the wooden grooves on the table, examining them carefully.

"You should check what's up there in the north. I think he's a senior commander." And he did not say it was a mistake, as you said. You do not even want to sit at the same table with me.

"You have to be careful of him, he's dangerous."

"We have to take risks, don't we? Aren't we at war?" I get up to go, and he repeats our traditional blessing.

"Take care of yourself."

"Take care of yourself," I answer before turning around and walking away. Slowly I climb the stairs leading out into the street, hating him and those words.

"Take care of yourself, you miserable Frenchie," I repeat the blessing the following nights before I fall asleep, trying to forget what his lips tasted like when he kissed me in the basement that time. It never happened. He will not embrace me anymore. I need to learn to stay away from him.

Invitation

It takes a while until I turn my attention to the next soldier in line, handing him the bag full of cookies, raising my head, looking into his green eyes, and freezing.

"I thought you used to send your assistant." Despite the showcase that separates us, I can smell his eau de cologne.

"I wanted to come and see the place where you work, the place everyone is talking about." He ignores the rudeness of my words while Simone closes the cash register and tries to listen, making herself busy.

"I work here when you don't surprise me." I show him the small space, full of chairs, tables, and cigarette smoke, trying to pull myself together while ignoring Simone as she bends to take something out of the counter but stays close.

"So you don't like to be surprised?"

"Not really."

"I don't like to be surprised either; I think we just found another thing in common." He smiles at me, and I manage to smile back.

"Sorry, Madame," he turns to Simone in French as she rises, smiling at the sight of his many ranks and decorations, as she first noticed him. "Can I borrow Mademoiselle Monique from you? I'd be happy if she could show me around the city."

"She'll be happy to join you." She smiles at him and nods at me to leave, and I turn to remove the apron around my waist, wondering what words Simone will use after I walk out the door. Will she tell Marie that she misses the respectable young French women? Those who can't be found in the city anymore?

"Thank you very much; she will get back to you tomorrow." He thanks Simone while opening the boulangerie door for me, putting his arm around my waist. We both know I am his property, what surprise has he arranged for me today?

"Is everything okay? Why are we getting inside?" I break the silence between us in front of the Tuileries Gardens' gate.

"I have a few hours, and I wanted to spend some time with you." Oberst Ernest stands at the sign to the garden entrance, pinned to the open iron gate: "Entry to Jews is forbidden." Left over from those days when there were still Jews in this city.

"I thought you wanted me to show you the city."

"Isn't this garden a beautiful part of the city?" He crosses the gate and steps inside while his boots crush the white gravel.

"What did you do in the army before you knew me?" I hesitate for a split-second but walk after him into the garden I have not visited in recent years. The round pool at the entrance is empty of water, and no one sits on the green iron chairs. Where did the marble sculptures go?

"I told you before, I do not want to talk about the East, it will not interest you. When I'm with you, I want to talk about Paris and art, not about the war."

"Why me?"

It takes him a while to answer, as if he is trying to think of the right words. Silently we walk in the almost-empty garden, listening to the noise of gravel under our feet.

"Because you are different, you are not like the others."

He folds his hands behind his back, looking at the Louvre Palace's vast expanse. "You are quiet, not loud like Violette or disrespectful like Anaïs, you are not trying to impress me, but you are willing to learn. Maybe you are like the French nation, lying in wait for someone to come and take you. And I'm going to be that someone." He smiles to himself at finding the words he was looking for, stopping and looking at me.

"Am I a symbol for the French nation? Triumph and victory?"

"Don't forget who you are; you were born in German Strasbourg, you are only called French because of a historical insult."

"I never forget who I am." I speak German and French, I also kissed him, and I also lick German boots.

"It's only fair that this palace belongs to us. It fills me with pride." He looks around at the Louvre's enormous wings surrounding us, while I wait patiently by his side.

This time, he does not try to kiss me or even give me a hand. Herr Ernest keeps walking towards the exit from the garden, as if stating that from now on, I belong to him, and I will continue to follow in his footsteps. The marble sculptures of the garden peek at me from the corner by the wall, they were taken out and moved, gathered together and wrapped in sandbags, probably for protection from air bombs, I wonder if they too would like to be somewhere else.

The small gravel is trampled under my shoes at the gate's exit and the sign: "Jews are not allowed."

"Let me invite you for cake on the avenue," he tells me, and I obediently follow.

"Do you like the cake?"

"The cake is delicious; thank you."

I look down at the plate in front of me, filled with a slice of sweet cake made of real sugar, careful not to raise my eyes to the avenue and the people passing us. Oberst Ernest leans back as he watches me, savoring a glass of champagne from a chilled bottle which stands in special silverware beside the table. Why has no one taught me how to behave with a man who invites me to champagne?

"You need to wear bright dresses; it will suit you."

"Thank you; I'll try."

"Since when do you draw flowers? Like then, on our trip?" He mentions that day for the first time, and I tense up.

"Ever since I was little."

"In Paris?"

"Yes."

"I thought you grew up in Strasbourg."

"I grew up in Strasbourg, but I received my first drawing notebook from Paris, Dad bought it for me in Paris, on one of his work trips." I carefully bite the cake, trying to stay calm. I must not make such a stupid mistake again, ever.

"To your flower drawings." He raises the glass in my honor, and I smile, tapping my glass against his, hoping he has not noticed my trembling fingers.

"Halt." Herr Ernest shout-whispers as he leaps from his chair, and I freeze in my seat. All the people in the café stop talking and look at us. Only the sound of a fork falling on the sidewalk breaks the silence, disturbed by the sound of Ernest's spiked boots.

"Halt!" He walks and places his hand on the back of a man who is walking down the street. The man stops and looks at him with a surprised look.

"What did you do?" Oberst Ernest stands above him, getting closer to the man's face.

"I didn't do anything," the man answers him in a weeping voice.

"Apologize to the lady." He leads him with his head lowered, slapping him on the floor at my feet.

"Apologize to the lady for spitting on the sidewalk."

"I apologize." He cries at my feet, and I look down but

close my eyes so as not to see him and burst into tears.

"Do you accept the apology?"

Yes, I nod to Herr Ernest.

"Get out of here, filthy Frenchman." He picks him up by the back of his head and pushes him from the table area back into the street. The man walks away quickly, not looking back, and my gaze follows him until he disappears among the passersby, becoming a blur.

Only then do I let my eyes wander around, seeing all the people who have been watching us start talking again. The waiters are running once more between the tables, and the noise of conversation fills the air. Even the small crowd that gathered on the street disappears as if it never happened.

"I apologize for what happened." Oberst Ernest sits back in his chair, picking his officers' hat up off the floor and placing it back on the table, where it was before everything started.

"Nothing happened," I manage to say something, looking at the sugar cake on my plate.

"They should be taught the meaning of respect." He looks around, and all the people of the café stop their stolen glances in our direction, returning to their small talk.

"I forgave him; he did not mean to."

"Do you like the cake?"

"Yes, very much, thank you." How can he think of the cake now?

"We didn't propose a toast properly." Herr Ernest again raises his glass in the air, and we tap our glasses again, before I bring the glass to my lips, drinking it all and ignoring the bitter taste of champagne.

Towards the evening he accompanies me down the avenue as I stare at the sidewalk, strolling beside him.

"I live in a hotel. Unfortunately, it is not appropriate for me to invite a companion to visit my room." I nod in silence and breathe a sigh of relief.

"But I would love to meet you again." He holds my neck and brings me closer to a kiss. His lips touch mine again, and his tongue penetrates my mouth before he says goodbye to me and I turn back home, hating myself a little more, the smell of eau de cologne staying in my nose.

The key's sound is the only noise I hear when I enter the dark apartment, passing through the dim living room and climbing into my attic. Lizette told me she would be out, and I am left with my private darkness within the four walls and the simple iron bed.

"Dear God," the words of prayer are carried as I lie in bed and look at the black ceiling, "please turn everything back; please turn all that has happened into a bad dream. Please return me to my house; I promise I will not quarrel with Mom anymore when she asks me to keep an eye on Jacob, please. I promise to be the best I can be."

But the next morning, I wake up in the same attic, without Mom's voice hurrying me to go stand in line for bread, and Lizette asks me if I'll drink coffee with her after I'm done tidying up the house. And I do not hear the sounds of Jacob's laughter and Dad reading the newspaper, explaining to Mom that even though the situation is tense, no war will break out.

The autumn rain does not stop on my way to work, wetting the fallen leaves on the street. And the Nazi flag on Rivoli Street, at the German headquarters, drips a trickle of cold water on my head as I cross the grey street below.

He is no different from the others when he enters the boulangerie in his grey-green uniform. He closes the door behind him and shakes his coat from the raindrops that have been falling since the morning, looking for me with his eyes, like many others.

"Mademoiselle Monique?" He turns to me, ignoring Simone and her disapproving looks.

"Yes, that's me." My eyes look at him in surprise; how does he know my name?

"This is a present from Herr Oberst Ernest." He places a package wrapped in purple tissue paper on the counter, clicking his boots as if preparing to salute me, and turns and leaves the store, gently closing the door behind him.

"Who is it from?" Simone asks and approaches me, as if to make it clear that she is in charge here and that I have to get her approval before taking the package from the courier, even though she was standing next to me and heard what the soldier said.

"From him." I'm trying to calm myself.

"And what's in the package?"

"I don't know." I hold it tightly in my hands, afraid she will snatch it and tear away the paper, determined to find out what present I've received from a German officer.

"Then open it."

My hands begin to unravel the white ribbon that envelops the package; my smile makes me feel guilty.

"Are you opening it?"

What has he sent me? And what if it's an intimate item, as I saw that time in the window of the shop with Violette? I hurry to the back room, sitting in the corner on a wooden crate where no one can see. What if he expects something from me? With a trembling hand, I remove the purple tissue paper, feeling its delicacy between my fingers.

"Marie, please call Monique, decent French women should not receive a foreign man's gift." But I ignore her.

My hands grip the fancy notebook, wrapped in a hardcover of black leather with the curved letter 'E' engraved, and I can feel it as I run my finger over the smooth leather.

"Monique, there's a customer."

I open the notebook and hold the white note, written in rounded handwriting.

"To Monique,

Have a diary to draw as many flowers as you wish.
I would be happy if you would join me on a two-day trip to Normandy two weeks from today, keeping me company, including an overnight stay at a hotel.

Herr Oberst Ernest."

"Monique, the customer is waiting."

I look at the note for another moment before I return it between the diary pages, shove it into my bag that hangs on the hanger behind the door, and hurry back to my place by the counter.

On the way home I stroll, wanting to get wet in the rain, feeling I deserve to suffer. Why did I smile more than I did on my birthday two years ago? When I received a box of chocolate from Mom?

Again Lizette is not there, and the house is empty, and I step into the cold attic. What does Oberst Ernest expect me to do? Is it that thing I'm so afraid of?

"What do you expect me to do?" I yell at Philip a few days later.

"I expect you to do your best," he answers me angrily as he gets up from the chair, moving it rudely.

"I promise to do my best," I answer him, and look at the simple cardboard notebook that lies between us on the wooden table, wondering why we started fighting at all.

I did not plan to hug him as I went down the stairs to the basement, I promised myself I'd get over him, but my hands couldn't stop themselves. I embraced his body, holding on so tightly and smelling his body odor, mixed with the smell of gun oil, unable to release him.

"Just one moment," I whispered to him, "I know we must not." And he hugs me in silence, enfolding my back with his hands, and stroking me gently.

"I brought you something," he whispers to me, and I hug him even harder.

"One more moment."

"Just to let you know, they liked the information you gave us the previous time." He keeps stroking me, and I can't stop clinging to his warm body, feeling my whole body like electricity; what are these feelings?

"Who wants me to know?" I'm thinking about his fingers caressing my back.

"The ones who got the information. We must stop; we said it never happened." And I release my hands and back up; it never happened again.

"Can I start my report now?" He doesn't even want to hug me from time to time.

"I brought you something." He pulls out a simple cardboard notebook, placing it on the table.

"What is it?"

"It's a regular notebook. You can write down secret information there. I'll teach you how to hide it between ordinary words so that whoever reads it will not understand that there is information hidden in it." Why is he moving away from me?

The notebook is on the table between us, wrapped in a rough cardboard cover, and rubbed in the corners as if used by someone else before me. Still, I dare not ask, although when I open it, I can see that several pages have been torn from it, and no greeting note is written on the first page.

"Thanks." Shall I tell him about the gift I received from Oberst Ernest?

"He wants to take me with him to Normandy."

"Who, your officer?" And I nod in silence and try to get closer to him, but Phillip walks away from me, sitting down in the wooden chair, looking at me.

"It's a good sign that he trusts you." That's all he says, why isn't he telling me something else?

"What should I do? Tell me what to do."

"You have to go with him," he answers me in a distant voice.

"I'll go with him. I have no choice."

"Maybe I really need to get you a camera so that you can take some pictures."

"Then bring me a camera." I stand up and get ready to go; please stop me from going.

"I apologize; I didn't mean what I said." Philip also stands up and looks at me, but I look aside and panic.

For a moment, it seemed to me that the silhouette of Oberst Ernest was standing in the dark corner of the cellar, watching us, wearing his green-grey uniform with the Iron Cross on his chest.

"What happened?" Philip turns around quickly, his hand already holding the grip of his firearm, ready to pull it out.

"For a moment, I got scared by the pile of pipes in the corner." And Philip looks at me again, his hands releasing his grip on his firearm.

"I worry about you." He softens his voice.

"What do you expect me to do?" I yell at him, still thinking about the basement corner.

"I expect you to do your best," Philip yells at me back.

"I promise to be the best I can be." My hands grip the simple notebook lying on the table between us, and I toss it towards him. "I already have one notebook, from the one who reads me poetry."

"From him?" he asks quietly, and gently grabs the old notebook, stroking it with his fingers.

"It doesn't matter."

And all this time, Oberst Ernest continues to stand in the corner, watching me while his green eyes twinkle under his officers' hat's visor.

"Let's go back and sit."

"I have to go. Get me a camera, that's how I'll be the best I can be."

He's trying to catch and hug me, but I cannot feel his touch when I keep imagining Oberst Ernest watching us. I have to get out of here; I hate this basement.

"Monique, I did not mean it; don't leave angry," I hear him say as I climb the stairs, and I regret that I told him about Oberst Ernest's gift, but I can't return to pick up the old notebook. I also did not tell him that we were going for two days; what would I do when Oberst Ernest wants me to get into his bed?

"Monique, I care about you." He runs up the stairs after me and hugs me tightly, but after a moment, I release his warm hands, continuing on my way out into the alley. He will not be able to understand.

"You probably can't help me with that."

"Come to me if you ever need help," she'd told me one of the times the three of us walked together, standing at Pont des Arts and watching the river flow leisurely beneath us.

"I will," I'd answered her at that time, not believing it would happen. What was she thinking of me, I thought while looking at her with combined feelings of reluctance and admiration. My gaze followed her as she leaned against the metal railing and blew the cigarette smoke upwards, ignoring the judgmental looks of passersby towards a smoking woman.

"You might learn something," she'd added, throwing the cigarette into the green-grey river.

And even though I feel that she was disrespecting me, I have no other choice, and I leave the boulangerie in the middle of the day, promising Simone I won't take long. I'm not sure Violette can help me, and I'm ashamed to ask Lizette, so I find myself walking down the main avenue near the Gallery Lafayette store, looking up at the fancy building numbers, searching for her workplace.

"Please wait here," the girl at reception orders while checking my simple dress, making me feel like a maid who happened to be here and would soon be expelled in disgrace.

"Don't pay attention to her." Anaïs arrives and grabs my arm, taking me to a room at the back. "Distinguished ladies from Germany came to our fashion house to buy the autumn collection, and she doesn't want them to feel like they're in the ordinary world." And I do not know if she is trying to encourage me or again insult and patronize me.

The back room is loaded with rolls of colorful fabrics in shades of cream, red and black, and when we are silent, I can hear the conversation in the next room with the German buyer looking for an evening gown for prom.

"She is the wife of a senior officer," Anaïs whispers to me in a contemptuous tone, "She came here specially, from Berlin. In a few days, he will take her to a concert at the opera wearing a dress we sewed for her, and she has no idea that her husband brought his mistress here a week ago, buying her several dresses."

"I don't want to disturb you at work."

"You are not disturbing me; there are so many seamstresses around her that they will not notice I've disappeared for a few minutes. They are hovering around all the time, 'Frau' and 'Frau' and 'Frau,' showing her one dress after another."

"Shhhh... they will hear us."

"Do not worry, they are full of admiration for the suspenders that are in fashion again this year; soon they will sell her a new morning dress."

"Don't you like them?"

"I like them a lot. They are providing work to Anaïs and access to fashionable clothes." She smiles as she takes a pack of cigarettes out of her work apron pocket and lights one for herself, not before offering one to me, but I refuse.

"So why did you come to visit?" She blows the smoke and looks at me. "You probably did not just come to talk or see a new outfit." And again, I do not know if she is towering over me.

"Herr Oberst Ernest."

"What about him?"

"I think he expects something from me."

"What?"

"Well... that thing." I approach and whisper to her. "I think he wants it."

"Getting into your panties?"

"I think." I can feel I am blushing.

"I think you're too innocent for all these things."

"I don't know what to do."

"And why did you come to me?" She blows the smoke again up, enjoying humiliating me a little more.

"Because I do not know who to ask, and I thought maybe you know." Why am I blushing?

"Anaïs will teach you." She smiles and grabs my hand, taking me with her through the reception down the marble stairs to the street, ignoring the receptionist who asks her where she is going.

"First of all, you need classy lingerie." She critically looks at me as she reviews my simple dress, alluding to the underwear I'm wearing, while we both stand outside a fancy store of bras and panties.

"Wait," I hold her hand, preventing her from entering the

store and embarrassed of myself. "What should I do with him? Shall I refuse him? Agree? What do you do when…?"

"You're so innocent," she looks at me with pity before she takes my hand and enters the store with me. "Do you really think you can refuse him?"

After we leave the store, she takes me to a café; I think it's out of pity, and I try not to think about the delicate feeling of the bra and the garter belt, the ones the saleswoman measured on me in the store.

"Does it feel good?" I finally find the courage to come up with the question that scares me.

"Sometimes it's pleasant, and sometimes it's not," she answers me honestly, "but it should not be pleasant, it should serve your goals."

"And what are my goals?"

"Let him be satisfied; if he is satisfied, he will give you what you want."

"And how do I know what to do?"

"Don't worry, he already knows, you're probably not his first." And I blush again.

"Is that how all men are?"

"Yeah, everyone's like that, they just want one thing," she answers me indifferently. What about Philip? Has he already gotten into other girls' panties? Does he even care about me?

"And what about you? Doesn't it bother you?"

"Doesn't what bother me?"

"To be with him when he is a..." And I cannot finish the sentence.

"German?"

Yes, I nod. "Doesn't that worry you?"

"Anaïs has to take care of Anaïs," she places the coffee on the table and continues talking, showing me at a glance all the German officers sitting around us eating and drinking in the magnificent café, which overlooks the Opera House. "No one asked me whether to start this war, and no one asked me how I was going to get food, so no one should ask me what I am going to do to survive."

I try to sip my coffee, but it tastes bitter to me, even though it's real.

"Do not worry," she puts her hand on mine, "you will be fine. Wear what you bought, lie on your back and let him do the work, everything will be fine."

"Yeah, I'll let him get into my panties." I bring my head closer to her and whisper, trying to speak bluntly and sound mature, but the words sound ugly to me.

"Just like that." She smiles at me, and also at two German officers sitting at a nearby table, looking at us with interest.

"What took you so long?" Simone asks me as I walk through the glass door, looking hostile at the shopping bag I'm trying to hide behind my back. "You said you were going out for a few minutes."

"I apologize, I had to help a friend with a difficult problem."

I will apologize to him for the last time; I need him to hold me before the two-day trip.

The guards on the Pont Neuf bridge ignore me as I pass on my way to the Latin Quarter. I need him to promise me that he will forgive what I intend to do, and never ask me about it.

I'm almost running into his arms, lowering my eyes so as not to stumble on that broken step right in front of the basement entrance. But when my eyes return to look for him, I stop abruptly, trying to walk leisurely again like a young woman.

Philip stands in his same position as always, his body ready to jump towards any noise, but his arms are on his hips, and he does not approach me.

"Monique, meet Robert." He introduces the man standing next to him.

I reach out my hand, embarrassed by his unexpected presence, and tries to breathe as usual. Why is he here? Why today?

"Nice to meet you, Monique."

"Nice to meet you, Robert."

"Sit down," Philip instructs me, and remains standing as the stranger sits in front of me, looking at me for a moment with interest and appreciation. Where to place my hands? On the table? Who is he anyway? What was his name? He's older than the two of us, about thirty years old; what is that brown leather bag hanging over his shoulder?

"Does she know that they will execute her if they catch her?" He turns to Philip standing next to him, keeping distance from me.

"Yes, she knows."

"And she still wants to do it?"

"She asked."

"Are you sure about that?" He finally turns to me, and I'm not sure what exactly he means by that.

"Yes, I'm sure."

"Well," he sighs and opens the leather bag which rests on his shoulder, pulling out a small metal box with buttons and a glass lens, placing it on the table between us. I reach out, and for the first time in my life, I'm holding a camera.

"Carefully, pick it up carefully." He speaks as my fingers glide over the magic of black metal and golden buttons.

"This is a Leica camera, small and compact, the best in the market. There is no substitute for the Germans when it comes to cameras." He sighed, and my fingernails gently scratched the eagle with the swastika engraved on the camera's iron body, feeling reluctant and nauseous. I have to put it back on the table, but I can't; I can't withdraw now, after he arranged a camera for me.

"Now listen, and listen well," Robert demands my attention, "there is no room for mistakes." And in the next minutes, he explains to me about photography, explaining the buttons, how to aim and where to click, what is a film, and how to load it, forcing me to stand and practice.

"You have to aim fast and shoot fast; you have to practice sliding the camera into a hiding place in your bag. You should also have a cover story, at least a basic one, although it won't help you if a German soldier catches you."

He keeps talking to me fluently as I stand in the small basement and turn the camera on, looking at Philip through the viewfinder, pressing the button, and getting used to the noise of the camera shutter opening and closing. Throughout all this time, Philip stands motionless in the room's gloom, looking at Robert and me, not intervening or uttering a word. He trusts me, I can no longer disappoint him, even though I want to change my mind about the whole thing. What did I bring down on myself?

"Monique, you can still change your mind; this camera could be your death sentence." Robert stops me when the tutorial is over, and I hold the camera and understand that it is my most precious possession from now on.

"Monique, you can still back out."

I'm trying to figure out how to hide it in my side bag and looking at Philip. What does he expect me to do? His dark eyes look at me from a distance. Why did I yell at him last time?

"I know it's dangerous," I answer Robert and shove the camera into the bag, trying to give my voice a tone of confidence, but my body trembles with fear. What happens if I fail or make a mistake? Will I let him down? What will happen if they catch me? Why does Robert not leave us alone?

Although I thanked him twice, he stayed to talk to us about cameras and photography, telling us that now he must only take pictures in secret and that he misses the days when he walked the streets and just photographed people.

'Go already,' I whisper to him over and over in my heart, but he does not hear as time goes by, and in the end I have no choice, and I have to say goodbye to them, feeling sad for leaving.

"Take care of yourself," Philip tells me with distant politeness, and Robert joins in too.

"Take care of yourself."

One tear flows from my eyes as I walk out into the narrow alley and look around. I could not apologize to him. The hug will have to wait for next time, if there will be a next time.

Normandy

Despite the coat I'm wearing, the cold of autumn makes me tremble as I wait for Herr Ernest in Place de l'Étoile, shifting my body weight from foot to foot and rubbing my hands.

The Arc de Triomphe monument standing above makes me feel that every time I stand like this in the square, waiting for the German car, the figures engraved on the marble monument despise me more, judging me with tormented looks.

The grey car arrives just in time for me, and Oberst Ernest gets out of it quickly, even ahead of the driver who hurries to open the door for me and stand up straight on the sidewalk.

"Let me." Oberst Ernest takes the travel bag I am holding in my hands, caresses my arm for a moment, and does not forget to compliment me on the dress I am wearing, the one Lizette helped me choose.

The night before, we'd packed the bag together for the two-day trip; I looked in the closet, and Lizette volunteered to help. I'd folded the clothes with a shaking hand, trying not to talk or lie to her.

"Did your girlfriend invite you to come sleep with her tomorrow after work?"

"Yes, she wants us to go out."

"Only one night?"

"Yes."

"And you love him?" She feels I'm not telling the truth.

"Yes."

"So why are you so worried?"

If only I could tell her, or change the characters, I was looking for the right words, but the fear that I'd slip up made me silent, as I tried to fold the same shirt over and over again.

"Give it to me." She smiled and took the bright button shirt from my hand. I did not want to hurt her; she was so important to me; she did not deserve it.

What will I do when Oberst Ernest tries to do it with me? Maybe I can imagine Philip in his place? My fingers tremble as I fold the white lace underwear, carefully placing it at the bottom of the bag over a pair of silk tights, which are so rare because of the war. Anaïs handed them to me. "A gift from me," she'd whispered as she entered the boulangerie for a moment, taking me into a corner and ignoring Simone's gaze. "A woman should look her best." She giggled and placed the soft bundle in my palm, and I had no choice but to thank her and quickly tuck them into my apron pocket, trying not to think what they were meant for.

Occasionally, when the boulangerie was empty of German soldiers, I put my hand in my pocket, feeling the delicate silk in my fingers and trying to ignore the dull pain in the bottom of my stomach.

Everything would be okay, I tried to convince myself, but the inconvenience continued even in the evening as we packed the bag by candlelight. Lately, the power outages in the city have been increasing.

"Take this dress; it's going to fit you." She pulled a warm grey dress out of my closet for the ride.

"How did you know when it was the right time?" I'd held the dress and checked myself in front of the mirror.

"I didn't know; you can never know when it's the right time."

"So when did you decide?"

"I didn't decide, I wanted to," she paused for a moment and lowered her head, "but I wanted it to be special for us, I wanted us to wait until we got married, I thought we should create a moment for us to remember forever.

But he had to join the army; there is always a war or something to fight about. So I told him we'd wait until he came back. Here, that skirt will suit you, too." She put on a dark burgundy skirt, and I thought of the man in the picture waiting for the right moment, so sorry for the last time, for the arrival of Robert, for not kissing him, for not waiting a few more minutes, even though it was already late.

"Do not be sad," Lizette put her hand on my arm, "it's just one story of an old woman, your man is waiting for you, you should be happy."

While the grey-blue vehicle heads its way west along the Seine river, Oberst Ernest notices that I'm cold despite the coat on my body, and instructs the driver to stop at the side of the road to close the tarpaulin roof. Quietly I sit in the car and look up at the tarpaulin, slowly closing us into the gloom.

"Now you will be more pleasant."

"Thank you; I love autumn."

"I like the grey color too. I told you we are alike." He smiles at me, and I smile back, concentrating on the big trees. Their yellow leaves are falling on the wet road, and I try to ignore his hand wrapped in his black glove, resting on my thighs.

"I brought you the poetry book you love, for the evening at the hotel."

"Thank you; I'd enjoy listening to you."

"I want this evening to be perfect, a moment that you will remember forever."

"Me too."

"On the way, I have to stop at a few places, check some things, military subjects; you'll have to wait for me."

"I'll be fine."

"Did you bring the diary I gave you?"

"Yes, thank you, it's beautiful. I haven't yet had time to thank you."

"You can draw flowers, as many as you like."

"Yes, thank you, I will." Will you also take the binoculars with you this time?

Oberst Ernest goes on to talking about the wonderful French wine, telling me about a new crate of bottles he's received especially from Bordeaux, and about the bottle he especially brought for tonight. I smile at him, putting my palm in his hand and thinking of all the women who crowded in line outside the grocery store in the Latin Quarter a few days ago. They were whispering that a shipment of flour had arrived while they waited patiently, hoping it would not end before it was their turn.

"You're quiet today."

"I'm looking at the river view, look at how beautiful it is."

"But today you are especially quiet."

"I thought you liked that about me."

"I liked that, but I would like to know more about you."

"What more would you like to know?"

"I'll be happy to know what's on your mind right now." His palm is still on my thighs as if guarding me, where can I run?

"I'm thinking about the grey clouds ahead of us," I point my head at the grey mass in the sky that awaits us above the horizon. "I hope it doesn't rain."

"Soon we will reach the seashore; you will love the open sea."

The autumn wind constantly shakes the bushes and weeds on the dirt road, which curves to the seashore. On our way from the nearest village, we pass two army checkpoints which block the beach for the local fishermen, and on either side of the road there are barbed wire fences and concrete bunkers from which machine guns peek out.

"They might come from here," Herr Ernest tells me once as I look out over the trenches, making myself calm and holding the side of the vehicle shaking on the dirt road.

"Why did you stop?" Oberst Ernest asks the driver who slowly slides the vehicle onto the road.

"Look." The driver nods at a brown rabbit standing peacefully among the bushes.

"It's time," Ernest whispers to him, "this time he is mine." Quietly he gets out of the car, and I turn my head to the other side and close my eyes tightly, waiting for the shot to come. But even though I'm ready, my whole body shakes when I hear the sound of gunfire, and I have to stop myself from screaming, leaving my eyes closed.

"Great hunting." I hear his voice and open my eyes, trying to look at the distant sea and ignore Oberst Ernest, who proudly shows the driver the brown, dirty red lump of fur.

"He is big." The driver admires the trophy.

"Yes, we will give it as a gift to the cook at the outpost; he will make lunch out of it." He laughs and sits next to me, slamming the door and signaling for the driver to drive. I can smell the blood.

"Did you see?" He asks me.

"I could not look." What does he expect me to say?

"Hunting is not for women," he puts his gloved hand back on my thighs, and I imagine the lump of fur lying next to the driver and his hand touching it, feeling nauseous.

"Here's the beach and the sea you love so much," he shows me as the driver continues on the winding path towards the scarred sand, striped with barbed wire fences and jagged iron pillars that extend into the stormy sea and the grey waves hitting the shore.

"Heil Hitler." I hear the loud call from the line of soldiers waiting for us in a parade, shouting when the vehicle stops in front of a large grey concrete bunker.

"Would you like to wait for me in the car? Or you can go for a walk around, draw some flowers in your notebook," he asks me as the local commander approaches and stands politely away from the vehicle, waiting for Oberst Ernest to put on his officer's hat and say goodbye.

"Can I go around and draw?"

"Yes, but do not approach the edge of the cliff or try to go down to the sea." He nods at the beach dotted with barbed wire fences.

"I will stay away from the sea; thank you." I tighten the coat around my body and get away from the vehicle, turning my back to the driver who shows the lump of fur to the soldiers. What did the rabbit think as it ate grass? Did it know that its fate was sealed?

"What are you doing?"

He is wearing a German soldier uniform, standing above me on the mound, watching with interest as I bend over and hold the camera, trying to quickly shoot a battery of cannons that are well-camouflaged and hidden inside a concrete bunker, dominating the beach.

"I'm taking a picture."

"Photography is not allowed here, who are you?"

I am a young woman who is soon going to end her life with severe torture because she was stupid, arrogant, and careless. My legs are shaking, and I want to scream, or start running and throw myself on the barbed wire fences surrounding the cliff overlooking the sea.

"I'm a photographer for SIGNAL, your army magazine, do you know it? So I'm allowed," I answer him in perfect German as I get up, trying to smile my most peaceful smile at him, praying he doesn't notice my trembling legs.

"Really? So why were you bending over?"

"How much can you photograph army stuff? Sometimes I also want to photograph flowers, come and see." And he lowers the barrel of the rifle which was pointed in my direction, hanging it over his shoulder, and approaches me suspiciously. I can smell his strong body odor mixed with the stench of cigarettes and sweat.

"It's beautiful. You have talent." He admires the drawings in my diary, speaking in poor German.

"Thanks."

"Where are you from?"

"Now Paris, before that Berlin, where are you from?"

Please let him be from another city.

"Now Normandy, before that Gdańsk."

"You were not born in Germany?"

"No, I'm Polish, I was recruited by force, they needed soldiers, and Slava needed food and cigarettes. It's always better to be on the winning side."

"Always better."

"Want one?" He offers me a simple cigarette, smiling toothlessly.

"No thanks." I smile at him; I have to get out of here.

"Wait here, don't move." He turns his back to me, disappearing beyond the mound, and my legs are trembling again; what to do? Where can I escape?

"Here, now take a picture." Slava returns, standing in front of me, trying to tuck his shirt into his pants and arrange his uniform while holding a bunch of wildflowers he just picked.

"Watch out for the barbed wire fences on the cliff; there are mines there." He salutes me goodbye with his toothless smile, leaving me alone among the hills, holding a bunch of wildflowers in my hand and sweating under my dress, despite the autumn wind.

"Monique, where are you? " I hear Ernest's call among the sandy mounds, and I freeze in place; this time, I pushed too hard. The camera is in my hand, and my little bag has been left behind, along with the open diary.

"Monique." I can hear him getting closer.

"Don't come here."

"Monique."

"Don't come here." How do I release the film? What did he explain to me in the basement? Which button to press?

"What are you doing?"

"What every woman should sometimes do in private." Is that the button? Now turn the knob? I'm not sure anymore, is that what he explained to me? I have to hurry.

"Are you alright?"

"Yes, I'm fine, please don't come here." Here, that knob, now take the film out of the camera, where's the release button? Please don't slip out of my hands; it's stuck, by force, release it already.

"I'm waiting for you here."

"Thanks, I'm already done." What to do with the film? Where to hide it? And what about the camera?

"Are you okay? You should not have gone so far; there are minefields around here, I started worrying about you." Herr Ernest approaches me as he holds my bag in his hand, looking politely to the side, as I step out from behind a bush and arrange my dress.

"I looked at your diary; I hope you don't mind." He hands me my bag and the open diary. "I enjoy them."

"Do you like them?"

"Are you okay? Your hands are dirty from the ground."

"Yeah, I'm fine, I stumbled when I climbed the hill, it's nothing." I rub my hands together and take the bag and the diary from his hands while smiling at him, hoping he won't notice that I'm sweating. The film's metal box is scratching my thighs, buried inside my panties.

"Have you finished your military things here? Are we going to the car?"

"You shouldn't have gone so far, it's dangerous, I'm done here, now we'll go to the hotel, it's already getting late."

On the dirt road back from the beach to the quiet village, Oberst Ernest and the driver are reminded of the rabbit. With shouts of 'Schnell, Schnell' the driver accelerates on the white road, chasing an imaginary rabbit. While Oberst Ernest smiles at me, I'm smiling back, thinking of the German camera which remains under a bush on the shores of Normandy, covered in a bit of dirt which I was able to stack with my palms.

"Are you excited about tonight?" he asks me. "I booked us a table for dinner."

My fingers gently hold the pink napkin as I wipe my lips and place it in the corner of the table.

"Did the meal taste good to you?"

"The meal was delicious, thank you."

"Shall we go upstairs?"

"Can we take a walk on the promenade by the sea?"

"It's dark outside and cold, don't you want us to go up? The room is waiting for us."

"I'll be happy to take a walk."

While we are leaving the dining room of the luxurious

hotel, I turn around and look back. All the tables are full of high-ranking German officers, accompanied by women like me; maybe Herr Ernest will see a fellow officer here who will be glad to start a conversation?

"Shall we go?"

The clerk at reception hurries to bring my coat at the sight of Oberst Ernest's hand, and I give a last look at the warm dining room, heading outside.

The cold wind on the promenade surprises me as we walk side by side silently, and I'm trying to hug myself, keep distant from him.

"Are you cold?"

"No, I like the winter wind."

We are the only ones along the dark beach, whether because of the winter or the war. Here, too, barbed wire fences stretch along the Black Coast, and only the sound of the waves can be heard in the distance.

"Heil Hitler," a guard emerges alert from a guard station, but when he notices Ernest's ranks, he stands still and salutes, ignoring me.

"Heil Hitler," Ernest answers him and releases him to his concrete shelter, leaving us alone again on the deserted windy boardwalk.

"Shall we go back to the hotel?" Herr Ernest asks after a few minutes. "The bottle of wine I brought is waiting for us in the room."

"Yes, let's go back to the hotel." My time has come.

The silk pantyhose repeatedly slips from my thighs as I try to close the garter buckle on it, getting tangled with my trembling fingers.

"Shall I pour you the wine?" I can hear Oberst Ernest from the bedroom.

"Yes, please."

I also don't like the white lace underwear, and I blush when I try to arrange it so that I am more comfortable, avoiding looking at myself in the mirror in the dim light of the bathroom lamp.

"Can you please light candles?"

"But this hotel has electricity."

"Please."

"The wine is waiting for us."

"I'll be out in a minute."

I hope he doesn't notice my hesitant steps, or my unsteady hand holding the wine glass, trying to sip it in one gulp and feeling a drop land on my white lingerie, probably leaving a red stain on it.

"You are so beautiful; I was waiting for you. Come closer to me; it will not hurt."

Philip, I'll think of Philip. I have memorized that dozens of times in the last days, but no matter how hard I try, Philip has disappeared from my thoughts into the darkness of the basement of the Latin Quarter. All I can think of now is a woman lying on her back in a fancy hotel room on the big bed, moaning from pain and his body weight.

That's it; I'm a French prostitute who has slept with a German officer.

A Puppet
End of November 1943

Secret

II/23/I943

From: Western Front Wehrmacht Command

To: Army Group France

Subject: Preparations for the winter

Background: Russian forces intend to launch a winter offensive in the east.

General: On the Führer s orders, all forces in occupied countries are to supply food from local resources.

Task:

I. Collect food and other supplies to maintain an adequate standard of living for the army units throughout the Paris area.

2. It is the army officers responsibility to take care of any shortages that may arise from local sources.

SS. Telegram 64I

The eighth arrondissement, the mistress on the fourth floor

"You were perfect this morning, dear, as always," Herr Ernest tells me after a few minutes, as I'm catching my breath. My eyes are fixed on the chandelier hanging on the bedroom ceiling, waiting for him to kiss me once on my cheek before he gets up and goes to his clothes, to get dressed.

"I enjoyed it too." My hand pulls the blanket up to cover myself once I am free of his body weight and can breathe freely. Even though he knows my body, I still make sure to hide my nakedness from his eyes whenever I can.

Whenever he arrives at the apartment, he leaves his uniform carefully folded on the chair by the bed before approaching me. But first, he places his army boots next to the dark wooden legs of the seat, leaving them standing as if they were two black Doberman dogs waiting for their master to return, alertly watching me the whole time we are together.

"I brought you some cans of corned meat."

"Thanks."

"And next time, I'll try to get some coffee. I saw you're out."

"Yes, I'm out."

Despite the cold in the bedroom, Herr Ernest dresses slowly, paying attention to every detail as he stands in front of the mirror hanging on the wall, tucking his shirt into his pants, and examining the medals on his chest.

"Aren't you cold? I'll make sure someone brings you new firewood."

"Thanks, but I'm fine."

"I do not want you to catch a cold."

"Would you like me to make you some coffee?"

"No, I'm in a hurry." He arranges his belt. "The wine you served last night…"

"What about it?"

"Is it the Château Lafite-Rothschild 1934 bottle I brought last week?"

"Is it okay that I opened the bottle? You did not tell me you wanted to keep it."

"No, it's okay, It's an excellent wine. I'll take care of a few more bottles."

"That will be great."

Herr Ernest bends down to put his boots on, and I hurry out of bed, covering my naked body with the pink silk robe I'd received as a gift, bending at his feet on the parquet floor. The tips of his spiked boots accidentally hit my thigh, hurting me for a moment as I help him force his foot into the neatly polished black boots, but I bite my lip. He never means to.

"Thank you, the robe suits you."

"Thank you."

"I booked tickets for the opera in three days. There will be a Wagner concert."

"I love Wagner, I'll enjoy walking together. I've never been to the opera."

He always informs me in advance, so I will have time to prepare for our meetings, making sure not to surprise me. Even when he arrives early in the morning for a quick visit, he usually sends the driver or his assistant to the boulangerie the day before, letting me know so I will be ready for him.

"I want you to buy yourself a dress for the evening." He pulls his black leather wallet out of his military jacket pocket, placing a few banknotes on the mahogany dresser.

"It's for the dress," he smiles at me, "I know you cannot afford to buy something fancy."

"Thanks." I smile back and walk him to the door.

By the entrance, I hold his grey-green coat while he brings the leather briefcase from the study, the room I am not allowed to enter.

"Thank you for an enjoyable evening. We will meet in three days, I will come to pick you up."

And with those words, I help him fasten his coat, button after button, arranging the leather bag strap over his shoulder before he heads out into the cold stairwell. When I hear his steps going down, I imagine the neighbor from the third floor peeking through the peephole of the door, examining Oberst Ernest on his way out. I know she's cursing me.

I keep my ear against the thick wooden door, listening to the sound of his hobnail boots going down the wooden stairs until I hear the noise of the metal door slamming at the entrance to the building. Only then do I allow myself to sit on the cold parquet floor at the entrance and start crying.

Nothing remains as it was after that night in Normandy.

The night wind blew through the big window facing the coast of the Black Sea. Despite the sound of his quiet breathing beside me, I couldn't fall asleep in the foreign hotel room that night in Normandy.

I wanted to go out into the cold night and run to the black shore and the frozen waves, to step inside and just disappear, but I couldn't. The barbed wire or the guards would stop me, bring me back into his arms. Slowly I got out of bed and stepped into the luxurious bathroom, closing the door behind me.

"Everything's fine. You did it. You were fine." My lips whispered as I scrubbed my skin as hard as I could, scratching myself painfully with the bath sponge and shivering at the cold of the water. Philip would never forgive me for sleeping with him, but I kept on rubbing myself, unable to stop.

Only when the cold water was too much to suffer did I walk back to his bed, shivering, covering myself with a blanket, trying to fall asleep, and looking out the black windows.

The next morning, the second time was easier. I thought about the flowers I'd drawn in my notebook and concentrated on the rain falling outside, dripping on the window glass, creating small paths of water. I even managed not to hear the sounds he made and to smile at him when it was all over.

Patiently I stayed down until he got up to get dressed, inviting me to breakfast, starting to get organized for the ride back. My gaze followed him as he stood by the window and looked out into the rain, wearing his neat uniform and humming a German song to himself.

"Did you enjoy it?" He was staring at the grey beach outside.

"Yes, very much, thank you."

"Our breakfast is in a quarter of an hour. I do not want to be late. We have another long drive to Paris." And I tried to cover myself in the blanket before collecting my clothes and going to the bedroom.

On the way back to Paris, my head rested on the closed window while I looked outside to the yellow trees and the river, feeling his hand touch my thigh.

"You're quiet."

"I enjoy looking at the river. So peaceful."

"Yes, so peaceful and faithful, you can always count on it, that's the secret of nature's power."

"I like to observe nature."

"I have noticed. Your drawings in the diary I gave you are lovely."

"When did you see my drawings?" The film box, where is it?

"At the hotel this morning, when you were in the bathroom, I allowed myself to open your bag and look at the diary. Is that okay with you?"

"I thought a woman should have some secrets." The film, had he found it hidden in the bag? He was playing with me and would soon ask the driver to stop the vehicle. Would I be able to cross the river by swimming in this cold?

"Are you cold?"

"Yes, a little cold."

"Should I ask the driver to stop for a few minutes?"

"No, I'm fine."

"Let me wrap you in my coat. You will be more comfortable."

I could feel his hand continuing to caress my thighs through his heavy military coat, wrapping around my body. Please don't ask the driver to stop.

"I brought us a bottle of wine, especially for the way back." He instructed the driver to stop on the side, and while the driver arranged the picnic blanket, I walked away from them by the riverbank and looked at the peaceful grey river. How cold was the water?

It was already dark outside as we entered Paris, and the almost-deserted streets were illuminated in dim light. The military vehicle stopped at Place de l'Étoile, at the foot of the silent Arc de Triomphe. I watched the policeman back away into the shadows of the monument, keeping a distance from Herr Ernest.

"It was a pleasant trip," Herr Ernest pulled my body to his and kissed me slowly, his hands holding my neck. "We'll meet again soon."

"I apologize for being so quiet on the way back." I took a deep breath in the cold evening air and tried to overcome my headache.

"I will want to see you more often."

"I'll be glad to." The film box? Did he find it?

Standing still, I waited and watched the military vehicle until it disappeared down the boulevard, leaving the smell of burnt gasoline in the air.

In the first alley, I stopped and, looking back carefully, making sure no one is following me, I slipped into a dark corner. My trembling fingers found it difficult to open the bag's metal buckle, slipping again and again as I looked at the entrance to the alley in fear. The diary was in the bag, and my hand dug through the soft fabric of the dirty lingerie, turning it over and over again, my heartbeat calming down only when I felt the metallic touch of the film box.

The pavement stones were hurting my knees as I leaned on the wall and vomited, feeling the sour taste of wine in my mouth.

After a few minutes I could stand again, breathe the cold night air and start walking home. Again I had to lie to Lizette and hide my true identity, I couldn't tell her that I was the French prostitute of Herr Oberst Ernest.

A few days later, Herr Oberst Ernest takes me to a fancy café in front of the opera and lets me know he has found me an apartment.

"Thank you for your concern, but I'm getting along with the woman I live with." I look around at all the German officers sitting with their companions. Do they also have their own apartments?

"I want us to have more time together."

"We can meet as much as you like." I must not push too far.

"I want my intimate time with you."

"I would be happy to visit your place." And be the perfect spouse.

"It's not appropriate for my companion to walk through hotel corridors." He ends the conversation.

"Officer's car special secretaries." I hear the soldiers at the boulangerie laughing among themselves, not before checking there is no officer around.

"But the senior officers receive special corridor girls," they sometimes add, smiling at me while waiting for their baguettes, referring to the hotels confiscated by the German army.

"The maids at the hotels have to separate the uniforms and the lingerie." It is the joke they like most.

"Tomorrow, we will go to see the apartment." Herr Ernest signals to the waiter and I sip my coffee in silence, ignoring the German speech and laughter all around in the café. What did I bring upon myself? How would I leave Lizette?

I could not say goodbye to Lizette. I could not experience another farewell. For days, I wandered restlessly in the boulangerie, lowering my eyes in front of Simone's judgmental looks, thinking of what I could possibly say after she treated me so warmly. The nightmares return, and I wake sweaty. Until I can't sleep at all anymore, and I run away.

I pack all my clothes in a big bag and leave the house while Lizette is out, leaving her a small farewell note. Carefully I place it under the picture of the dead man in the silver frame on the fireplace, lowering my eyes and unable to watch his. But he continues to follow me with his proud gaze until I close the door behind me.

Why didn't I stay to hug her one last time? Why didn't I wait to hug Philip that time in the basement? What is wrong with me?

"Do you like the apartment?" Oberst Ernest asks as we walk around the abandoned and furnished place, holding the keys and looking at me.

"Who lived here?"

"It belonged to a family that left France," he answers casually, checking the study, "now it belongs to the German nation."

The creaking of the parquet under my feet feels foreign as I follow him into the study.

"Monique," he looks at me, "this will be my study. You will never enter here." And I turn and go out with a downcast look, concentrating on checking the pantry, my fingers examining the wooden boards.

"I'll make sure they clean here." He follows my fingers. "Do not worry about the dust."

I enter the living room and looking around.

"And I will also take care of new paintings instead of the ones that were taken," he adds as he notices my gaze on the bright spots on the walls. Once there were works of art hanging there, but they are gone.

"Do you like the apartment? I think it will suit you."

I have been living in an apartment that suits me for two months now. I usually wait for him in the evenings, and he comes when he can. I can hear the sound of his hobnail boots on the wooden stairs as he comes. A moment later, he opens the heavy door with the key he has, and I wait for him by the entrance, taking his coat.

"I brought you some boxes of meat and sausages." He hands me the heavy paper bag.

"Thanks, but there is no need. I have enough."

"Any cheese left from the last time?"

"Yes, there is."

"I'd be happy if you serve it for dinner, with the red wine I brought."

"Will you stay the night?"

"Yes." He caresses my side with his hand.

I exist for those times. For those nights when he falls asleep after he gets off me, lying in bed.

Quietly I roll up the blanket and carefully walk on the wooden floor, searching in the dark for his brown leather bag lying in his study, the room I must never enter. Listening to every noise, I carefully open the bag, feeling like I'm putting my hand into a monster's mouth as I pull out a pile of documents and take them to the bathroom. Behind a closed door, and by candlelight, I read them. Names of army units, dates and movement orders, fortification instructions, and situation assessments. When I finish, I shove them back into place, exactly in the same order, smelling the leather scent of the heavy bag monster lying on the floor, mixed with the scent of fear coming from my sweaty body.

Then I return to bed with quiet steps and lay beside him. But it is difficult for me to get to sleep again, wondering if tomorrow morning Oberst Ernest will discover what I did and put me by the wall for the last time. Only in the morning, after I hear the building's front door slam, do I allow myself to sit on the cold parquet floor by the entrance and hug myself for a few moments.

Since Normandy, Philip has not hugged me again.

The basement

"You are late." Philip leans against the basement wall, wearing his old leather jacket.

"Someone was standing by the steps of the metro entrance, watching the people. I had to wait for a group of women to pass. I didn't want him to start asking me questions."

"We need to change the method; it's starting to get dangerous."

"The method is fine. I just have to be careful. I know how to be careful."

"I worry about you."

But he does not show it anymore. He just looks at me from a distance, and all I can smell is this damp basement.

"Your hugs never happened," I whisper to myself.

"What did you say?"

"Oberst Ernest is constantly busy fortifying and preparing for the American invasion. They call the barricades 'The Atlantic Wall.'"

"How do you get along with him? And with Simone at the boulangerie?"

"Right now, they estimate the invasion will take place in the next spring. That's what their intelligence claims."

"And where do they think the invasion will take place?"

"They are concentrating on the Pas de Calais area. The shortest distance from Britain. They have moved another armored division there."

"What about Normandy?"

"It gets secondary priority in their army orders."

"And how do you feel? Aren't you taking too many risks?"

"They are transferring less efficient units to Normandy.

Some units are comprised of soldiers forcibly recruited from Poland."

"Does that mean they have a shortage of manpower?"

"It does not seem to me that anything will cause a shortage for the Germans. They always can decide to conquer some nation or piece of land."

"Do you have everything you need?"

"Yes, I'm not missing anything. I have a full pantry. Oberst Ernest is taking care of me." Philip takes a step in my direction, but after a moment, he returns to leaning back against the wall, folding his hands. He can't understand me, it is not his job. It's also not his job to hug me, not after what I'm doing with Oberst Ernest.

"Do you remember the photo film you gave me, from Normandy?"

"I've already forgotten about it."

He was so angry with me then, when I returned from Normandy.

"How could you lose the camera? What will I say to Robert? It took so long to convince him. Do you know the efforts I made to convince him?" He'd walked around the basement shouting at the wall, and I'd stood embarrassed in the corner, ashamed of myself and of what I had done with Oberst Ernest.

"I was not careful enough." I'd tried to stop my tears as I handed him the film I had taken out of my coat pocket, my fingers gripping the small metal box nervously. I'd guarded it for days, afraid of the man in the black coat at the stairs to the metro. Would he choose to search my body?

"Take it, it's for you." I'd approached Philip in fear, wanting to apologize, and did not find the words, but he just put the film box in his jacket pocket and walked away from me. Not even slightly touching my fingers, leaving me waiting to feel warm hands, that time after Normandy.

"London loved the material you photographed; they really appreciate what you did."

"I manage to read a telegram."

"They asked me to relay their appreciation."

"The telegram indicates that the Germans are debating how to deal with the invasion." And I explain to him the movement of forces and units as I remember them. He can pass all that information to those anonymous people living in London. I, too, have no identity. I no longer expect him to hug me anymore.

"Is there anything I can do for you? Can I take care of something for you?" I look at his simple clothes.

"No, thanks. Herr Ernest takes care of everything I need." All Philip cares about is the stuff I bring him.

"Do not forget who you are. You are one of us." He's not trying to hug me.

"I do not forget." I'm a French whore that everyone leaves. You will also abandon me in the end. Luckily, I did not fall in love with you.

"I just don't like you mentioning him."

"I belong to him."

"You are one of us." His fingers are playing with the pencil he is holding.

"I need to go. I have an evening gown I need to purchase." My fingers touch the hem of my coat.

"Take care of yourself." I manage to hear his voice behind me as I climb the stairs leading out of the basement to the rainy street, but I do not turn back.

"Take care of yourself," I whisper as I walk down the alley and wipe away my tears, passing a woman in a grey dress and her daughter, both standing in the doorway of their old shop, watching me walk in the rain. I have to hurry. I have a dress to buy.

"I need your help," my lips whisper to Anaïs, trying to make sure the receptionist won't hear me.

"She's with me," says Anaïs to the girl behind the mahogany desk, as she pulls me after her to the back rooms of the fashion house, the space that holds all the rolls of fabric standing against the walls.

"How are you? Tell me, how is he?"

"He's polite."

"Is he gentle?"

"Yes, he is very considerate."

"And does he hurt you?"

"No, never. Does your Fritz hurt you?"

"Sometimes, he has a hard time expressing his real feelings, but I know how to take care of myself. I'm a woman."

My fingers gently caress her hand, but she turns her back to me and lights a cigarette for herself, turning again and exhaling the smoke, closing her eyes with pleasure—the smelly grey-bluish smoke lingers between us. "The most important thing is to know how to take care of yourself. No one else will do that for you."

"I know."

"So, to what do I owe the honor of your visit?" She again looks at me, and I'm sorry for not visiting her before, inviting her to a café, sitting and chatting together. Someday I will, I promise myself.

"I need a dress."

"So let's go buy you a dress. I'm just going to get my bag."

"No, I need a dress from here."

"From here?"

"Yes, I need a dress for the opera."

"Are you going to the opera?"

"Yes, Herr Ernest wants me to be his companion for the opera."

Anaïs looks at me, smoking in silence. Suddenly, she seems smaller and more vulnerable.

"The dresses here are expensive. Do you have enough money?"

"Herr Ernest gave it to me." I put the rolled bundle of bills in her hands, asking anxiously: "Will that be enough?"

"Yes, that will be enough." She slowly examines the bills, returns them to me, and puts out her cigarette. "Not only does Anaïs know how to take care of Anaïs, Monique also knows how to take care of Monique. Follow me."

"Anaïs, come here, please," the fashion house manager calls her from the back room. She apologizes to me, asking me to wait a moment.

While standing in the center of the fitting room, I try not to look down at the seamstress kneeling at my feet. They have arranged the red dress wrapped around my body, examined the straps, making sure they do not fall when I bend over.

"Anaïs, please help the lady in the red dress."

The windows of the measurement hall are covered with dark curtains. They probably do not want to stand out in front of the poor city outside.

"Anaïs, please bring the lady a pair of high heels to match the dress, the closed shoes from the winter collection, what is your size?"

There is a stack of wooden chairs in the corner of the room, placed on top of each other. When German women arrive, do they sit comfortably and watch the entire collection? I mustn't look down.

"Anaïs, please arrange the hem for the lady."

"I think it's okay." If only I could run away from here.

"No, we need it to be at the perfect height, Anaïs, please fix that."

Maybe they cover the windows because of the nighttime regulations against bombers? No, they surely don't want to show off.

"This dress looks perfect on you. You're perfect. Thank you, Anaïs, you can go back to the sewing room."

"When do you need the dress?"

"The concert is tomorrow." My eyes follow Anaïs' back, watching her disappear into the back room, closing the door behind her with a slight click.

"Excellent, our courier will bring you the dress tomorrow morning, give the address to the receptionist."

On the way out, I want to go and say goodbye to her, but the salon manager accompanies me to the exit, kisses both of my cheeks goodbye, and I'm too ashamed to go back.

One day I will visit her, and we will both go for a walk in the street, passing the fancy café and watching the opera house. Tomorrow I will enter it for the first time in my life.

Pompeii

"Did you get wet?" Herr Ernest asks when we get out of the car, hurrying up the marble stairs leading to the magnificent entrance.

"No." But Herr Ernest turns to scold the boy holding a large umbrella, and opens the arriving car's doors.

"It's okay."

"No, it's not okay. He needs to know how to do his job." Herr Ernest goes down the stairs and speaks to him in his quiet voice, and I turning away, looking up at the big red flags with swastikas in their center. They hang at the building entrance, drizzling rain onto those coming to the concert.

"Shall we go inside?" His hand holds mine. "Be careful not to slip on the wet marble stairs."

At the entrance to the hall, I stop in place, overwhelmed by the golden wealth surrounding me. The crystal chandeliers illuminate the spectacular ceiling paintings and shiny gold sculptures, as if there are no power outages throughout the city. Waiters in black suits and bow ties move quietly among the guests, holding silver trays with champagne glasses. The war did not cross the threshold of the opera, except for the guests, German army officers in pressed uniforms with various ranks and decorations.

"Please, for you." Herr Ernest hands me a clear yellowish glass with small bubbles while bringing his lips closer to my ear, so as not to shout in the bustle of noise all around us: "What do you think?"

"Wonderful." I want to run out of this place, feeling so prominent in my red gown.

"The dress suits you so well." He holds my arm, like all the other German officers traveling in the hall in their uniforms, proudly presenting their female companions wearing their prom dresses, as if they were a valuable prize.

"Come, I will introduce you to some of my colleagues." He leads me to the center, under the huge golden chandelier.

"And how come a young French lady like you is interested in Wagner?" A senior officer in a black uniform and visored hat turns to me in French, looking at me mockingly.

"There are young ladies who love his music and his opinions," I answer in perfect German, looking at the skull decorating his hat.

"You did not tell us she speaks German." The officer turns to Oberst Ernest while appreciatively looking at me, and everyone laughs.

"Be careful. Maybe she is a spy." Another officer answers him, his helmet also decorated with a skull, and the sounds of laughter increase.

"It's clear to me she's a spy." Oberst Ernest smiles at him. "Therefore I will keep her close to me, so you can't snatch her. You all know the German rules. What we hunt belongs to us."

"Never trust French women unless they are accompanied by a German officer supervising them," I answer the officer in the black uniform in my perfect German, smiling a perfect smile with my red lips, but my stomach hurts from tension.

"To the beautiful and loyal French women." The officer in black raises his glass in my honor, and I feel the hand of Oberst Ernest tightening around my arm.

"To the thousand-year Reich." Another officer raises his champagne glass, and we all cheer.

"And to the pleasures of Paris," adds another officer.

"And to staying here forever, to never be sent to the Russian front."

"You can trust the Americans who are preparing for the invasion. They will keep us here." The sounds of laughter continue, though no one dares raise his glass.

"To our Führer."

"To the Führer."

"Where are you going?"

"To the ladies' room."

"Hurry up. The concert is starting soon." He releases my arm, and I cross the hall slowly, having a hard time walking on luxurious high heels while knowing that all the officers' eyes are fixed on my back, examining me.

"Are you okay?" she asks me in French as I wash my face in the luxurious restroom.

"Yes, thank you, I was nauseous for a moment."

"It's the champagne. You're probably not used to it."

"Yes, it must be champagne."

I hear the bell ringing in the hall, calling everyone to enter the concert. Oberst Ernest is waiting for me in the emptying lobby, and I watch the column of men holding their colorful wives. They slowly climb up the marble stairs, and I think of the man from the railway company, that time in Drancy, when he told me about the rows of people climbing into the train carriages.

"Are you enjoying the evening?"

"It's a wonderful evening. Thank you for taking me."

When he stays the night in my apartment after being inside me, I sit quietly in the bathroom and read military orders. The Russian winter offensive has begun. Therefore the Final Solution to the Jewish Question must be accelerated.

"What is the Final Solution to the Jewish Question?"

"I don't know. How are you? How do you feel?" Philip tries to get closer to me, but I walk backwards until the basement wall's rough stones stop me.

"Check with your Communist friends about the Final Solution."

"They are not just my friends; they are your friends too. If they were not, you would not be here." He keeps his distance. When will he get tired of me?

"The Germans are losing on the Russian front; they've taken huge casualties, whole units have been dissolved."

"I'll give them that; how are you?"

I do not want to tell him how I am. It won't change anything anyway.

"Here in Paris, they are afraid they will be transferred to the East. They are talking about it amongst themselves."

"And what are your feelings, and how is their morale?"

"Their morale is still high, especially here in Paris where they enjoy all the pleasures of the city, holding French women like me in their arms."

"You are different, you are not like them; you don't have to think of yourself like that."

"I know I'm different from them." Really? What's the difference? That I'm telling you what I read at night? Believe me, I'm licking German boots just like Anaïs and Violette. They at least believe it will help them.

"You are one of us, important and precious."

"I'm aware of that." One of you? One of the resistance? One of the Communists? One who betrays her dead girlfriend? One that everyone abandons in the end? I will stop being one of you as soon as it does not suit you. I know exactly how precious I am.

"I'm worried about you. You're taking too many risks."

"I can take care of myself. Please check with your Russian friends about what I asked, this matter of the Final Solution to the Jewish Question. I have to go."

"Monique, wait." He calls after me, but he no longer chases and hugs me on the stairs. He too has got used to the cold.

On the narrow street where old crates are thrown on their sides, I go to the shop entrance on the other side of the alley, take out a sausage packed in a paper bag and serve it to the small dirty girl who always stands in the doorway, looking at me. She snatches the bag and runs inside the dim shop, disappearing from my sight.

I have learned not to cry.

"Darling, what do you want to do this morning?" Herr Ernest asks me a few days later after he gets off my body, and I cover myself, wiping away a tear with the tip of the blanket.

"What were you thinking of doing?"

On Sundays he tends to stay with me until later, looking for something to do for himself and his companion whore.

"Maybe we can go see some art?"

As we go down the building's stairs, passing the third floor, I hear a rustle from the neighbor's apartment door. She peeks at me from the peephole every time I go downstairs. Once, I asked her who owned the apartment I live in, but she refused to tell me and just looked at me with hatred in her eyes, slamming her apartment door in my face.

"Put on your coat. It is cold outside." Herr Ernest holds the front door for me.

In the grey street, his driver faithfully waits for us in the military vehicle, and I wonder if he sat like that all night inside the frozen car.

"Good morning," Oberst Ernest greets him as the engine chokes from an effort to start at low temperatures. "Please take us to the Tuileries Gardens."

"I thought we were going to the Louvre."

"The Louvre is almost empty. The ungrateful French managed to hide away all the paintings. We don't know where."

"I thought you knew everything."

"We Germans have the patience to discover everything about traitors like them." He smiles at me. "And you are one of us, you were born in Strasbourg, remember?"

"I remember."

"I'm happy you are not like them." He puts his gloved hand on my thigh. "You're like us." And I look out the car window and think he is right. I'm like them. I eat German food, warming myself in the cold winter with firewood his driver brings me, and I'm being driven in a German military vehicle on a Sunday morning, watching the almost-empty streets.

"Can you bring more candles the next time you come over?" Power outages have intensified recently, causing a shortage of candles.

"Already finished? I thought there were enough." Even Simone allows herself to smile at me more often, occasionally asking if I can bring her some.

"I used them up."

"Yes, I'll bring you some. Is anything else missing? Stop

the car here by the plaza," he instructs the driver.

"No, nothing more."

"Wait for us here, please," he instructs the driver as he opens the car door for me near the entrance to the Tuileries Gardens. Several other military vehicles like ours are already parked next to ours. What exhibition is this?

"This way." Herr Ernest hurries to wrap me in my thick fur coat.

The only sound I can hear as we pass through the gardens' large gate is the gravel under my leather boots, the ones he bought me. The wooden sign is still hanging by the entrance, but I'm not stopping anymore, just looking at the white letters beginning to peel, revealing a rotting wooden board beneath.

"Here." He holds my arm and points to a hall in the corner of the garden.

A couple is approaching ahead of us, holding a wrapped package, and while the officers salute each other with 'Heil Hitler,' we, the mistresses, examine each other's coats with embarrassed smiles.

"What's this place?"

"It's time to keep my promise."

"What promise?"

The guard at the entrance to the hall salutes and taps his heels, but I am used to it and no longer get tense, just smiling at him politely, hurrying to escape from the cold wind outside, into the hall full of framed paintings.

"What exhibition is this?" I look around. There are thousands of paintings hanging on the walls, in piles on top of each other, or just standing in simple wooden crates in the center of the hall. "Who do these belong to?"

"We came to purchase some paintings," Herr Ernest

addresses the older man who approaches us, nodding politely and turning to me.

"What style does the madame like? Or maybe the gentleman decides?"

"The madame decides at home," Herr Ernest smiles and does not scold him. "What style do you like?"

"What is this here? Who do all these paintings belong to?"

"This is a painting store," Herr Ernest answers me. Like us, several German officers walk around, some with their spouses, some with an assistant who follows them, holding open notebooks and writing down the names of paintings they point at.

"And the price, how much does it cost?"

The older man takes a few steps aside out of politeness, patiently waiting for us to finish the discussion and decide on the style I like.

"These are paintings for sale at an excellent price," Herr Ernest is staring at me with a blank look.

"Who sells these paintings here?" I lower my eyes, but I can't hold myself back. I should be quiet.

"These collections belong to families who wanted to get rid of them, or did not need them anymore, so they sold them, this is a real opportunity. I promised you I would buy you some paintings for your apartment, and I keep my promises." He smiles at me. "What style of art do you like?" He signals to the older man in the suit that the discussion between us is over, and orders him to come close again.

"What would the madame like me to show her?"

"I have to see myself," I answer him hesitantly.

At first, I walk step by step between the paintings, quietly examining the richness that lies before me, raising my eyes and looking at the walls around me, or lowering them and watching the piles that lie on the floor. But then I start to hurry, going through the paintings, checking them one by one, and removing pile after pile while the older man in the suit helps me examine the ones at the bottom, box after box. He is gasping from the effort but keeps calm, and all that time, Herr Oberst Ernest accompanies us in silence, patient with my crazy behavior.

"I want that one," I finally point to a drawing of a smiling dancer, raising her arms high above her head.

"I can see madame loves modern art. You have good taste," the older man compliments me and turns to Herr Ernest for his approval. "It's a painting by a well-known painter."

It seems to me that Herr Ernest is not happy with my selection, but I insist, and he approves with a nod of his head, signaling to a young man standing aside to come take the painting for payment and packaging.

"Is that all you want?"

"Yes, that's all I want, now it's your turn."

Herr Ernest walks slowly, pointing with his finger at the old man to follow him, and chooses a large drawing of a horse race and a painting of hunters hunting a fox in the woods. "It will be perfect for the living room and my study," he explains when the man in the suit marks the paintings for packaging.

As we go out to the car, followed by two employees carrying the paintings we purchased and keeping a respectful distance behind, I give Herr Ernest a hand and thank him for the new purchases.

"You're welcome, my dear. It will make your apartment more pleasant."

The driver standing next to the grey vehicle hurries to

open the door, and I wait outside in the chill wind for the store workers to put the packaged paintings in the car.

"Be careful," I ask them, not before looking one last time at the garden gate and the peeling sign. I'm so glad I did not find the painting that hung in my bedroom.

Mom and Dad had given it to me for my tenth birthday. A dancer bending forward, tying her ballet shoes. I'd once wanted to be a ballet dancer very much.

The nightclub dancers raise their legs high in the air, stomping to the beat of the loud music, and I watch them through the cigarette smoke that fills the crowded place, trying to look in another direction.

"Try it. You'll love it," Anaïs yells as she brings her lips close to my ears, trying to overcome the noise of the band playing and the crowd loudly talking around us.

"Herr Ernest will not be pleased with that," I answer as I lean towards her, looking through the smoke at the line of dancers on the stage.

"What will he not like?" Violette joins, grimacing as Anaïs points to the pack of cigarettes lying on the table.

"Everyone should have at least one obscene habit," Anaïs laughs, "it will make you feel good, try."

"They say it will soon be impossible to get cigarettes," Violette is almost shouting to overcome the noise.

"It will always be possible to get cigarettes. You just have to know the right way to get them," Anaïs leans back and lights another one for herself. "For what purpose were soldiers invented?"

Oberst Ernest and the two Fritzes sit on the other side of the table, bending towards each other with their backs on us, looking at the dancers and talking, maybe about the war.

"I don't think they're talking about your cigarette stock right now." I laugh with Anaïs.

"They surely are not. They are wondering how high the dancers will lift their legs, and how much they will be able to see." She points with her eyes to the black garters that occasionally flash under the fabric of their dresses.

"It's disgusting."

"You have to get used to it. That's how it is with men. They can sit with you, reading poetry and talking about art and culture, but when they are alone, they go to peep shows in Pigalle."

"Do you think they go to strip shows in those clubs?"

"Even though you were taken to the opera, you remain a little innocent, aren't you?" She blows the cigarette smoke into the dark hall and smiles.

"I think they are talking about the situation in Russia," I try to change the subject and shout in her ear, even though I do not believe it. For a while now, Oberst Ernest has not been talking about the great victories in the East. The rumors about the success of the Russian winter offensive have reached the city's grocery stores, giving the people standing in the endless lines something to gossip about. Even the few people walking on the streets, curled up in their coats, believe that the Germans are in retreat.

"Do they talk about Russia?" asks Violette.

"Yes, but he says we have nothing to worry here in Paris." I answer.

"I want to experience the culture of this city," Herr Ernest pulls me outside almost every evening he comes. "We must be strong against false rumors," he adds as we drive through the cold, dark streets.

The cafés are still full of soldiers, even though some are not heated, and I have to sit wrapped in the fur coat Herr Ernest bought me, looking back at the people outside when they watch me. What does it matter if they spit on the sidewalk? It is wet from the rain anyway.

The telegrams I read at night about the eastern front tell of crushed German armored columns on the sides of roads and frozen soldiers dead in the snow. Even the French-language German army newspaper, still sold at a stall on the boulevard, has stopped reporting on the German army's strength, concentrating on articles about fighting spirit in battle.

"I promise you they are not talking about Russia unless the dancer in front of them was born in Moscow," Anaïs approaches as if whispering a secret. "Maybe they want to start practicing their Russian." She bursts out laughing, looking at us dismissively.

"What will happen? I'm scared of the Communists," Violette asks, not smiling tonight at all.

"What are you afraid of?"

"Fritz treats me so nicely, I'm afraid they'll send him to the east," she approaches us and tries to whisper, though her whisper sounds more like weeping. "I heard terrible things are happening there."

"They will not send him to the East," I place my hand on hers, trying to calm her down, "they need him here in

France."

"I'm afraid it will end one day."

"It will not end," Anaïs answers her, and smiles at me as she puts out her cigarette in the ashtray. "We were promised a thousand-year Reich, weren't we?"

"Sorry, we neglected you." Fritz hugs his Violette, who clings to him tightly, putting her head on his shoulder and looking at us with a smile.

"We thought you were more interested in the dancers," Anaïs answers him, making us laugh.

"Are you going to strip shows?" I bring my lips to Herr Ernest's ear and ask him, trying to be quiet, but he just smiles at me and doesn't answer. Why does Anaïs know such things that I don't? Are all men like that? Does Philip also go to such clubs in the Latin Quarter, ending the night in the bed of a sweaty cabaret dancer? What does it matter at all?

"I want to try," I shout across the table and reach for the cigarette box placed between us. The music bothers me, and in my eyes, the dancers are ugly.

"It's not for you," laughs Anaïs, snatching the box away, "it's just for simple women like me."

"Give her a try. I'll get you more," her Fritz says, but one look at Herr Oberst Ernest silences him, and he places his hand on Anaïs' arm, turning her towards him and kissing her passionately while she strokes his fair hair with her fingers.

"To Paris." I lift my glass of champagne, covering the insult, and everyone joins.

"To German-French friendship."

"To the thousand-year Reich," Anaïs raises her hand, and we all drink again.

"Pour me more," I shout at Ernest. Trying to overcome

the noise of the band and the dancers' footsteps in their black garters. At least he allows me to drink.

If I drink a little more, I may be able to stop all my fears and feelings of shame.

"Shall I stop?"

"No, it's okay, you can go on."

I can hear the roar of American bombers in the distance. The German searchlights are probably traveling through the dark sky, looking to aim their anti-aircraft cannon batteries and hunt down bombers.

"Does it feel good?"

"Yes, don't stop."

I'm sprawled on the bed with an awful headache. I drank too much tonight.

The whimper of the alarms sounds every few minutes, and the roar doesn't stop, like a muffled gurgle that shakes the window and the parquet floor, causing the iron bed to creak with a shrill sound. But perhaps these are all the movements of Herr Ernest lying on top of me while I close my eyes.

"They are looking for Renault's factories in the suburbs. They will pass us," he whispers hatefully as he continues to shake the bed, and I groan, thinking of the pain that awaits an anonymous young woman now soldering metal plate for a German truck on Renault's production line, somewhere in the suburbs. She doesn't know that in a few minutes, her fate will be sealed. Which of us will hurt more?

"Don't stop." It doesn't matter; death will come for both of us, sooner or later.

───※───

"Mademoiselle." They approach me the next day on the street, near the opera square.

"I'm in a hurry to the metro, he'll stop working soon, and I have to buy Christmas presents."

"Do not worry about the metro," the tallest smiles, "what do you have in the bag?" And I want to scream.

"I have nothing in the bag." I hand them my ID card with shaking hands, also because of the cold.

"Monique?" he asks in good French, sifting through the certificate, comparing the picture to my face. They stand close to me, hiding me from the other people on the street with their black leather coats. Those few who take a quick look continue walking, thankful for their good luck. I knew it was coming. It was only a matter of time before they got me.

"Were you born in Strasbourg?"

"Yes."

"Date of birth?"

"Fourteenth of December nineteen twenty-five."

"Where did you live in Strasbourg?" He compares the details to the notebook he has taken out of his pocket. What is written there? What does he know about me? Is he just trying to scare me?

"What did you ask?"

"Where did you live in Strasbourg?" He raises his eyes from the notebook, looking at me.

"Rue de Barr, I think, I was a little girl. It was by the river. We went to the river on Sundays." Never be too confident in yourself. You are not a notebook of information in which everything is precisely written as it happened. They always suspect someone who knows all the answers accurately, as if memorizing them. Philip told me that, in the old warehouse south of town, and I think that was the moment I started to trust him.

"Is it close to the river?" The tall one keeps looking at me while his friend examines my tremors with his hand hidden in his coat pocket. What does he have there?

"I think so. Dad used to carry me on his shoulders. I remember there was a playground next to a slide."

"Are you cold?"

"Yes, I do not have a warm coat like yours." If you feel they are starting to suspect you, show some aggression, but not too much, people who feel guilty do not tend to be aggressive. Philip put me in front of the wall and approached me, role-playing with me, and I smelled his body odor for the first time, mixed with the smell of gun oil and the printing ink from his fingers.

"Do you speak German?" The other man asks me in their language.

"Yes, certainly, from childhood," I answer them in German.

"So why didn't you answer us from the beginning in German?"

"Because you approached me in French."

"And why are you not in Germany, with all those now helping the homeland?"

"I help here, selling delicious food at a boulangerie to soldiers who come tired from the front lines. I know how hard it is for them, especially those who fought the Communist monster that wants to destroy us." If you run out of ideas, invent, Philip briefed me, and I sat fearfully in front of him and thought there was no way I could ever invent anything.

"And what's in your bag?" He takes my bag without asking.

"A notebook. I draw sometimes."

He lets the other man hold my certificate while carefully examining the notebook, flipping through the pages, and reading the titles.

"Do you like Normandy?"

"Yes, very much, but we cannot go there now." Be careful not to slip, providing them a piece of information they may check and verify that you are lying to them, like places you have been to or dates. Make sure you stay as general as you can. Philip remained standing close to me, but since then, because of me, everything was ruined.

The short man gives one last look at the diary before closing it and returning it to me.

"Have a good day, Frau Otin."

"You too."

I start walking away, trying to keep calm without looking back, as if nothing had happened, but after a few steps, he calls me again, and I stop, turning back to him, filling the pain in my stomach.

"Frau Otin?"

"Yes?"

"I enjoy strolling the beaches of Normandy."

"The Strasbourg River of my childhood is more magical."

What do they know about Normandy? Why did he say that?

"How are you? Is everything okay?"

"Yes, everything is fine." My trembling hand looks for the pack of cigarettes in my bag.

"How was the road here?"

"Nothing special. The same Gestapo men standing on the steps of the metro, examining the people, it's cold to stand like that in the snow for so many hours."

"I worry about you more every time."

"You do not have to worry about me. I know how to get along." I take the matchbox out of my bag, trying to light a cigarette, but my fingers are shaking, and the match is broken, so is the next one. Philip takes the matchbox out of my hands, and gives me a lit match. I inhale the smoke with a look of relief.

"You started smoking?"

"Yes, such an obscene habit." I blow the smoke up, lean back, and look at him.

"I hope you do not smoke next to Ernest. I don't think he would like a woman smoking. It is not feminine."

Is that what interests him? What Herr Ernest will say?

"I manage Herr Ernest. Don't worry about Herr Ernest. Monique knows how to take care of Monique."

Philip examines me, watching with his dark eyes, searching for what to say. It's cold in the basement, and we're both wrapped up in our coats like we'll soon be out of here. Philip notices my eyes looking at his torn gloves, and he folds his arms, trying to hide them, and I want to take off my new leather gloves, another gift from Oberst Ernest. I inhale again. The heat of the cigarette smoke in my throat provides me some comfort.

"You have changed," he says.

I inhale the cigarette again and look at him. I so want to hug his body and promise him I've stayed the same, me and all my thoughts at night. I want to move this distant table that has been standing between us for so long and rest my head on his shoulder, whispering for him to hug me. But I know it's too late, I'm with Herr Ernest, and he has his resistance and maybe a cabaret girl he shares his nights with, getting into her panties like all men.

"Yeah, I've changed, but we did not come here to talk about me, we came to talk about the Germans and the material I have to tell you, didn't we? So let's start."

And he keeps looking at me in silence as I describe all the information I can remember, sketching out a new defense plan I was able to see one night.

"This is important information. I will pass it on."

"Excellent."

"You're doing a great job."

"Excellent." What am I risking myself for, bringing them all this stuff? Why don't they do something with it? What are they waiting for? For them to catch and torture me? For Herr Oberst Ernest to find out who I am? Why aren't they already invading and winning this war?

"What happened?"

"Nothing happened." I stand up from the small table, lighting another cigarette. Suddenly this basement feels too suffocating for both of us.

"You look angry." Philip gets up with me, trying to get closer, but I walk away from him, blowing the grey smoke in his direction.

"I'm not angry. I'm doing my job excellently. Even you say that."

"So why are you so distant from me?"

"Because I'm already tired and because you chose."

"What did I choose?"

"To send me to him."

"Because I had no choice."

"So I'm with him, and everything's fine."

"You must go on. There is no other choice." He tries to get closer again, but I don't want him to, feeling the basement wall scratching my back.

"I'm getting along great." The cigarette is tossed on the floor, and I crush it with my shoe. The air here is compressed and damp. "I deliver good information, and you keep me alive, a great deal."

Philip pauses, furiously looking at me. "Do not forget who you are."

But I'm tired of everyone trying to explain to me who I am. I don't know who I am anymore, who I'll be when it's all over, and how it will end. I'm not able to change anything anyway.

"Besides, you can ask your fellow Communists to take down the sign that forbids Jews from entering the Tuileries Gardens. It bothers me on my trips with Oberst Ernest, and there are no Jews left in Paris anymore."

Philip looks at me angrily, and for a moment I think I've

gone too far, and he will hit me, but he just balls his fists, approaching me and holding my body, biting my lips tightly and making me stop breathing. His hands grab me as he continues to kiss my lips, trying to spread them with his tongue, and for one moment, I allow him to, no longer able to stop myself.

"Merry Christmas." I push him away from me, scratching his neck with my fingers, and escape, knowing that if I stay another moment, I will never be able to return to my apartment in the Eighth arrondissement.

Tonight Philip will probably go out with his cabaret dancer and leave me alone with Oberst Ernest.

At least I can look for the little girl in the alley, giving her two cans of meat that I kept especially for her, for the new year.

The snow that has fallen in the last two days has painted the city white, covering the quiet streets in white shrouds. Only a few people are walking in the cold, leaving deep grey footprints in the snow. But most of them remain in their homes as they try to heat the small apartments with some old newspapers or some firewood purchased on the black market, in exchange for ration slips for flour and oil. Some German army truck crosses the boulevard at a slow pace, leaving black streaks on the road as it melts the snow, but the rest of the vehicles disappeared from the streets months ago. There is no fuel. Even the big market has returned to using traditional wooden carts, harnessed to tired horses.

"Merry Christmas," Simone greets us as we wrap ourselves in coats and huddle near the back door of the boulangerie. She even allows herself a moment of sentimentality and hugs us before we head out into the wet and white streets. I have to hurry home. Herr Ernest has informed me he will be coming today.

My cold fingers dig in my bag, searching for the apartment key when I hear a noise from inside, and I freeze.

Is Oberst Ernest early? Are they waiting for me inside? What should I do?

My feet quickly carry me down the stairs as I run out to the street, almost slipping and falling on the wet marble stairs at the building entrance. Panting in the cold air, I keep running to the street corner, ignoring my footprints left behind in the snow. Where shall I go now?

The street is empty, no black car is waiting to pick me up, and I can't see car tire tracks in the snow on the road. Only my steps seem so visible to anyone who wants to chase after me. What should I do? One woman strolls at a distance, bent over, carrying a bundle of wood or rags on her back. She doesn't seem to be one of them. Could I be wrong? Maybe Herr Ernest is in the apartment waiting for me. Shall I wait for him to arrive?

The street is getting dark as I stand and rub my palms together, trying to move a little and ignoring an older man passing by. He is probably wondering why a woman is waiting like this on a street corner when it's snowing outside. My feet hurt from the cold, but I try to keep on walking, trying to hide from passing cars that might be looking for me. I can't bear it anymore.

I have nowhere else to go. How much longer will I live in such fear?

Slowly I climb the wooden stairs, carefully open the door, release the key, and hold it between my aching fingers, ready to fight as much as I can or turn around and escape. The house is warm and cozy.

"Where have you been? You're freezing." He walks over to me, helping me remove my coat. "What took you so long? I sent my driver into the street looking for you. I brought us a Christmas tree to celebrate, like in the homeland. Are you okay? Why are you so quiet?"

"I'm cold." Just taking off my shoes and wet socks, and warming up a little by the fireplace, that's all I want now.

At the end of the living room the tree stands proudly, and Herr Ernest goes around it slowly, placing string lights and silver orbs that twinkle cheerfully. It's nice to watch the fire burning in the fireplace, concentrating on the flames that light up the walls and the hunter painting that Herr Ernest bought, a man shooting a running fox, and Mom lights candles. We all sing Hanukkah songs, laughing at Jacob who can't manage the strange Hebrew words, and I whisper the words quietly because I'm ashamed they'll discover who I am, and Dad is touching my shoulder: "Monique, Monique."

"Monique." Herr Ernest whispers to me, gently touching my shoulders, and my eyes look around, trying to figure out where I am and who this man is with the cropped yellow hair and green eyes. "It seems you fell asleep." He looks at me.

"Did I say something?" I straighten up in an armchair in front of the fireplace.

"No, you just mumbled something strange." He continues to examine me. "Look, I made us a Christmas tree, to feel like home."

"It's beautiful. The most beautiful I've ever had."

"I also brought you a present." He points to the box under the tree.

"I'm so sorry. I did not buy you anything. I thought you would return to your family in Germany." I'm looking for a reason. "Do you have family in Germany?"

"I'm an army man. My home is where my boots are." He walks to the Christmas tree and brings my present. "Merry Christmas."

My fingers gently remove the colored ribbon and peel off the paper, grabbing the cardboard box and opening it.

In horror, I examine the brown leather case inside the box, looking at the black metal box with the golden buttons and lens. My fingernails gently scrape the iron eagle engraved on the camera body, holding a swastika with its claws.

"What is it?" I'm looking at him.

"It's a camera. It's your present, the best on the market thanks to our Führer, a Leica camera."

Even if I wanted to get up and run away, I couldn't. My feet are paralyzed. Why did he buy it for me?

"Why?"

"Because it suits you," he is not smiling at me, "you love to draw, and I thought of giving you a present, you should have thanked me for your present."

"I'm sorry." My legs manage to carry me as I stand and approach him, trying to lift my arms and hug his shoulders. "You just surprised me, and I've never had a camera, what do you do with it? Can you show me?"

And Oberst Ernest relents and sits down in the armchair, begins to explain to me how to hold the camera and how to aim and which buttons to press to shoot or pull out the film.

And all that time, I'm kneeling at his feet on the carpet in the living room, asking questions, and making myself interested while trying to warm myself and looking at his fingers holding the metal box. What does he know about me, and how long will I be able to hide myself?

"Next summer, I'll take a few days off from the army, and we'll drive to the beach, maybe to the south of France, and then you can take a picture of us." He looks at me.

"Please pour me some wine," I ask.

"Will you make us dinner? I brought groceries. They're in the kitchen." He strokes my hair as I kneel on the carpet.

"What did you bring?"

"Some things for the holiday." He continues to stroke my hair. "Too bad you don't have pure German blood."

I look up at him questioningly.

"In order to have a legal spouse, an officer in my position must find a German woman with certificates."

"And what about me?"

"After we win the war, you could come with me to Berlin."

My lips are silent as I rest my head on his knee, thinking what to say that would fit, wondering what he would think of my racial purity.

"Merry Christmas." I kiss his knee, feeling the rough pants on my lips. I have to get up and make dinner, and then I can drink the wine he brought. Tonight he will probably let me drink as much as I want to.

"See you tomorrow, and watch out for the snow," Simone says goodbye a few days after the new year, and I'm starting my way to the apartment by foot, blowing on my frozen fingers. The metro is not working.

When will this snow end? Maybe it would have been better for the snow to last forever and paint this grey city white. No one will wrap me in white. I will never wear a white dress. I will not even be like the same French woman I saw a few months ago, who married a German officer in the church of La Madeleine. I'd passed by and glanced at them for a moment. All his fellow officers stood in two straight rows on the steps, creating a passage of applause for them while the hem of her white dress disappeared in the church. Even Herr Ernest doesn't want me, and if he knew who I was, he would have killed me already.

I'm looking at the boy near the newsstand. He is shaking and waiting for me in the snow. What's the point of all this? The war will never end.

In the end, the Germans will defeat all of us, the Russians, the Americans, the resistance, me, I know that. The maps of the beaches I see at night, while waiting to be caught, tell me this. The never-ending lines of German soldiers in the boulangerie tell me this, even the food and wine Herr Ernest brings me every time he comes tell me that.

"Cigarette pack, please." I stand at the stall, moving from foot to foot to keep warm while the seller looks sideways nervously.

"The price has gone up. Are you paying in Francs or Reichsmark?"

"Whichever suits you," I pull my wallet out of the bag and pay him in silence, then start walking towards the bridge, lighting a cigarette to warm up a bit.

The soles of my shoes are already worn, and the cold from the pavement freezes my feet, but I hide it from Oberst

Ernest, not wanting him to rush and buy me a new pair or to put German money on the dresser again.

By the bridge, I pass a hunched family, wrapped in old coats and torn blankets. Where is my family? How come I haven't heard yet from Mom and Dad and Jacob? At least they do not know where I ended up and what I had to do to survive. Mom would yell at me, and Dad would shut up, but the look in his eyes would tell me how disappointed he was in me.

"What's the point?" I crush the cigarette with the tip of my shoes, and after a few minutes I light another one, my fingers shaking from the cold. The only white dress I'll be wearing will be the snow that will cover my grave, like Claudine's. I should start getting used to it from now on, and I stand in the cold before entering the alley, letting the snowflakes fall on my hair.

We have not met for so long. What does it matter what he says?

"They are building new barriers here and here." My fingers show him the places on the crumpled map he pulled out of his coat pocket, carefully flattening it with his fingers. "If your American friends do not hurry, they will have no place to invade."

"We have to be patient. We have no other choice. I promise you they will come, is everything fine? I'm worried about you." Philip puts down the pencil with which he marked what I said, never letting me write. If someone gets their hands on the map, it could be a death sentence for me.

"No, you are not," I snatch the pencil and begin to fill in the map of the beach with the barrier lines. Perhaps my time has come.

"What are you doing?" Philip tries to stop me, holding my hand.

"No, you are not," I shout and scratch his hand, continuing to write, even though I no longer know what.

"What am I not?" His hands grip me tightly, and I can hear the creaking of the wooden table and chairs on the floor of the damp basement space.

"You are not worried about me at all. It's the telegrams you care about, that's all I'm worth for you. He's making me a Christmas tree and talking to me about Germany and family, and you are interested in telegrams. You didn't even ask our Communist friends what happened to my family."

"They are in Auschwitz. Your Ernest and his friends sent them to Auschwitz," he shouts back at me, looking at me with anger and hatred.

"I know they arrived at the Auschwitz camp."

"No one comes back from Auschwitz, and more and more trains with people are going there. Do you understand what that means?" I can hear his shouts echo in me from the walls closing around, unable to believe what he is telling me.

"So why didn't you tell me when you knew?" My breathing is heavy. I have to sit down, inhale. This basement is suffocating me. "Why didn't you tell me?"

"How could I tell you such a thing?" He tries to hug me while his voice breaks. "How could I tell you?"

I can't be here anymore. Where's the door outside? I have to breathe, where are the stairs?

"Who will want me?" I've been left alone, let me get out of here, don't touch me. My hands push him. Please, stop staring at my tears running down my cheeks over Mom and Dad and Jacob and the name that makes me sick of Auschwitz, and Herr Oberst Ernest, and me, for all I did when they were no more. I feel sick.

"I want you."

"No one will want me, don't you understand?" I try to fight him off. I have no more Mom and Dad.

"I will want you, it will end one day, and I will study at the Sorbonne as I once did, and we will all return as we once were." He insists on hugging me.

"The past is dead, gone, even you once said it," I shout at him and cry, "no one can fix it."

"But I still want you." He refuses to release me.

"I do not want to see you anymore. Find yourself a replacement, someone whose fingers have no stains of paint and the smell of gun oil." I get up from the hard floor and search for the stairs.

"Please, don't go."

"Don't you understand? I do not want to see you anymore, ever. Get out of my life. I'm like the rats in the Nazi movies, everyone I touch dies or leaves. I spread diseases. I slept with a German officer; you will never marry me. I am an infected Jew."

To Live

March 1944

Secret

3/5/1944

From: Western Front Wehrmacht Command

To: Army Group France

Subject: Preparations for an attack in the West

Background: Army units subordinate to the Western Front must be on alert for an American-British invasion attempt on French shores.

General: France s citizens are expected to show signs of ingratitude towards the German army and may attempt to provoke rebellion in anticipation of the coming liberation. Army units must impose severe discipline on the population and search for ungrateful civilians.

Tasks:

1. Army officers should be alert to treason attempts by locals.

2. It is the army officers responsibility to instill the German army s power in the local population.

SS. Telegram 93

The Sewing box

"My dear, I lost a button on my uniform. Will you sew it back on for me?"

"Certainly, my dear." Herr Ernest hands me his grey-green shirt, the one with the black iron cross, and remains in a white tank top. Carefully I take the metal button from his hand and walk to the bedroom, searching for a sewing kit. We have not met since that time in the basement three months ago.

It's better for me that way, trying not to think about him anymore. I even stopped wandering the streets aimlessly, smoking, looking to punish myself, strolling without direction until the curfew hour. The sketchbook pages are full of new intelligence, hidden in code names among all the flower drawings. But all the information I received didn't change anything, and even if I wanted to contact him, I don't know how. It's better for me, without looking at his fingers or remembering the smell of his shirt.

"Darling? Did you find a sewing kit?" Herr Ernest's voice coming from the study takes me back to reality, and I sit down by the bed, opening the dresser drawers one by one, searching for a sewing kit. I remember seeing one when we moved here, along with the few things that were left in the apartment.

The wooden box is hidden in the third drawer, between white tablecloths. It is made of mahogany wood, and I place it on my lap, looking in the small drawers for a green-grey thread, comparing the small spools to the shirt spread out on the bed. Another drawer opens, and another, as I rummage through with my fingers, pulling from the bottom, and suddenly I notice them and freeze.

Like a snake bite, I quickly close the box. The sound seems to shake the whole room.

"Is there a thread in the right color?"

"I found something similar." My voice is shaking. Did he notice?

Slowly, carefully, I open the small wooden drawers again, gently pulling the spools and trying to peek, quietly praying that I am wrong, but they are there, in the bottom drawer, under some burgundy spools of thread.

I send my fingers out, touch them, pull the spools aside, expose them to the warm air in the room, gently feeling the yellow cloth with my fingertips, and drawing the outline of the letters 'Juif' in the center of the Star of David.

"My dear, I'm in a hurry. I have an appointment."

"I just found it. I'm sewing it right now. I almost forgot how to sew."

"A good woman never forgets," his voice came from the study.

My trembling hands fail again and again to insert the grey thread into the eye of the needle. It is pushed aside with each tremor, refusing to lock itself, and the tears are interrupting it as well.

"I'll be done in a minute."

My fingers sew quickly, pushing the needle firmly into the stiff, rough cloth, ignoring the pain of stabbing it into the shirt, loop after loop, non-stop, like an emotionless machine. Still, in the middle of sewing, I can't anymore. I toss the shirt aside, gripping the wooden box and pouring all its contents onto the bed with a great noise, not thinking what will happen if Herr Ernest loses his patience and comes to find the source of the noise. My fingers rummage through the box, checking to see if there is anything left in the empty wooden cells, but there is almost nothing else there. Just the two yellow badges and one light brown photo of a family by the sea. A father and mother and two children sitting on the small stones, and on the other side, it is written in pencil: "Us, June 5th, 1939, the hotel in Nice."

"Were you crying?" he asks as I stand at the study entrance, handing him the ironed uniform with the button back in place.

"No, I just rubbed my eyes. I couldn't get the thread into the needle."

"Well, thank you very much. Too bad it took you so long. I have to leave now. The driver is already waiting outside."

"Will we meet in the evening?"

"Yes, Please wait for me." He reviews himself in the hall mirror, making sure the button is back in place. His presence in the small entrance hall is too dense for me, but before I can breathe, I have to wait until I hear the door slam shut behind him and the sound of his footsteps moving down the stairwell. I must go out and feel some air that is not in this apartment, a place that does not have a German officer's presence and the smell of eau de cologne.

But I can't return the yellow badges in my pocket to their hiding place in the sewing box, nor the light brown photo.

"May a loving man give you a flower," my lips whisper as I pretend to place a flower on her grave, my hand empty. I couldn't find any flowers. The older woman wasn't standing on the corner, and I do not know what happened to her. Maybe she did not survive the winter, or perhaps she went looking for loving couples in another place. Who would buy flowers when there was no money for food, and the German soldiers were at the front?

The square overlooking the Eiffel is also deserted. The smiling German soldiers and the French girls like me, hanging on their arms, have gone. Only a few army trucks pass through the square in a slow drive, rushing to their destination on the western front, not stopping to buy flowers for anyone.

The cemetery is quiet, and I clean the stone with my hand, brushing it as hard as I can even though the winter rain has washed it clean.

"Sorry I haven't been here for a long time. I'll tell you everything," my lips start mumbling as I try to stop my tears, but I cannot tell her. I can't say the words out loud. Even the yellow badge hiding in my dress pocket does not give me enough courage.

"Exalted and hallowed be His great Name," my lips mumble the prayer to the souls of Mom and Dad and Jacob, and I do not know more than these words. I do not know if I am allowed to pray because I am a woman, and it is not acceptable, and I'm committing a great sin, as Dad used to tell me when I refused to light candles on Friday night, yelling at him that I was French and did not want to be Jewish, but I do not care.

My lips repeat the few words I do know in a whisper, over and over, as I hold the yellow badge firmly in my fists, my eyes closed.

"Sorry, Claudine, I have not visited you in so long. I will

come more," I apologize before I walk away from the grave. For a moment, my gaze is turned back as I struggle with the urge to leave the yellow badge on the stone, but it's too dangerous. I must return it to its hiding place.

I have to see someone I'm running away from; maybe she will agree to take me back.

What if she refuses to open the door for me? I stop at the avenue and look around. Maybe I should stay here? Between the cafés I'm already familiar with?

The German laughter from last spring has disappeared, and only a few soldiers are sitting at the empty tables, served by bored waiters. Maybe I'll sit for a few minutes? Perhaps it's not a good idea to go to her?

What could I tell her? After I ran away from her without saying goodbye? Packing my few belongings and disappearing from her life without explaining, I have not even called her since, even though her luxurious apartment has a telephone. I tried to pick up the phone and ask for her several times, but once I heard the operator's voice asking me for the number, I slammed the black tube back into place.

I have to hurry, Oberst Ernest will come soon, and he doesn't like to wait for me. Recently, his green eyes have become cold, and his voice sounds sharp, making me even more nervous. I quickly cross the boulevard, looking away from the Arc de Triumph and the Nazi flag flying overhead.

The narrow streets have not changed as I walk through

them; even the large metal door at the entrance remains as it was. What will she say to me? Maybe I'll go back and return another day?

My fists clenched, and my nails pressing hard into the palms of my hands, I wait by the door after ringing the bell. My stomach hurts.

She's not there. I can go now, at least I tried. But the door opens, and she is standing and looking at me.

"My girl, you have grown so much." I hear her voice as her hands wrap around me warmly, and I let the tears come out.

"I'm a Jew," I sob in the stairwell.

"Shhh... shhh... it's okay... be careful that no one hears." She pulls me inside, and closes the door behind us.

"I am a Jew, and they sent my parents to a place called Auschwitz in the east, and probably killed them." I can't stop whimpering and crying.

"It's okay, my girl, it's okay," she continues embracing me. "They're watching over you from above, hugging you from there."

"I miss them so much, and I'm with a German officer. I live with him. I'm so ashamed. He brings me food." My face is red and wet from the tears, and my body is shaking and whimpering, vomiting out all the shame I've carried inside for so long.

"Shhh... shhh... it's okay." Her hands continue to stroke my hair, trying to calm me down.

"I just wanted to stay alive and look where I ended up..." My voice choked.

"Shhh... my beautiful girl... no one wants to die..." She continues to hug me as I calm down, and only my breaths are heard inside the luxurious guest room.

"Shall I make us a cup of tea? Or coffee? I think I even have some real coffee left."

"What will I do?" I ask her sometime later, as we sit in her living room, sipping the tea she made for us. Now and then, I still have to wipe away a tear, but I am not shaking anymore.

"Move on, just keep moving on. You have to stay alive."

"I cannot live like this. I can't go back to him."

"Can you leave him?"

"They will catch me and kill me."

"So you must go back, for yourself, for your parents who are watching you from above, for Claudine, for Philip, for all the people who care about you. You are not alone. Even if sometimes you feel you have no one, you must live for them."

"How will I do that?"

"Just keep moving on the best you can, the liberation will arrive, the Americans will come."

"I no longer believe they will ever invade. The Germans always win in the end."

"The war will be over, you must believe, if not for you, for them."

"And what about you? Do you believe the war will end?"

"Sometimes it's hard for me too, but then I imagine what he would do or say," she smiles at me sadly and looks at the man in the picture above the fireplace, "so yeah, I probably keep living for him."

We say goodbye with a warm hug, and I hurry home, knowing I'm late and that Oberst Ernest will be angry with me. Why did she mention Philip? How does she know about him? But I do not have time to think about it; he sent me to her house, and Lizette surely heard about him. I have to hurry, Herr Ernest is waiting for me.

"I need to move on. The war will end soon," my lips repeatedly whisper as I speed up my steps. The apartment is already close.

"Where were you?" He looks up from the documents placed in front of him, lying on the massive oak desk in his study, the room I am not allowed to enter.

"I was delayed. I apologize."

"I'm waiting for you, we'd made plans to go to a show, and I came especially."

"I know, I'm sorry."

"I have a lot of work to do. War is not a distant concept. It is approaching us. You have to understand that."

I silently dress, not wanting him to be angrier at me than he is already. The drive to the theater passes silently with his gloved hand resting on my thigh.

"It is always such a pleasure to again meet the French mademoiselle who speaks perfect German," the senior officer smiles at me in his black uniform with a skull on his visored hat, as we stand at the theater hall entrance.

"Germany above all," I answer him in perfect German.

"I am always happy to meet a loyal French citizen."

"I hope not in the building on Avenue Foch," another officer joins, and everyone around laughs, but Herr Ernest says nothing.

"Where are you going?" Oberst Ernest asks me when I turn my back and start walking.

"To the ladies' room."

Don't be afraid of him. He is just flirting with you. He knows nothing. I wash my face with cold water, but it doesn't help. I have to go back. They are waiting for me.

"Sorry, I had a nauseous moment." I return to the group of officers again, hoping Herr Ernest won't smell the cigarette I smoked in the restroom.

"We hope you are not cooking us a little German kid," an armored officer winks at me, and I get close to Herr Ernest, holding his arm.

"Well, about that, you'd have to ask my Herr Ernest." I smile a perfect red lipstick smile at the officer. Even though everybody is laughing, Herr Ernest is looking at me with his green eyes and not smiling.

I'm not pregnant. Anaïs already taught me how to be careful, when I still had to learn what to do. "Take this, it's for you, so you won't have to donate a child to the Führer." She placed a pack of rubbers in my hands, explaining to me how to use them as I blushed and hurried to hide them in my bag. "I'm just making sure you don't come to me later, asking for my help." She laughed and lit a cigarette for herself, then, before I started to smoke.

"Here's to German women who devote their wombs to the Fatherland." I fake a smile.

"Here's to German women." The officers around me agree, smelling of cologne, and even Herr Ernest raises his glass.

"Let's go inside." Herr Ernest holds my arm as the announcer rings the bell, and we all head to our seats.

"I look forward to our next meeting," the black-uniformed officer kisses my hand politely as I tightly hold Oberst Ernest's arm, waiting for the lights to go out.

Soon the war will be over. Lizette promised me that. But I have not seen Philip since I shouted at him in the basement.

A few days later, I'm walking by the newsstand when I notice the boy is back. He is arranging a pile of newspapers and whispering to me about the meeting point, and my heart is pounding. It's been so long.

I must not think about Philip; I have to concentrate, make sure I am not followed in the streets. What about my fears of Herr Ernest? Shall I tell him? Will he calm me down after all the horrible things I said to him?

The road to the Latin Quarter does not end as I pedal the bike, hurrying as fast as I can, looking down in shame as I pass a long line of women. They are waiting quietly at the grocery store entrance, hoping to buy some food with their food ration stamps.

I will tell him everything, even if nothing will ever be between us, and even if all he is interested in is the information I'm bringing. I don't care; he is waiting for me.

The stairs leading down into the basement seem dark, and I stand and arrange my breath, my dress, the bag strap on my shoulder, and I brush my hair with my fingers; I am ready, despite the dull ache in the bottom of my stomach. Will he hug me?

Without thinking, I quickly go down the stairs, stopping on the last step, looking at him and freezing. He is not Philip.

"Hello, Monique," the stranger standing at the basement entrance reaches his hand out. "Do not run away."

The Stranger

Where's Philip? What did they do to him? Did they catch him? Is this man German? I want to scream, and my stomach hurts. What should I do?

Think fast about a cover story. My hand quickly goes into my dress pocket, but all I have is a yellow badge. Why didn't I put it back in its place? They will kill me. Where's Philip?

"Everything is fine," the stranger raises his hand in a calming motion and tells me his name, but with all the screams in my head, I can hear nothing.

"Monique," he tries to approach.

Slowly, I go back up the stairs.

"Do not run away. Everything is fine. I'm one of ours. I'm replacing Philip."

Everything is not fine, and I do not believe him, where's Philip? My hand stays tucked in my dress pocket, holding the yellow badge tightly; maybe he'll think I have a weapon, while my eyes follow his movements, ready to run away, even though he will probably shoot me if I turn my back.

"Everything's fine, do not be afraid, I'm replacing Philip, and I'll work with you from now on." He smiles at me, but I can hear noises outside in the street upstairs.

"Where's Philip?" I slowly approach the wooden table waiting for us in the basement, watching him come closer and raise his hand again.

Then, in one movement, I kick him as hard as I can, turning around and escaping up the stairs. Between my breaths, I can barely hear him groaning behind me, and the sound of a falling chair, but I'm not stopping; I must run out of here.

Like a bullet, I burst into the street and start to run as

fast as I can, almost tripping over the smooth street stones, trying to pass through two merchants arguing, holding wooden carts, and shouting at each other for the right to cross the narrow street. I don't have time to look back.

In one of the alleys, I hide and rest for a few minutes, leaning against the cracked brick wall and trying to catch my breath. What was that? What happened to Philip? Did they ambush me? I carefully peeked into the main street, but everyone seemed suspicious. The man dozing on the bench and the woman standing in the store's doorway, and what about the young man slowly pedaling his bike, looking to the sides, is he looking for me?

My head is down as I return to the main street, trying to walk calmly. Running earlier was a mistake; it surely attracted attention. I don't want them to find me. I promised Lizette that I would stay alive.

"What arrived today?" I ask the last woman in line as I stand behind her, waiting on the street to enter the grocery store, hoping I'm not arousing suspicion with my modern dress.

"They say he had bread and oil, but there is not much left."

"I hope something will be left by the time we get inside," I smile at her while looking to the sides of the street.

"He does not accept the old coupons, only the new ones. Do you have the new ones?"

"Yes, I have."

"Would you like to exchange coupons?" she whispers to me, not wanting the others standing in the line to hear us. "I can give you cheese coupons in exchange for meat coupons, is it right with you?"

"Yes, sure." My fingers rummage in my bag, searching for

the ration card as I turn my back on her and carefully tear off the stamps. I don't want her to notice that my ration card is almost unused, it will arouse her suspicions, and she will start poking around, asking more questions. The street is empty, maybe I've managed to escape from them.

"What a fool I am. I've run out of oil coupons. I'm standing here for nothing." I make a sad face.

"Never mind, I'll give you one of mine," she smiles at me. "We women must help each other. Otherwise, how will we survive this war?"

The sun has already set as I cross Pont Neuf towards the east bank, holding a paper bag with a loaf of bread. The metro has already stopped operating at such an hour, they are trying to save electricity, and I will have to walk all the way to the apartment. At least I insisted on giving her some meat stamps from my ration card, knowing they are priceless, and I do not need them anyway. My pantry is full of German army meat tins.

On the way home, I occasionally stop and look back, making sure I am not being followed. Sometimes I sit on a bench in the avenue, resting and looking around, but I avoid smoking, even though I need it so much. A smoking woman always draws attention.

Carefully I approach the building and carefully climb the stairs and listen outside the door. The apartment is dark and empty. No one is waiting to arrest me, not even Herr Oberst Ernest. He informed me he would not come today. He's been coming less recently.

I wake up at night, hearing someone outside on the building stairs, but no one knocks loudly at the door, shouting at me to open up. What happened to Philip? Maybe

I'm wrong, and everything's okay? Perhaps he's replacing him? I did not even manage to hear the stranger's name.

Next time I will be more prepared.

───※───

The next day, on my way out from the boulangerie, the boy is waiting for me again, and I have to go back to the Latin Quarter. I'm ready this time.

Step by step, I carefully go down the stairs, my hand resting in my dress pocket, my fingers firmly holding the knife's handle. The yellow badge was returned to its hiding place in the sewing kit. I must never repeat such mistakes.

Along the way, I was still hoping it was a mistake or a bad dream and that Philip would be waiting for me this time, but it wasn't a dream. The same stranger is waiting for me in the damp basement.

"Hello, Monique."

I remain standing on the last step, nervously examining him, and say nothing. I must know what happened to Philip.

"Hello again." He tries to get closer but notices the tiny movement of my body stepping back, and stops where he is, afraid I'll run away or try to kick him again. My fingers hold the knife's handle tighter.

"I am listening."

"I'm replacing Philip."

"And why does he need a replacement, and where is he?"

"I can't tell you."

"So why should I believe you?"

"You have to believe me. Look, he gave this to me." And the stranger takes the map of the Normandy coastline out of his pocket, places it on the table, the same map I tried to draw the last time we met. I'm so sorry for what I said to him.

"Did you replace him because of what I said to him?"

"What did you say to him?"

"Doesn't matter."

"Are you ready to get closer?"

"Will he meet me again?"

"I do not know. It doesn't depend on me."

"What is your name?" I ask him in German.

"I do not understand," he answers me in French. Shall I believe him?

On the way back to the city's east bank, I choose to return through Pont des Arts. The river's grey water flows quietly under the wooden boards, and despite the chill wind, I sit on one of the benches and light myself a cigarette. A couple of adults standing not far from me are looking at me and whispering, but I ignore them, feeling the hot smoke in my throat. I have already done much worse than smoking. Am I falling into the trap of the Gestapo? Did they infiltrate the resistance? Doesn't he want to see me anymore?

"Do not cry, my dear. He will return." The older woman who looked at me with anger earlier is approaching me. "Everything will be all right."

"Thanks." I smile at her, wiping my tears with the handkerchief she's handed me. He will come back, he must come back, I will bring the best information I can get, and I will stay alive, telling him how much I miss him.

Before they walk away, the older woman turns to me,

smiling one last time for encouragement, and I smile back at her, wiping my tears again. I have to stop this crying; Herr Ernest will arrive at the apartment soon. He wants us to go out with his officers, and I need to continue acting like everything is perfect.

***

The dark night sky is filled with the lights of anti-aircraft trace ammunition slowly climbing up, until they disappear between the clouds.

"Stop the vehicle," Oberst Ernest instructs the driver as we hurry to get out of the car, rushing to the side of the street and looking up.

I can't see the American bombers in the dark night, nor the German searchlights traveling between the clouds and looking for them, but I can feel them there, in the sky above me.

Their monotonous noise and the echoes of explosions in the distance make me sweat and cower in fear while I cover my head with my hands.

The street is entirely dark, the few lamps that are still on at night have gone out, as ordered, and I kneel on the dark, cold sidewalk.

"Come on, hurry up," he calls to me, and I continue in the direction of his voice, clinging to the wall, waiting to feel the heat of the bombs, but they do not come.

The sirens' howls don't stop, tearing at my ears, but the anti-aircraft batteries aren't heard at all at a distance. Only their death bullets are seen, painting the skies in red stripes. The bombers are probably just passing by.

"You can get up. It's over." Herr Ernest reaches his hand out after a few minutes, supporting me as I get up from the sidewalk, arranging my evening dress. "Your friends went to bomb other Frenchmen."

"I'm with you, and they're bombing me too. I do not support the Americans."

"I know you are loyal to the German nation." He opens the car door for me; did he mean what he said?

The rest of the ride passes quietly, with the car's headlights making their way through the dark streets to the nightclub, but his hand does not rest on my thigh.

"I thought you would not come," Anaïs hugs me and shouts in my ear, trying to overcome the noisy music.

"Slight delay," I smile and point up with my finger.

"Yes, soon they will arrive, and then we all have to learn English." She smiles her knowing smile.

"I'm not going to replace what I have." I place my hand on Herr Ernest's back, as he is busy talking to the Fritzes. Even though we have not exchanged a word since the unplanned stop on the street, I must have him trust me.

"We will see." She laughs at me and hugs her Fritz, whispering something in his ear, and he takes a cigarette box out of his pocket, lighting one for her.

"How are you?" I try to shout to Violette, who is sitting quietly on the other side of the table, but she does not answer me; she just smiles sadly.

"Lately, Fritz doesn't give her attention at all," Anaïs volunteers to tell me the latest news, ignoring Violette who is sitting beside her. "She's afraid he won't take her with him to Germany." And I feel sorry and want to hug her. She looks so lost to me.

"Do not worry, Violette, he will stay here with us until the end." Anaïs hugs her instead of me. "Look what the city has to offer him," she points to the stripper dancing in front of the men. She is wearing panties and shaking her breasts, which are bound in a purple corset, to the cheers of the crowd. "No one else will be able to provide him with such pleasure."

Anaïs' evil surprises me, and I look for something to answer her, but Violette gets up and walks towards the restroom, pushing between the crowds, women in nightdresses and men mostly in German uniforms.

"She does not need you, she needs to face reality," Anaïs grabs my arm as I get up, intending to follow her. "She needs to learn how to take care of herself, like us."

"I'll be right back." I smile at her, hurrying after Violette into the dim opening on the side of the stage, apologizing to the people around the tables as I pass. I'm running out of friends to lose.

"He's ignoring me," she cries in front of the filthy mirror, and her whole body trembles as she searches through her little bag, looking for a pencil to fix the makeup around her eyes. "He tells me I don't support him enough and that he's busy."

"Maybe he's busy?"

"A few days ago, he returned to town, and we haven't met since then." Her sobs continue.

"Men are like that," my hand touches her shoulder. "They like to play in the war." The feeling of the mature woman who should encourage another is strange to me.

"He was not like that at first. At first, he had time to hang out with me, promising me things."

"That's the way it is. First they promise you things until they get into your underwear, but after that, they are not interested." I try to speak with a funny tone, but Violette just cries more.

"What will they do to me?" She turns to me with a scared look, her cheeks dirty from her smeared eye makeup.

"Who?" My hand continues to caress her shoulder, even though it feels strange to me.

"Everyone, the French."

"I don't understand."

"What will they do to me if the Russians or the Americans come?" I stop caressing her.

"They will not come, they have been fighting for four years, and they have not come yet."

"I was so scared today when I heard the bombers coming. I didn't want to come at all, but Fritz insisted."

"The Germans are strong. They will beat the Americans if they come. Nothing will happen to you. Your Fritz will protect you."

"And the Russians?"

"They will defeat the Russians too."

"It all happened because of the Jews who control the world's economy. They influenced the Russians with their money, and now the Americans too." She wipes her face with a handkerchief she pulled out of her bag, looking at herself in the mirror. She has never really been my friend.

"I heard that the Germans have done unspeakable things as well." I can't stop myself.

"Those are just rumors. I do not believe that my Fritz would harm someone; he is so polite with me even when he is angry, not like French men." She fixes her lipstick and, unhappy with the result, removes it with her handkerchief, applying it again.

"They are probably just rumors. They will not come. You will stay with your Fritz forever, you will see." I force myself to hug her a little for encouragement, waiting for her to finish fixing her makeup, but she already wants to return to the club. Suddenly the noisy club feels intimate to me, despite the loud music, the applause, and the cigarette smoke filling it.

"Did you hold her hand while she was fixing her makeup?" Anaïs whispers as we sit down at the table. "Don't worry," she brings her mouth close to mine, making sure I hear her over the noise, "I hosted a company for everyone instead of you. What are best friends for?"

But it does not seem to me that the men are paying any attention to her at all. Though she never stops stroking her Fritz's back, the men's eyes are focused on the almost-naked dancer on the stage. She slowly removes her skirt to the sounds of cheers and whistles. No one from the crowd cares anymore about the dark planes that passed over our heads earlier tonight.

Later, in the apartment bedroom, I wonder if, like all men, Herr Ernest lays on me but imagines the stripper shaking her breasts in front of his eyes and mostly smiling at him, impressed by his high rank. When he was in Russia, did he own some woman? Doing horrible things during the day and being polite to her at night? The same politeness he shows me?

The sound of Herr Ernest's breathing disturbs the silence in the room as I sneak into the forbidden study. I must find better information, to see Philip again.

Fissures

"The Germans are moving more forces towards the coast and splitting headquarters. There is an argument between the generals."

"What kind of argument?"

"Something about unit sectors, I could not understand."

"And how do you know that?"

"I heard a phone call."

"Monique, you've done a good job so far, but these are things that we are less interested in. I need you to get me plans, photos, not rumors you maybe hear in a casual phone conversation."

"I'm bringing anything I can get my hands on."

"Monique, you need to work harder. We need every bit of information for the coming invasion, not just pieces of small talk. I need you to get me maps, telegrams, real material." His finger knocks on the wooden table that separates us, making me cringe. It seems to me that he hasn't forgiven me for the kick he received at our first meeting. I can apologize to him, but he's still scaring me.

"When will Philip return?"

"I'm replacing him. You're working with me now."

"Yes, but when will he return?"

"What does it matter to you? Are you working for Philip, or the resistance and the liberation of France?"

His black eyes angrily stare at me as I curl up in my chair, lowering my gaze slightly and examining his clean grey button-down shirt.

"I am working for the resistance."

"You should forget about Philip; for you, he no longer exists."

My fingers tighten around the knife handle in my dress pocket, unable to release the grip and place my hands on the table. But he is also sitting in front of me with his hands tucked deep in his pants pockets, taking them out only when he wags his fingers and scolds me. Why does Philip not want to meet me anymore? I have to find him.

"Monique, you are not listening to me."

"Sorry, what did you say?"

"That you must be more efficient, certainly if you want to go back and work with Philip." His finger is raised again in front of my face.

"I'll be more efficient, I promise." But I keep my hand in my dress pocket.

On my way out, I look for the little girl from the shop in the alley. I have two cans of canned milk that Herr Ernest brought me. She will probably relish the white sweetness; surely she needs the milk more than I do. The girl in the torn shoes and dirty dress approaches me in hesitating steps and stares suspiciously at my hands holding the two white cans, on which German eagles are printed, holding black swastikas.

"Take it," I whisper to her, and she snatches them from my hand and runs from me, laughing as if she doesn't care about the war and the Germans spreading fear.

I don't remember myself laughing. I think I forgot how to laugh when I saw my first German soldier a few days after the occupation. He stood on our street corner and ordered Dad to bow to his hobnail boots before we could continue walking. We were on our way home, and I held Dad's hand and smiled awkwardly at the soldier.

"What are you laughing at?" The huge soldier shouted at me in German, waving his arm and threatening me as I looked up at him and choked.

"It's okay," Dad whispered to me, humiliated and bowing before the soldier let us continue our way, not before throwing Dad's hat on the pavement, forcing him to kiss the ground.

"Let's go home. Mom made you something delicious." He tried to cheer me up, but from that day on I did not laugh anymore.

"Don't cry," Dad tried to soothe me. "Mom's waiting for us at home." Our home with the red carpet in the living room and the kitchen that was always full of cooking aromas. The house that must have been taken over by a German officer housing his mistress.

Is one of the rooms set as his study, which she is not allowed to enter, but she does by night?

My fingers quickly go over the pile of documents in his briefcase as I carefully pull them out and carry them with me to the bathroom. Quietly I sit on the floor and read them by candlelight, trying to understand the assessments for protection from a telegram allocating barbed wire fences to various shorelines.

The noise of the bathroom handle makes me jump out on the floor, and I manage to blow out the candle.

"What are you doing?" I hear his voice through the closed door.

"I'm in here." What to do? I'm dead, my hands hold the candle, what to do with it? And all the telegrams?

"What are you doing in there?"

"I need to be here."

"I've been lying awake in bed for a long time, waiting for you." What to answer him? What about the pages? My hands search in the dark, looking for somewhere to tuck them in. What if they wrinkle? He will kill me.

"Please don't come in. I'm so ashamed. I ate something bad." My fingers grope and carefully push the papers behind the radiator before I go out and quietly close the door behind me.

"Please do not go in, I beg you." My eyes try to examine his silhouette in the darkness of the room, but after a moment, I choose to turn my back on him and quietly walk to bed; he mustn't think I am trying to stop him from entering the bathroom.

With every step, I wait to hear him open the door or grab me by the hair and throw me on the floor for turning my back on him, but when I lie in bed and finally stop shaking, he joins me.

Only hours later, when I'm sure he is well asleep, I get up again and carefully return the telegrams to his leather bag, praying he will not notice that they are more wrinkled than they were before. I won't do that anymore. It's getting too dangerous.

"Are you okay? Aren't you sick?" Simone asks me the next morning.

"No, I'm okay, everything is fine."

"Then why are you late again? The fact that you are living with a German officer doesn't give you special privileges. Ordinary citizens have more to struggle with than you. Look at Marie. She is always on time."

I apologize to Mrs. Simone and hurry to stand behind the counter, waiting for the day to end so I can go back to the apartment, put my head down, and get some sleep.

The sound of the vase shattering on the floor wakes me in a panic, and I sit up in bed, trying to figure out what's going on. My eyes are wide open, but I see nothing in the dark room. In the distance, there is a muffled noise of an explosion followed by a flash of light from the window, penetrating the room's curtain, followed by a much louder explosion that shakes the iron bed and the window. I bend over and scream, covering my head with my hands. What's going on?

Another flash from the window, followed by a deafening explosion; I can hear the sobs of sirens from a distance, and the cups in the kitchen shattering on the floor. As I stumble from the bed to the floor, I cover my head with my hands, clinging to the wooden floor, making myself as small as I can, trying to disappear inside the parquet. I do not want to die.

Another explosion shakes the house while I crawl towards the window, getting on my knees and opening it. What's going on outside? The explosions blast wave immediately blows the window from my hand, slamming it against the wall, pulling back the curtain, and all the sounds of hell enter the room. The next house's windows sparkle with orange light, fire reflected from a distance, and the skies are lit in red-orange colors. Anti-aircraft batteries are firing lines of red tracer ammunition in a monotonous rumble, painting red dots towards the orange sky, but above all, there is the noise of growls and explosions.

Like a deep gurgle that does not stop for a moment, the noise of the aircraft bomber engines in the sky fill the air as they pass in an endless stream of invisible monsters above me in the darkness, growling incessantly with a muffled voice of rage.

Another explosion shakes the air, and I am thrown back, screaming. Please don't hit the house. While crawling on the floor and ignoring the porcelain shards of the vase wounding me, I manage to find my nightgown and make my way in the dark to the front door. Another flash, followed by an explosion, illuminates my way for a moment. I must escape.

My hands fight to unlock the door, sliding them by force, but the key falls to the floor with a sharp sound of metal, and I grope for it with my wounded hands, crying for them not to kill me. Please move on; throw your bombs elsewhere, just not on me. Another explosion shakes the house as I try to insert the key, looking for the keyhole with trembling hands.

Through the open door, I crawl down the stairs, groping in the dark and leaning against the railing. From the stairwell window, I can see the orange light of distant fires and more explosions, painting the air with shards of light that fly to the skies, making me cringe in my place on the stairs. I must reach the bottom, where I will be safe.

She is kneeling near the third-floor door, and I almost stumble and fall when I hit her, screaming in fear, but bending over and touching her body. She is silent even as I'm trying to shake her, feeling her body trembling under my touch.

"Are you okay?" Another flash of light from the window highlights her open eyes that are looking at me.

"It's the Americans," she answers in a hollow voice.

"Are you okay? Are you injured?"

"They're bombing me."

"Are you okay? Injured? Can you get up?"

"It's the Americans."

"Come, get up, lean on me."

"They're bombing me."

"We must hurry."

"It's the Americans."

"Get up," I scream and slap her, cringing again at the noise of the glass in the stairwell and the never-ending growl of planes. Stop it already. We're both going to die here.

"Get up," I slap her again, and finally, she slowly rises, leaning against my body, and we both go down the stairs, hiding under the staircase at the entrance. While hugging her, I whisper to the planes to go, asking them to leave and cringing with each explosion, knowing the next bomb will hit us.

Long after the growl has gone and disappeared into the night, and only the light of the fires in the city paints the clouds in the night sky grey-orange, we slowly start climbing the stairs again. Occasionally I hear people running in the street, or a fire truck's siren whimpering and disappearing between the buildings in the distance, painted yellow.

"Here, this is your door," I say goodbye to her at the front door of her apartment. "Do you have the key?" Maybe she will hate me less.

"The Americans bombed me." She refuses to let go of her grip, holding me firmly, and I have to take her to my apartment, seating her in the kitchen and making her a cup of tea. I already want to be alone and curl up in bed, even though I cannot fall asleep.

"Are you okay?" I put the cup of tea in front of her.

"Was I scared?"

"No, you were not afraid. You were just fine."

"You have a lot of food." Her gaze wanders to my pantry shelves, filled with cans wrapped in light brown paper and marked with the sign of the German eagle.

"Want some?" And she nods her head. I do not need so much anyway.

"Have a quiet night," I say goodbye to her later at the door of her apartment, helping her down the stairs and supporting her, holding the food I gave her. But after the door slams shut, I am left to sit in the darkness of the stairwell, unable to go up to my apartment alone. I can occasionally hear people outside shouting in the street, or the whistling sound of a passing car.

"A barbaric American bomb hits Paris, the French and the German nations in a partnership of fate!" the boy selling newspapers shouts as he walks down the street and holds the Paris Soir newspaper above his head. For a moment, I want to stop him and tuck a coin in his hand, and take the thin newspaper, which contains government propaganda insults towards the Americans, but I'm not sure I can read about people like me who ran out of luck last night.

The city is quiet this morning; fewer people walk the streets, looking to the sides, being careful not to stumble and get hurt by the glass scattered on the sidewalks—even the car traffic, which has been low lately, is hardly noticeable this morning. Here and there, I can hear a fire truck rushing to a fire that has not yet been extinguished; its horns howl as passersby quietly look at it.

One man stands inside a shattered window in the avenue, quietly collecting the glass remnants into a bucket of tin, gently removing them from the luxury clothes that hang on the dolls in the window, and estimating the damage to his store. Further down the street, several people gather and talk excitedly, recounting the experiences of the previous night, and I stop for a moment.

"I heard the Eighteenth Arrondissement was hit the hardest," one woman babbles to the crowd gathered around her, and I get closer, even though Simone is waiting for me.

"They tried to hit the railroad tracks and hit innocent people," another man adds. "A lot of them got killed." And the crowd nods in approval. I'm already late, and I have to stop listening to them. What if they come again tonight? Or tomorrow?

The sky above is still full of grey smoke, and the burnt smell fills the streets and intensifies as I get closer to the opera and the boulangerie. More people are crowding in groups around the newsstands, reading the headlines and talking excitedly, but I just pass by and do not stop to stand in line. Since yesterday I haven't stopped thinking about Philip. Has something happened to him?

"Thank God you're fine," Simone hugs me as I walk in the door, and I am embarrassed by the touch of her hands. "I was already afraid something had happened to you. What is going with these Americans and the British? They are unable to come free us, so they decided to try and kill us?" She's trying to be funny, telling a joke I'd heard from someone before on the street, at one of the gatherings.

"They are trying to expel everyone from Paris, so that the city will remain only for them when they come." I also try to contribute to the humor, feeling that I am not succeeding; the boulangerie floor is full of porcelain fragments.

"Come and help me. We'll start cleaning." She hands me the apron and broom, but after consulting with Martin the cook, she calls me to the back room.

"Monique, the butter delivery did not arrive this morning. I do not know what happened to the delivery truck. I want you to go to the market and try to get butter. I will give you our confirmation letter."

For two years now, I have refrained from approaching the massive market building.

For two years, I have circled it or walked the streets around, avoiding the market, fearful that maybe one of the sellers might recognize me from those days I ran from them. Still, Simone refuses to send Marie instead, and I have no choice, I must go there.

I approach the arched structure at the city center, looking down and peeking to the sides. The market is as noisy as ever, though the trucks that used to park on the side streets are gone, and horse-drawn carriages have replaced them. The piles of crates are smaller, or maybe they just stayed huge in my memory as I hid between them, waiting for the night to sneak out for a moment. But the smell of pickled vegetables mixed with cheese and meat has not changed. And the noise and sellers' shouts remain the same.

"My name is Monique Autin," I whisper as I get close to the two policemen standing under the entrance gate of the cheese area, trying to examine their faces. Will they recognize me? But they seem excited, talking about yesterday's bomb with a small man stacking crates of vegetables on a cart, not paying attention at all. They surely are not looking for a single girl who escaped from them two years ago. I take a deep breath and pass them in a steady walk, raising my eyes only when I'm inside and watching all the sellers and the merchandise guards. Step by step, I pace down the first aisle, breathing slowly and pushing between all the people, forcing myself to look around and searching for our butter supplier. My hand tightly holds the confirmation paper that allows him to sell butter to the boulangerie. I mustn't lose it.

"Mademoiselle, he's not here today." The salesman at the next cheese stall returns the crumpled paper to me as he looks at me intently, trying to remember if he knows me.

"Thanks." I snatch the paper from his hand and quickly walk away.

"Maybe he was killed at night, no one knows. Have you bought from him before?"

"Never mind, thanks."

"Mademoiselle, I can sell to you."

"Thanks, I'll manage."

"Mademoiselle, no one else will sell to you, especially after what happened in the night."

What shall I tell Simone? The selection is meager at the cheese stalls, and he is right. They all refuse to look at the paper I'm holding, explaining that their butter is already promised to other stores. Maybe the big man will help me? The one with the filthy tank top and the sour smell of cabbage, who saved my life two years ago and disappeared?

What happened to him? Is he with the resistance? I look around, but there's no way I'd recognize him. The market is huge, and I no longer remember where I ran and hid. The rows of stalls and piles of crates look the same to me in every direction my eyes look. And if I find him, will he recognize me and want to help me again?

Finally, I return to the cheese seller with a downcast look, handing him my order and making sure to look around, just not at him, but he keeps examining me as he slices the chunks of butter, as if trying to refresh his memory.

"Thank you," I hurry away from him with the packages on my shoulders.

"You're welcome, come again," he shouts after me, but I no longer answer him.

Only at a safe distance from the market and the two policemen at the entrance do I return to my usual walk. It was just my imagination. There's no way he recognized me from those days I ran hungry between the aisles. I must hurry; Martin is waiting for the butter, but it is difficult to walk down the streets with the stuffy smell of fire all around.

"That's all I've got. It's not enough." I place the baskets in front of Simone.

"I knew I should have sent Marie to do that job. God knows where she disappeared to a few minutes after you left, go and search for her."

"Is everything okay?" I sit next to Marie outside the back entrance of the boulangerie.

"I saw them hitting one of the planes, and the fire coming out of it," she says quietly. "I didn't know where to run."

"They are fighting to set us free."

"I didn't think you would say such a thing." She looks at me.

293

"Yes, I know what you think of me." I take out a cigarette and light it, smoking in silence, thinking of the American soldiers in the burning bomber who came all the way from overseas to set me free.

"New York, San Francisco, Statue of Liberty," I whisper the magical words of freedom; Dad once showed me postcards from America.

"What did you say?"

"That we need to get back to work. Simone is looking for us." I throw the cigarette and step on it. "Don't worry; they will not return tonight."

Paris is not bombed the following nights, but the planes still pass in the dark over the town. I sit in bed and listen to the monotonous noise of their engines, my body tense while I wait to hear the explosions. "Los Angeles, Montana, Niagra Falls," I try to whisper, but my body doesn't stop shaking. Only in the morning do I manage to fall asleep, imagining Philip's warm hands hugging me, like that time in the basement.

There is still a faint smell of fire on the way to work, but they have already cleaned the glass from the streets, and the cracked shop windows are covered with strips of sticky paper. I try to work as hard as I can in the boulangerie, distracting my mind from the nights to come.

The boulangerie door opens, and I notice Violette coming in, her eyes red.

"Good morning," I say, but it's been hard for me to smile since the last time we met at the club about two weeks ago.

"I need to talk to you."

"What happened?" I ask, already guessing that the answer has to do with her Fritz.

"I cannot say." She looks at the soldier waiting in line for his order and watching us.

"Wait. I'll be right with you." I pack his croissants and hope she hasn't gotten Fritz involved in that female problem. Did Anaïs also place a package of rubbers in her hands? Her Fritz probably brings them from German army supply; he wouldn't want to harm his Aryan race's purity, mixing it with some simple local mistress.

"Monique, you are daydreaming. The honorable soldier is waiting."

"Sorry I only gave you only three croissants; we are limited in quantities." I hand the bag to the soldier. Supply shipments have become irregular in recent days, but it does not really matter. The flow of soldiers in grey-green uniforms has filled the small space with loud speeches, and cigarette smoke remains only a distant memory. Only a few of them enter these days. Everyone is at the front, waiting for the invasion, hardly visiting Paris anymore.

"Sit down; I'll join you in a minute." Or maybe Fritz abandoned her, decided she was not right for him. We had not met since that evening at the club, I was comfortable keeping a distance from her, afraid I would be tempted to say nasty things. I've never been like this, maybe I learned from Anaïs, or maybe too much time has passed, and I have become one of them. Surely this is what Simone thinks of me. Even Marie no longer wants to go out for a walk with me on the boulevard, as she wanted to when she was new.

"What happened?" We sit down at one of the empty tables, and even Simone does not make a face. Maybe more customers will enter when they see that people are sitting by the boulangerie tables.

"I can't go on like this anymore."

"What happened?"

"I do not sleep at night, Fritz hardly comes and when he does, he is stressed, there are almost no food rations at the grocery store, and you do not come to visit me."

"I was busy; I apologize." I touch her hand.

"When will they invade?"

"They will not invade."

"I'm scared," she holds my hand. "Why can't we be like we used to be?"

"What do you mean?"

"Back then, when we went to the river, sailed in boats, laughed and had fun, or when we were going to cafés on the Champs-Élysées, and no one cared about when the Americans were coming. I hate this summer."

"The summer has not yet started. We are only at the beginning of June," I answer her, and wonder when exactly, in all this time she was enjoying, Fritz's friends killed my family in Auschwitz. I want to stop stroking her hand, but I hold myself back.

"I already hated this summer before it began," she smiles a little. "I like to feel your fingers, they're warm, I'm lucky you're my friend."

Two more armored German soldiers enter the boulangerie, laughing and saying they need something sweet before they leave Paris on their way to the staging areas, and Simone clears her throat. I have to get up and serve them.

"Do not worry; the Americans will not come." I give her

one last hug before I walk up behind the counter, wondering whether she would have stayed my friend had she known who I really was. "How can I help you?" I ask the two soldiers in the mottled uniforms with a polite smile, the ones who would try to kill the American soldiers if they came to set me free.

On the way back to the apartment, I stop for a few minutes and light a cigarette, walking into one of the small streets, far from the reproachful looks of men seeing a woman smoking, but on the way to the metro, I see several people in long black coats scanning the crowd, and I decide to walk home on foot.

Oberst Ernest informed me that he would come tonight, and I no longer know what scares me more, his presence or the bombers passing through the night sky.

What does it matter, I think to myself when I stop and light another cigarette. My end will be the same.

※

"How was your day?" I kneel at Herr Ernest's feet, trying to help him take off his boots, but he ignores me and enters the apartment, examining it with his eyes.

"What happened to the wine glasses that were in the living room?"

"They were broken a few days ago by the bombers."

"The American and British bombers?" He lets me help him take off his boots.

"Yes, the American and British bombers." I look down at the floor, holding his dirty black boots.

"They are destroying all our achievements, coming at night like thieves, afraid to invade and fight the German army."

"I hate them." I place his hobnail boots by the front door.

"But all the people in the streets cheer when they come."

"I don't think they are cheering for them." I get off the floor and help him remove his coat.

"No, they are spying for information, that's what our intelligence says. They are ungrateful for our efforts to stop the Communist monster coming from the East, destroying the world together with the Jews."

"I hate the Communists."

"The French people always surprise me, supporting the wrong conqueror. Our intelligence reports that the resistance is passing information to England, helping them destroy France."

"I'm with you. I don't want Paris to be destroyed." Is he setting a trap for me? What should I answer?

"Aren't you more French than German?"

"I'm with you here, isn't it the answer?" What should I do? Why did Philip not prepare me for this?

Slowly I hand him back the bottle of wine he brought with him, praying he won't notice my trembling legs, looking into his green eyes and whispering to him in German: "If that doesn't suit you, I can go." Then I turn and walk to the bedroom, getting ready to start packing, my whole body tense and shaking.

Did I do right? Should I have fallen on my knees and begged?

"Take your clothes off."

But I keep walking, turning my back on him, knowing that he is a German officer and he can do whatever he wants to me. He can kill me. No one will even bother to investigate or even ask why he did it. The noise of my footsteps on the parquet floor is jarring to my ears as I keep walking, thinking about my breathing. I don't know what to do, did I made a mistake?

"Please take your clothes off," he gently says to me.

Later, when we are in bed, and he is catching his breath, he apologizes for not reading me poetry for a long time.

"I would love for you to read me poetry. I love German poetry."

"A weak woman would get down on her knees and beg me to forgive her behavior. I hate weak people. Like back then in the East, when I could smell their fear," he whispers, as if to himself, before he gets off me and falls asleep.

The open window and the growl of the planes passing over us leave me awake all night, repeatedly turning restlessly on my side of the bed. Although he is fast asleep, I am too scared to get up and go to his study. Can he smell my fear?

The smell of fear is all around me in the next days at the almost-empty boulangerie. I clean the same plates repeatedly or try to get out the back door, sitting in the sun for a while, but Marie never stops talking to me.

"They say the Russian soldiers are the worst. What if they come?" she asks. "The German army radio says we must unite and fight against them."

"Marie, they will not come, they are far away, and

according to the German radio, the German army hasn't stopped winning." I lose my patience with her. Even the newspaper headlines keep on publishing German victories, but I don't believe them anymore.

"And they say the Americans will invade Belgium and that the Germans will destroy Paris, just as they destroyed every city before withdrawing."

"Marie, the Russians are in Poland, the Germans are in Paris, they will not destroy Paris. Otherwise they will not have cafés and boulangeries with fresh croissants. Everything will be fine." I get up and enter, waiting for the end of the day. But the boy is waiting for me again at the newsstand. I have to go meet him.

I'm just too tense. I stop for a few minutes over the bridge, trying to calm myself down and checking the people around. It's just the tension that makes me imagine something's wrong. I've been in this costume for too long. It makes sense that I'm scared, especially with all those rumors around, everyone is wondering if there will be an invasion and when.

Everything's okay, I just need to relax.

I carefully go down into the dark entrance to the basement and get ready to meet the man in the grey button-down shirt who is waiting for me. For a moment, I imagine Philip will be standing there with his quiffed hair and old jacket, but I know it will not happen. He will never want me after what I did and said.

"Good afternoon, how are you?" He approaches, wanting to hug and kiss me on the cheek, but I hurry to sit down at the table, feeling more secure with the old wooden board separating us.

"Good afternoon, how are you?"

"I'm good."

"What did you bring with you today?"

"I do not have much information. My officer rarely comes, and we almost don't meet."

"Still, didn't you see or hear anything?"

"They are arguing among themselves whether there will be an invasion or not."

"You told me that last time, we need more information."

He leans back and looks at me angrily. What does he want from me? Doesn't he know that I'm trying? He does not care about all the nights I do not sleep, wondering when they will catch me. About the Gestapo building on 84 Avenue Foch, that I dare not think about at all.

"I will try to do better." My fingers firmly hold the knife in my dress pocket.

"What's your officer's name?"

"Didn't Philip tell you?" He's not my officer, he's German, and I'm scared of him, I'm scared of you too.

"No, Philip told me you would provide me with all the information I would ask for."

"Why are you asking me all these questions?"

"Because the people above me want to know."

"Then ask Philip."

"Don't be rude."

"Sorry."

"And what is his rank?"

"I think he's an Oberstleutnant."

"You do not even know his rank?"

"Their ranks are really confusing. They have so many."

"You are not helping me. What's his last name?"

"I think he's an armored officer. I do not know exactly what unit. I think he's in a Panzer tank."

There is a long moment of silence as we sit on either side

of the table, looking at each other. I lower my eyes, trying to think if there is another detail I can tell him that he'd like. Where are his hands? Why does he always keep them in his lap, not putting them on the table as Philip used to do? I have to look up and smile at him, the problem is with me and all the surrounding tension.

"Is that all you know about him after a year of being together?"

"He does not tell me anything, he is silent."

"You must bring us more material, even if it involves taking more risks."

"I promise I'll try." I choose not to tell him about that time in the bathroom, when Herr Ernest almost caught me.

His dark eyes continue to examine my face and body as if researching me.

"Well, we'll see what to do with you and your poor material." He ends the meeting between us after a few more moments of silence, signaling with his hand that I can go.

"Thanks."

I'll be better. I promise, I want to tell him when I get up, but I say nothing, just turning my back and searching for the stairs. How could I be so wrong about Philip?

The grey light at the end of the stairs seems to invite me to leave this suffocating basement, and I hurry to get out into the open air, feeling his eyes on my back, and letting out a sigh of relief as my feet touch the sidewalk of the alley.

I look for the little girl from the store, wanting to give her a chocolate bar that I brought with me, especially for her. A real chocolate bar, flavored with sweet sugar and bitter cocoa, such that my mouth fills with saliva when I close my eyes and imagine its taste. Even in the German army, they now give chocolate to pilots alone. A few days ago, Herr

Ernest brought some chocolate bars with him, placing them in the pantry beside the wine bottles.

But the girl does not peek out the store door, and despite the dripping summer rain, I am ashamed to approach and look inside, preferring to stand and wait for her. I have a bad feeling that something will happen to her and that this is the last time we will meet. Maybe a bomb will hit her, and perhaps something will happen to me.

I need to relax. I will meet her many more times, the sun will soon set, and I have a long walk to the apartment. Herr Ernest has informed me that he will arrive tonight.

All night it drizzles, forcing me to close the window. Despite the silence in the dark apartment, I can't fall asleep. My eyes are wide open in the dark room as I listen to his breathing, trying to force myself to walk to his study, but I'm too afraid to get out of bed. The ringing of the phone from the study wakes me up, I must have fallen asleep. While I'm trying to understand what happened in the middle of the night, Herr Ernest is already hurrying to the ringing phone, listening for a moment to the sounds coming from the black tube, putting it in place, and quickly starting to get dressed.

"What happened?" My hands are busy tying my bathrobe.

"Nothing special, usual military alert, go back to sleep." He finishes zipping his coat, collects the papers from his desk, perhaps waiting for me as bait even though I did not dare approach them. Herr Ernest stuffs them in his leather bag and walks out the door, barely saying goodbye.

The rain has stopped, and I open the window and peek into the dark street. A military car passes and stops for a moment, picking him up and continuing on its way. The sound of wheels is heard on the wet street stones, but after it disappears behind the street corner the city returns to its peaceful night.

On the way to the boulangerie, the street traffic is usual while the morning sun dries the wet sidewalk. Still, inside I hear Simone's angry voice, talking to Martin the cook, barely noticing as I walk through the door, despite the bell ringing every time it opens.

"This is the fourth time in the last two weeks that we have not received butter. How do they expect us to make croissants? With their terrible substitutes?"

"Monique," she turns to me, "please note in the vendor book: June sixth, and no butter has arrived again." I go behind the counter, take out the heavy supplier's notebook, writing in perfect handwriting: "June sixth, 1944, no supply of butter."

"Monique, I want you to go to the market again to try and get butter." But I manage to convince her to send Marie, using the excuse that she must gain experience talking to vendors, and soon a lot of soldiers will come, even though the boulangerie is almost empty in recent days.

The morning hours pass lazily by as I help Martin clean the back room when the doorbell rings, and I hear Simone's usual shout in the direction of the baking room: "Monique, you have customers."

My clients are two transport soldiers. I recognize them by the unit badges on their uniforms.

"Good morning, how can I help you?" I ask the two transport soldiers in French, and a minute later, two more soldiers from another unit enter, exchanging greetings, and one of them asks if they heard the radio this morning.

"No," the taller of the two answers, smiling at me flirtatiously.

"The Army radio reported that the enemy has begun an invasion on the beaches of Calais, but we managed to push them back into the sea," the transport soldier tells them and smiles. After a moment of excitement, everyone looks at me and falls silent.

"Have a nice day." I address him in poor German, serving him the bread.

"Thank you." He takes the paper bag from me with a suspicious look.

"How can I help you?" I turn to a soldier who previously tried to smile at me and is now no longer doing so.

"When were the cakes made? This morning?"

"No, unfortunately, they are from yesterday, we have not yet received butter this morning."

"Well, never mind, I'll come later." He and his friend walk out the door.

"What did they say?" Simone asks me the second after the door slams shut.

"They said that the German radio reported an American invasion attempt in the Calais area this morning, and that the attempt failed," I say, and watch the grey morning clouds outside.

"Well, that fits Americans, they can do nothing properly. Where's Marie? Why is she so late?" Simone goes to talk to Martin in the back room, and I think she's wiping a tear away as she passes me.

"All roads from Normandy are blocked," Marie reports excitedly when she finally returns from the market empty-handed. "No delivery truck has come from there since last night, and everyone is whispering that the beach is full of American ships, and there is a war there."

"But the German radio reported on Calais, and you also failed to get butter," Simone silences her.

"That's what they say in the market," Marie apologizes and heads down to the back room in tears.

The rest of the morning passes in silence. A military truck occasionally passes by the boulevard, full of German soldiers. Simone and I accompany them with our gazes and return to cleaning the empty boulangerie tables with cloths.

"Monique, please take care of the cash register. I'll be back soon." I stand behind the cash register excitedly. Simone never leaves the money drawer, she always makes sure to stand and keep an eye on the rustling coins and bills. "I'll replace you," I tell her quickly, not sure she heard me through the slamming door.

My fingers repeatedly polish the porcelain plates with the white cloth, arranging them in a pile, deciding to clean them again and placing them in a new stack.

Simone walks in and quietly closes the boulangerie door behind her, and I look up from the porcelain plates into her shining eyes as she approaches me and lowers her voice. "The BBC radio reported that the invasion has begun in Normandy. They said that the Americans and the British have taken over the coast."

My trembling hands keep wiping the plate I'm holding again and again. I'm thinking of the cannon battery in Normandy and the Polish soldier in German uniform holding flowers. Now they are shooting at Americans and

British soldiers storming the barbed wire placed on the coast. Will they survive?

"Statue of Liberty, New York, America," I whisper.

"What did you say?" Simone asks.

"Nothing." I wipe away a tear.

Nemesis

August 1944

Secret

8/2/1944

From: Western Front Wehrmacht Command

To: Army Group France

Subject: Preparations for the defense of Paris

Background: The U.S. Army has established units on Normandy's shores and is trying to break through the German defense line in order to occupy all of France and Paris.

General: French citizens should be treated as enemies rather than collaborators as in the past.

Tasks:

1. All Gestapo units and S.S. divisions should intimidate the civilian population in order to prevent insurgency and harm to German soldiers.

2. The Gestapo units will work to exterminate the resistance fighters without regard for innocent civilians.

3. All German female soldiers will be immediately evacuated from the Paris area in order to prevent the possibility of their capture.

SS. Telegram 483

The grey helmets will fight till the end.

"Certificate, please." The German soldier standing in front of the guard post gives me a hostile look, keeping a safe distance, while his friend's submachine gun is aimed at my body.

"Guten morgen," I hand him my ID card and wait patiently. Although they see me every morning, they no longer smile as I pass their checkpoint on my way to work, crossing the wooden guard post and the barbed wire fences they have placed near the German Headquarters on Rivoli Street.

The soldier carefully examines the cardboard paper, looking at me and comparing my face to the photo attached, checking the stamps with his finger to make sure they are not fake.

"Monique Otin?"

Monique Moreno, I want to shout in his face that has almost disappeared under the grey metal helmet.

"Yes, it's me," I replace the shout with a polite smile.

"Have a nice day." He hands me the worn-out cardboard, returning to look at Concorde Square's wide roads, alert for a hidden enemy that might suddenly emerge.

I keep walking down the street and put the certificate back in my bag, not looking back. Since the invasion, I've been taking it out so often at the checkpoints all over the city that the cardboard has become faded, wrinkled under all those hands that examined it, and the eyes that stared at me.

A black car is coming towards me on Rivoli Street, and I stop walking, watching its silver lights aimed in my direction, getting closer.

"Guten morgen," I stop walking and say to a bored

soldier standing next to one of the vehicles left in front of the headquarters.

"Bitte?"

"Do you have a light?" My hand searches for the cigarette pack in my bag while I turn my back to the black car as it slows down, and only the sound of the engine is heard on the empty street.

"Sure." He pulls out a metal army lighter, marked with the SS symbol, and I get close to his hand, smelling his scent of cologne mixed with grease.

"Thank you." I inhale the smoke. Did the car stop? I must continue walking. Otherwise he will start to suspect.

"Have a nice day." He returns the SS lighter to his pocket, and I have to keep on walking, my eyes following the small rear lights of the black car until it disappears around the corner. I'm safe this time.

I must not think about the horrible building at 84 Avenue Foch, but for a moment I have nausea, and I throw the unfinished cigarette into the street before I continue on my way, trying to breathe the clean morning air.

Above my head, I can hear the big red Nazi flag flying quietly in the morning breeze, as whispering above. Still, I look forward to the Louvre Palace, trying to count cars in front of the headquarters and getting away from the German soldier. Only a few of them left, and I do not know if they're all at the front or have started evacuating back to Germany.

A long convoy of trucks full of soldiers crosses the street on their way to the western front, in the direction of Normandy, and I follow them with my eyes, counting them and trying to identify the unit. The soldiers are crowded quietly and do not whistle in my direction, asking me to show them the city.

To my surprise, the boulangerie's front door is locked, and I have to walk by the alley around to the back door, stopping and looking over my shoulder to see if someone is following me. But Martin, the cook, is sitting inside his kingdom on an empty wooden crate, looking at the almost-empty pantry.

"She must have forgotten to open," he says, and I enter the boulangerie from the back.

At first I do not see her, but then I notice that Simone is bending behind the counter, opening the bottom drawer where we keep the tablecloths, pulling out a red-white-blue flag and kissing it carefully.

"You have arrived," she quickly turns as I place the bag on a chair.

"Good morning."

"It's just in case the Germans withdraw, but it's not going to happen." She hurries to return the flag to the bottom drawer and closes it.

"It's okay."

"Why didn't you enter from the front door?"

"It's okay. I will not say anything."

"I miss those days when women had values, and weren't peeking behind my back." She passes me, going to talk to Martin. I want to whisper in her ear that we are both on the same side, even if she is disgusted with me because I'm licking a German officer's boots, but I know she wouldn't believe me.

I also know she is listening to the BBC radio news, an offense worthy of execution by the black-coat Gestapo people. "I heard it from the neighbor," she tells me, but I do not believe her.

"Monique, Supply has not arrived again. You will have to go to the market and try to get some."

"Maybe Marie could go? I went yesterday and Tuesday."

"No, I want you to go. I do not trust her."

Despite my requests, she does not let me off the hook this time, and I get out and walk as fast as I can. I try to stay off the streets, and it's not just me; everyone is trying to avoid being outside while the Gestapo is searching for the resistance.

In the first days after the invasion, the city was waiting for the Americans to arrive, people made flags, and there were also brave ones who spat at German soldiers as they passed by. The German female soldiers, those who were called "grey mice" behind their backs, have completely disappeared from the city streets and are no longer seen walking down the Champs-Élysées holding cameras, as if they were on vacation.

But the days went by, and the German soldiers are still in the city, standing in the streets and checking people. What's going on at the front lines? Was the German counterattack successful, as the German army radio reported?

On the way to the market, I cross the newsstand, but even it can't tell me any news. The German army magazine and the daily newspaper are the only ones on display, yelling loud Nazi propaganda, which is limited to four thin sheets of paper.

"Papers, please." Two German soldiers are stopping people in the street, and I lower my eyes to their hobnail boots.

"Are you tense?"

"No, I'm not." I look at his dirty, greasy fingers.

"Bitte." He hands me back my papers, and I smile at him politely, walking as fast as I can, but there are three men in black coats near the market entrance.

"What took you so long?" Simone asks as I close the door behind me.

"The seller in the market said that since the invasion, there are barriers around the city. They are hardly letting supplies get in."

"And you brought nothing?"

"He said he didn't receive anything today."

"You should have argued with him."

"I did."

"You needed to do more. We do not have the privilege of not being loyal to the Germans and stopping providing them with what they want."

I look down and apologize, hurrying to put on my apron, and returning to the empty space behind the counter. Again I polish the porcelain plates and pray that it will all be over. Soon I'll hurry to the quiet apartment. Herr Ernest almost doesn't come anymore.

At first, when I close the thick wooden door behind me, hanging the bag by the apartment entrance, I do not notice anything unusual. But Oberst Ernest's voice from his study causes me to tense up, and I cross the hall into the living room and stand there.

The study door is open, and Herr Ernest sits in his leather chair, leaning in front of his documents and looking up at me like nothing has changed. Still, all the paintings on the walls, the ones we bought together, and others I have never seen, have been removed and concentrated at the side of the room, ready to be shipped. Besides the painting, there are several nailed wooden crates of wine and champagne, and maybe even cheeses and other foods that I cannot identify.

"Good afternoon, how are you?" He looks up from the documents in front of him but does not stand.

"I'm okay. How are you?" I stay at a safe distance from his study door.

"I'm fine, thank you, can you please make me something to drink?"

"Why are all the paintings off the walls?"

"I'm transferring them to the homeland," he says and returns to his writing.

"Why? I thought you were defeating the Americans."

Herr Ernest stops writing and looks at me.

"We are defeating them, and we are not preparing to leave Paris, certainly not without a German mark that will be remembered for eternity."

"What will you do to the city?"

"We will find a worthy solution for this city, just as the American bombers are destroying the cities of Germany."

"Are you going to destroy Paris?"

Herr Ernest examines me for a moment.

"I thought you were on our side."

"I'm on your side and think you'll stay here forever, so I do not understand why you're taking the paintings."

He raises his eyes again from the papers in front of him, and I fear that I've said too much, but he just smiles and goes back to reading.

"And what about my painting? The one I chose?" I can't stop myself, watching my dancer placed by the wall, near his hunters' paintings.

"Can you smell the fear of the people around us?" Herr Ernest raises his eyes from the document he is reading, looking at me with his green eyes. "I don't smell it anymore. Maybe it's time for a lesson about loyalty and betrayal, don't you think so?"

"I know I'm loyal to you," I place my trembling hands behind my back.

"I know you are loyal to the German nation and me. I was talking about the French nation and the price they are going to pay for their disloyalty." He smiles. "Why did you think I was talking about you?"

"Will you leave my painting here?" Is he trying to set me up?

"The painting must go to its new homeland. It is valuable. I cannot leave it behind. It is already German property. Please prepare a drink for me." He looks at me angrily.

For a moment, I want to ask him if I too am considered property for German use. Occupied property that will make its way into the thousand-year Reich's borders, but I prefer to look down and examine my painting, which lies by the wall. My dancer is still tying her ballet shoes, lying on her side, and it seems like her pink skirt is flying high, exposing her body to Herr Ernest's eyes if only he would look at her.

"Please leave the painting to me, just as I'm staying with you."

He looks at me in silence for a moment, as if debating whether to push me into the corner or let me go, at least for now, playing with me for his pleasure.

"I appreciate your loyalty and the remnants of German blood in your veins, but my dear, I'm the one who decides when you stop being with me."

The way he looks at me and says things makes me cringe,

but I smile at him and keep holding my hands tight. I am his personal property, as long as he wants me.

"What would you like to drink?"

In the kitchen, I rest my hands on the sink, close my eyes, and take a few breaths. For a moment, I have a desire to open the knife drawer and examine its contents, but I stop myself and light a fire to heat the kettle. It's too dangerous to walk down the streets with a knife, especially now with all the surprise checks. I just have to stay alive, just a few more days, until the Americans succeed in breaking the German defense lines and come.

"After you're done with the coffee," his voice comes from the study, "I'd be happy if you brushed my boots." I want them to shine for tomorrow morning.

Even though the window is open to the night air, I can't sleep beside Herr Ernest, and my eyes are fixed on the dark ceiling. I know I have to go to his study, but I can't. I'm too afraid, feeling stifled between the rooms and his shining hobnail boots guarding the entrance door, keeping me and my dancer painting from running away into the street.

The next morning, as I walk down the avenue, I see them emerge from a black car and stop in my place. I grip my handbag tightly in horror.

Like a black raptor, the vehicle arrives at a fast pace and stops next to a man walking in front of me down the street.

He does not notice what is happening, continues to walk. And I want to shout at him to run away, but it is too late.

Three people in black coats jump out of the vehicle and grab him by force. Even though he tries to resist, they point a gun at his head and drag him into the car. In seconds, the doors are closed, and the vehicle continues to drive, disappearing behind the street corner.

Keep on walking, do not stop walking.

All the other people continue on their way as if nothing happened, turning their heads to the other side, only the ringing bell of the boulangerie door calms me down a bit. Here I'm a little safer.

"Monique, it's good that you're finally here. You're delayed just like all the farmers who are unable to supply flour."

I have no answer for her, and I hang my bag on the hanger, but it falls to the floor.

"What happened? Did you not sleep at night, that you have no strength?"

"I'm okay." I bend down to pick my bag from the floor with my shaking hand.

"So you'd better hurry, maybe some German soldier will come by chance and you can serve him."

"I'll be right there, I'm sorry." My fingers get tangled with tying the apron.

"Let me help you." She approaches me. "You are like the Americans. You need help with everything, unable to do anything properly. Is everything okay?"

"Yes, everything is fine."

"Do not cry. I did not mean what I said. It's just all this tension and the waiting for the Americans to arrive." She finishes apologizing and goes to the back room, probably scolding Marie.

When will the Gestapo arrive at my door? I try to make myself a cup of disgusting coffee substitute.

All morning the boulangerie is empty, and I pass the time listening to what Simone thinks about the British and watching the street, searching for black cars. Still, by noon, I notice Violette standing outside the glass door.

"Can I take a break?" I ask Simone, already taking my apron off.

"Did you hear? The Americans have also invaded the south of France. They conquered Nice." Violette enters through the door. "They say the German army is collapsing."

"Paris is not in the south of France, and it has nothing to do with us," Simone answers her. But she too is gripped by excitement. Without noticing me standing next to her, she bends down to the bottom drawer behind the counter, sliding her hand over the hidden flag, but quickly rises when she notices my gaze, wiping her face with her hand.

"Go, go. I need to re-fold the tablecloths," says Simone, "but don't stay outside for long, it is not safe anymore." And I hurry to remove my apron, going out into the summer sun outside.

"What is going to happen?" Violette asks in tears. "The Germans are retreating. They will not be able to protect Paris."

"No, they will not succeed, they will probably retreat soon."

"You promised me there would be no invasion and that the Germans would win."

"Yeah, I was wrong, I was wrong about so many things, I'm sorry."

We both stand on the Pont Des Arts, watching a group of

German soldiers laying down sandbags on the bank, to the shouts of a nervous sergeant, preparing defensive positions for fighting throughout the city.

"Everything is falling apart, everything we had." She starts crying. "All I had."

"Do not worry, everything will return to normal." I watch the green water flowing leisurely. "We will continue to sit in cafés and drink fine coffee, strolling down the avenue." But deep inside, I know nothing will return to what it had been.

I had Dad and Mom and Jacob, who disappeared without me even being able to hug them one last time. How could everything go back to normal? I have nothing left, only Philip, who will never love me after what I did. And I don't even know if he is still alive or captured by the Gestapo. What world will I have after the Nazis go?

"At least you have your Fritz." I touch her hand for encouragement, but the touch is unpleasant for me, and after a moment, I return my hand to the metal railing. "Everything will be back to the way it was before the war, don't worry."

"Before the war, I was a simple girl without a spouse to walk with on the avenue." She continues to cry. "Even you have tears."

"Yes, even I have tears."

"See you tomorrow," I say goodbye to Simone. I have to hurry to the empty apartment, it is not safe in the streets, but the child is waiting for me by the newsstand. I have to go.

"Just a few more days." I kiss Violette on both cheeks. "Don't worry."

Just a Few More Days.

"St. Joseph Street," the boy whispers to me, and I start walking. It is too dangerous to set a meeting point in the opera area. The place is full of Gestapo and people avoid entering the metro stations in the area.

But when I enter the quiet street, it is empty, and no one is waiting to accompany me, on foot or by bicycle.

"Get in the trunk of the van and wait," a man in work clothes passes by and whispers, disappearing behind the street corner and leaving me alone, watching the grey van parked and abandoned at the side of the alley. What's happening here?

As if by itself, my hand goes down along my dress, looking for the pocket, but there are no pockets in this dress.

The street is quiet, and there is no one around. Everything's okay. I breathe quickly and enter the trunk, closing the door behind me, wrapping myself in darkness. Breathe, everything's fine.

I can hear the car doors open and close, and the engine starts, and I breathe slowly, fighting the urge not to open the door and escape. I have done this before. I have to trust them.

How long have we been going? I've lost track of time. Are we still in the city? The vehicle changes direction every so often. We are probably still in Paris. Is the meeting at the place I met Philip for the first time? Will I meet him this time?

Suddenly the vehicle stops, and I tense.

"Shut off the engine," I hear a voice in German and want to scream.

"What?" I can hear a muffled sound.

"Shut down the engine," says the voice in bad French, and the monotonous engine rumbling stops. I must be quiet.

"Certificates, please." Rustling and then quiet.

"What do you have in the trunk?"

"It's empty. We're back from the market."

"Open the trunk."

Breathe, breathe, breathe, my nails scratch my thighs, breathe.

"No need, it's empty."

"Open it now." The voice in poor French is getting louder.

A barrage of gunshots, and footsteps, and more shots and a door slamming and shouting in German. My body is cramped in the dark as I bend my head and shove my fist into my mouth, stifling a scream.

"Run away." I hear a woman's shout, and another barrage of gunshots and my trembling hands grope for the trunk door handle in the dark, opening it and sending my legs out, stumbling for a moment on the road. The afternoon sunlight dazzles me, but I manage to stabilize myself and start running around the corner of a warehouse, running non-stop.

Run, run, run, do not look back.

My whole body hurts from the effort, the sweat, my heavy breathing. Keep running, another corner, hide behind it, now behind the hill, do not stop, ignore the pain of running, keep running, even further, between the bushes, do not stop running, further and further.

Only later, as I hide among the shrubs and try to catch my breath, I start to recall what my eyes had seen. The man in the black coat lying on the road in a strange position, looking at me with a hollow gaze as I burst out the back door and almost stumbled over him, the shouts in German that kept echoing in my head: "Shoot her, shoot her." And the strange, whistling noise passing me as I ran. What happened there? I have to hide and wait for the darkness. It doesn't matter what happened there.

The darkness is already falling when I dare to get out of my hiding place under a large bush, walking quietly on the path and listening. I have to keep walking. It did not happen to me, it happened to someone else, not to me. I was never there in the van.

My hips are scratched from the bushes, and I am already tired of walking. In what direction is the city? I must not be mistaken. Every time I see car lights approaching in the street, I hide until they pass. I walk through the abandoned warehouse area, hoping I'm going the right way, and the lights in the distance are directing me. I need to warn the man in the grey button-down shirt, something happened and I did not get to the meeting, he must know. There were other people there, and something happened to them too, what happened to them? I'll tell him.

I don't know what time it is when I reach the east bank, but it is clear that the curfew has already started and I must not be caught on the street.

Carefully I take off my shoes, ignoring the pain in my feet, and start walking barefoot so as not to make noise. Now and then, I hear the sounds of a German patrol's hobnails boots, and I hurry to hide in the alley or at the entrance to a stairwell, waiting for them to pass before I can continue walking. Was it planned? Did anyone betray us? I must know.

Near the apartment, the street is quiet. No car is waiting for me there, nor in the neighboring alleys, just a cool summer breeze and a single streetlight that shines dimly. Should I go upstairs? Are they waiting for me there? I have no other place to go, I must not stay in the street, it's too dangerous.

After waiting for long minutes in the stairwell, I carefully open the front door, afraid to enter, but the apartment is empty. No one is waiting to kill me as I scan the rooms in the dark, holding the kitchen knife tightly in my hand and moving suspiciously. I have to eat something.

My hands tremble as I struggle with the opener, unable to get it into the metal lid of the meat tin, trying again and again, opening it as much as I can and starting to hungrily swallow the greasy pulped meat. In the light of the candle, I notice the eagle stamped on the tin, its wings spread, and I remember the hollow look of the man in the black coat and the woman's shout: "Run away."

My legs no longer hold me up as I collapse on the kitchen floor, vomiting, and starting to cry.

"You're late again. I will not give you extra privilege for living with the Germans." Simone raises her eyes from the money drawer the next morning when she hears the doorbell. But I can explain nothing to her. I cannot explain all the times I looked out the window last night, checking if a vehicle had arrived and people were coming to stand me by the wall. In the early morning hours, I woke up in a panic to loud noise, standing up, and noticing that the knife I'd held in my hand while sitting prepared at the chair in front of the entrance door had fallen out.

"I apologize. I will try to arrive on time." My hands take the apron from the hanger, tying it in mechanical motion. "What do you want me to do?"

"The usual, nothing has changed since yesterday."

"Yes, madame Simone." I will stand behind the counter as if nothing has changed from yesterday. What happened there?

I must meet and inform the man in the grey shirt that something happened. Are they looking for me, or was it a coincidence? Did I make a mistake, had they discovered my identity?

Some German pilots come in, pointing to the bread in silence and patiently waiting for me to pack it for them.

"Monique, you are not focused. They are in a hurry."

What could I have done that exposed me? Did Herr Ernest discover who I am, and sent his Gestapo dogs after me, wanting to hunt his French boot-licking mistress? My eyes rise, and I watch through the window, will a black car stop here in a few minutes?

"Four Reichsmark, please." I notice for the first time their buttoned grey uniforms, full of medals.

Did someone betray me? What does he know about me?

My name? Does he know the name of Herr Ernest or the place where I work?

"Monique, they are waiting for the change."

"Danke." They thank me indifferently, slamming the door on their way out and causing me to tense from the noise.

"Monique, I need you to go to the market."

I'm too afraid to walk by myself, but I can't say 'no' to Simone. Slowly I take my bag and head out, closing the door behind me and scanning the street.

─── ⁂ ───

"It took you a while to visit me after the last dress you bought." Anaïs picks me up from Reception. "What happened? Do you need a new evening dress again?"

"I apologize. I was busy."

"You should buy one, the German ladies have stopped coming, they are scared, you will receive a big discount."

"I did not come to buy a new dress."

"So why did you come?" She takes out a cigarette and offers me one, but I refuse with a nervous smile, and she lights the cigarette for herself, inhaling the smoke with pleasure.

"So why did you come? Even cigarettes are hard to receive these days. Fritz stopped bringing me any."

"I came to ask how you are. I'll bring you cigarettes." I take the pack from my bag, offering it to her, but she refuses with a bitter smile.

"How am I? I'm fine, waiting for the Americans to come."

"And aren't you afraid?"

"What should I be afraid of?" She exhales the smoke into the air.

"The Germans, your Fritz, all this crazy war around us, the Americans."

"Anaïs knew how to get along with the Germans, and Anaïs will know how to get along with Americans," she answers indifferently and looks at me. "Are you scared?"

"Yes," I admit. "I'm afraid of everyone, of the Americans who want to kill us, of the Communists, of the Gestapo driving in the streets."

"You are the spouse of Oberst Ernest. You have nothing to fear from the Gestapo. As for everything else, we'll have to see." She smiles at me. "I'm sure the U.S. military has officers too."

Finally I say goodbye to her. She has to go back to work, and I have to go back to Simone, telling her that I couldn't find any butter at the market.

"See you soon," I say, but I'm not sure it's going to happen anymore. Soon they'll probably catch me.

On the way back, I hide every time a car passes on the street, waiting at a building entrance with my heart pounding. I have to relax.

"Revenge." The headline screams in black print on a poster pasted to a building wall on the street, and I slow down and try to read the text.

"They did a big operation yesterday, killing and capturing many of them." Two women whisper behind my back, and I keep standing, making myself continue to read the poster.

"Who? The Gestapo?" the other one asks.

"Yes, they say there was a traitor among them."

"May God protect the resistance. Let them survive," the

other answers and crosses herself as they continue walking down the avenue, and I follow them with my eyes.

Philip, is he alive? I must know, I must talk to Lizette, she is the only one that might know him. And I start walking as fast as I can to the metro station, forgetting that the Gestapo is waiting at the entrances, checking the passersby.

"Lizette, open up. It's me." I knock hard on the door. I'd tried ringing the bell for a long time, waiting patiently and trying again before knocking. But the door is still closed. She does not usually go out at such hours. "Lizette, open up. It's me."

"She's not here." The neighbor from next door opens her apartment door, peeking out as if ready to slam it at any moment.

"Excuse me, where is Lizette?"

"She's not here."

"Where is she? I must find her."

"Don't you know?"

"Know what?"

"Wait, aren't you the girl who lived here a year ago? I used to see you on the stairs, Monique?" She opens the door and approaches. "Don't you know?"

"Know what?"

"Lizette is gone, she was killed, the Gestapo killed her, the other neighbor said she tried to escape from a vehicle they'd stopped."

While running down the stairs, I can hear my pounding footsteps hitting the marble stairs as if drums were beating in my ears, and the neighbor's voice calling my name from a distance, but all there is are the drums in my head and the sharp metal sound of the building door when I burst into the street.

My hands grip my ears tightly as I bend down on my knees on the pavement, trying to silence the voices but failing. They do not stop, swirling loudly and making a strange whistle as they pass through my body. What did I do? Why is everyone dead instead of me? Even the embracing arm of the neighbor trying to hug me can't stop the screams, and I rise and run away from her, whispering to her as I get away: "Do not touch me, anyone who touches me dies."

The telegram.

"Why did you light those candles?" Herr Ernest asks when we sit at the table.

"I thought there might be a blackout." I watch the four candles standing in the cabinet. Do the Christians light memory candles?

"Now blow them out. After we regroup north of Paris, there will be a lot of blackouts." He hungrily bites the canned meat I served.

"I thought you would stay with me forever." I rise from the chair and approach the candles, putting out the fire with my fingers, ignoring the heat and pain.

"We must retreat from Paris. There are traitors among the French, passing information to our enemies. Return to your seat, aren't you hungry?"

"I'm not hungry today, I apologize. Would you like my meat?"

"But we are going to get revenge. They thought we wouldn't find them. We will catch them all. The ones that escaped, hiding in their holes like dirty rats. They won't stop us anymore. Is there wine left?"

"No, all the wine is gone. Is it okay if I go to sleep? I'm a little tired."

"Yes, you may. Thank you for a lovely dinner."

Later that night, with Herr Ernest beside me, I can't sleep. I feel the pain in my fingers and think about the man in uniform, the one in the silver-framed photo at Lizette's house, and I can't stop the tears.

Quietly I get out of bed and walk barefoot to the study.

Top Secret

8/16/1944

From: Division 44

To: Engineering brigade 7II2

Subject: Preparations for destroying Paris monuments

1. 7II2 Engineering Brigade will mark key sites and bridges in Paris prior to their demolition.

2. Maps and charts of the sites will be taken from the municipality of Paris.

3. Explosives will be supplied by Supply Battalion 422I, which is located at Le Bourget airport.

4. Destruction will take place after a direct order prior to retreating from Paris.

SS. Telegram 9I2

My eyes pass quickly over the telegram by candlelight, my fingers flipping through the other papers, searching and trying to read the most important ones before carefully putting them back in his leather bag, quietly returning to bed. What should I do with this information?

I must forget what I saw. The Americans are on the way. I just have to stay alive, wait for their arrival. I must not risk myself anymore. They are searching for me.

Even if I wanted to, I have no one to pass the information on to. I don't trust the man in the grey shirt with the buttons, and I can't find Philip.

My hand wipes the tears away in the dark room while I constantly hear Herr Ernest's breathing beside me in bed. Soon the morning will come, and he will wake up.

I will pass the information in the diary on to someone. I don't know how, and I don't know to whom, but I will find a way.

―――

The alarm clock rings early in the morning, and I sit up tense, hurrying to put on my silk robe and rushing to the kitchen to make him coffee, there is some left. But Herr Ernest gets dressed in silence and hurries out, leaving me alone in the kitchen in front of the boiling kettle. "Please don't come back," I whisper after I put my ear next to the wooden door, hearing the building's front door close behind him and going to get dressed. I have to hurry.

The boulevard is silent, and no German army vehicle crosses the road with rattling engine noise. Even the metro exit in the large square in front of the opera is empty of people. Only a few passersby stand and look at the posters hastily attached on the billboard during the night. "Popular uprising," shouts the headline. "The policemen and railway workers for Paris."

Another poster is calling for revolution, printed in black ink on the billboard.

"We are going to pay in blood for this." One man expresses his opinion and makes room for me as I push between them, trying to read the rebels' instructions.

"They're already running away, like mice in their grey uniforms," says another, and I look around.

The magnificent café in front of the opera, which was always full of German soldiers, is closed, and no black-coat Gestapo is standing at the metro entrance. The streets are empty of Germans as if waiting for the change to come, but the Nazi flags still hang in front of the opera house, and as I hurry to the boulangerie I see two German armored vehicles passing by in the middle of the boulevard. The soldiers are standing alert, wearing round helmets and holding machine guns, ready for battle. With a stone-cold stare, they watch the empty streets while driving slowly, making me stop and hide in one of the houses' entrances, feeling the rumble under my feet and waiting for them to disappear

'They will not run away like mice,' I whisper to myself and accelerate my steps. They are still here, and no one has yet been able to expel them, neither the Americans nor the resistance, not with any of the information I passed to Philip or his replacement.

The diary is at the bottom of my bag, and despite its light weight, I feel the leather strap cut into my shoulder, leaving a red mark on it, and I have to fight the urge to turn around and run away. I have to pass that information on. I owe it to Lizette.

Why did you kill her? I want to scream at the red flags hanging in front of the opera building, but even though the street is empty, I'm afraid someone will hear my cries.

Now Lizette is with the charming man who waited for her patiently, looking at her for so many years from the picture above the fireplace. She hugs him non-stop, wrapping him in her warm arms, as only she and Mom knew. I need to hurry, and I almost stumble because of my wet eyes.

Two more German armored vehicles in camouflage colors pass through the boulevard, their chains creaking noisily and the soldiers holding machine guns aimed at the sides of the street, the bullet chains ready to fire, waiting to send the copper bullets out on command. I must ignore them.

The newsstand is almost naked of all the newspapers that covered it in the past, exposing wooden boards carelessly painted in peeling colors. Only a simple government newspaper glorifying German victories is still for sale.

"I've run out of cigarettes," the salesman is looking to the sides, "even the simplest ones, try in a few days."

"I'm not searching for cigarettes. The boy, I need the kid."

"Which kid?"

"The boy with the grey cap, the one who is sometimes here and arranges the newspapers outside, at the back."

"I do not know such a boy."

"I need to find him. I have something for him."

"Mademoiselle, you have to go," he looks sideways apprehensively, examining whether I came alone and not calming down even when he notices no one is around.

"Please, I must find him. I know you can help me."

"He has disappeared, never come here again, ever." He lowers his gaze and turns to deal with his affairs, ignoring my presence. What to do?

"Please."

But he no longer answers me.

Simone rises towards me from behind the counter at the sound of the doorbell, but the boulangerie is quiet and dark, the wooden door to the back room is closed, and the trays in the display case, which were always full of pastries, are empty.

"Good morning." I gently close the door behind me.

"Good morning, Monique."

"What happened?" My eyes look around, trying to get used to the gloom.

"It is impossible to open today. We are closed."

"We are never closed."

"As of today we are closed, there were no groceries, and the market is closed, we can do nothing, we will have to wait until everything is over. Go home, I have already sent Martin and Marie away."

"What about you?"

"I will stay here, at least for now. I will wait for them here."

For a moment, she seems lonely to me in the dark boulangerie, and I would like to say something encouraging to her, but she never liked me too much.

"I'll help you arrange things, and then I'll go."

We both work side by side in silence, occasionally looking up the avenue at the sound of a German armored vehicle passing by in slow motion, shaking the road stones, and making us tense.

"What will you do when it's all over?" she asks me, taking the tablecloths out of the drawer and folding them again, even though there is no need.

"I don't longer believe it will end well."

"For women who collaborated horizontally, it will definitely not end well." She gives her opinion, and I know she means me. It doesn't matter anymore whether I live or not. What I did can no longer be changed.

"I have to go."

I quickly collect some leftover chocolate chip cookies. They are not fresh, but they are the last ones in the jar, and I have no other plans to pass on the information I have.

"When it's all over, if you want to continue working here, you're welcome," she says when I go to open the door, probably for the last time.

"Thanks." She does not really mean it.

"Monique."

"Yes?"

"Be careful, take care of yourself."

With a slight slam, I close the door behind me and hasten my steps to the Latin Quarter, armed with a diary full of crowded lines in my handwriting and a paper bag of chocolate cookies.

"What do you have in your bag?"

"A woman's belongings."

The soldier standing in front of the Pont Neuf Bridge military outpost looks at me indifferently while his friend examines my body with an eager look, moving his eyes from my dress to my feet. The policemen at the guard post have disappeared and been replaced by soldiers in grey and green uniforms, standing beside a machine gun position and barbed wire fences.

"Can I see the bag?"

"Please, it's for you." I take out the cigarette pack from the bottom of the bag, pull it out, and serve it to him.

"The whole pack?"

"The whole pack."

With a gesture, he puts the pack of cigarettes in his uniform pocket and instructs his friend to let me pass.

Don't look back, keep on walking, your eyes straight ahead, don't give him time to regret.

I ignore the soldiers measuring the bridge and the officer pointing with his finger, giving orders to a soldier who kneels at the bridge's center, painting white crosses on the old stones with a paintbrush.

Keep walking, enter the alley, only there will you feel safe. When I walk into the narrow street, I allow myself to stand for a few minutes and wipe my sweaty hand holding my bag and the diary inside.

The old alley walls are full of posters, urging citizens to revolt and take up arms. A few people gather around the entrance to a grocery store, talking to each other and pausing as I pass, scrutinizing me, reviewing my new dress.

I'm one of you, help me, I want to shout at them, but I know they will not believe me. Who will believe a young woman dressed elegantly in a poor neighborhood? After all, I cooperated horizontally with the Germans.

The basement entrance is also closed with a metal door, locked with a large padlock, and there is no one around to help me. Only the girl from the store smiles at me.

She looks at me with sparkling eyes through the old shop door, and I approach her hesitantly, wanting to give her the cookies I'd kept, especially for her.

"Get out of here," her mother whispers angrily, pulling her inside the store.

"I need you to help me." I follow her. I have no one else left.

"Get out of here and don't come back." She picks up a wooden stick.

"The man who was here a long time ago in the basement," I put the diary on the filthy counter. "Give this to him." And I turn my back and run away before she can say anything, before I regret it, before she looks at what is written inside and goes straight to the police or the Gestapo.

On the way back to the east bank, I notice that I forgot to leave the bag of chocolate cookies for the girl, but I don't have the courage to return, and I sit on a bench, eating them and watching the Notre Dame Cathedral and the soldiers measuring the bridge. I have to talk to someone. I need to calm down.

"Anaïs no longer works here," the receptionist answers me with a smile of victory as I stand in front of her, asking to call her.

"What happened to her?"

"She did not come to work, disappeared, so she was fired. Can I help you with something else?"

"No, thank you, I was searching for Anaïs."

"If I were you, I wouldn't worry about her," she continues in her arrogant tone. When I go down the marble stairs, I think of Anaïs taking care of Anaïs, wondering which soldier her next occupation will be. With a perfect smile, she will show him all the treasures of Paris.

I can look for her at the apartment where she lives, she once told me the address, but I have a feeling she may not be there either, and worst of all, when I go down the street and start walking down the avenue towards the Lafayette Gallery, a few shots are heard.

A group of armed soldiers stands at the entrance to

the big store, quickly running into battle positions, taking shelters behind the tree trunks. What should I do? All the people disappeared from the street when the shouts began, leaving me standing alone on the sidewalk.

Where to run and hide? I manage to run to a nearby advertising column, bending and trembling at its feet. Who is shooting? All I can hear is the German shouts from the soldiers lying in the street. Where are the shots coming from?

Minutes pass on the street, no car passes, and only the sounds of tree branches in the wind is heard on the avenue.

"Everyone on your feet, keep on moving," the sergeant shouts in German at his soldiers, and they all rise and keep on marching down the street, looking around with weapons drawn and suspicious looks. As they pass by, I bury my head between my hands, cramped by the sound of their hobnails boots on the road.

"Are you okay? The danger is over. You can get up." A gentleman in a suit touches my shoulder and holds my hand, helping me up.

"Thanks." I look around, rubbing the dirt from the sidewalk off my knees. The soldiers have already moved further down the street.

"Go home. It is dangerous on the streets." He makes sure I'm fine before he walks away, and I hurry to the apartment. I have to stay there and wait. Soon everything will be over. Just a few more days.

Paris, Eighth arrondissement, August 18, 1944 evening.

All afternoon I am shut up at home, trying to read a book I took from the bookshelf, but I'm unable to concentrate, finding myself reading the same paragraph over and over again and losing concentration. Occasionally shots are heard through the open windows, making me cringe in the little living room armchair. What's going on outside?

The hot summer air penetrates the apartment, and only in the evening does a cool breeze enter. I peek out of the window and see people running, wondering if the Germans have abandoned the city, but a few minutes later a truck full of soldiers stops, and they quickly jump out of it, spreading in the street, causing me to withdraw from the window.

Have they come to arrest me? Did the woman in the store pass the diary I gave her to the Gestapo?

At first, as I'm trying to listen through the entrance door, the staircase is quiet. But suddenly I hear footsteps of hobnail boots climbing the wooden stairs, and I push my feet as hard as I can to block the door as they come. I will not give up without a fight.

"Monique? What are you doing?" I hear Herr Ernest from the other side of the thick door, trying to push it open.

"Sorry, I was scared. There were shots in the street today, I did not know if you would come back." I open the door slightly, trying to see if he's come alone.

"We evacuated the hotel. We're moving north, so I came to say goodbye." He stands in front of me, and I look up at him, checking his green eyes.

"You came to say goodbye?" Will I stay alive?

"Yes, I came to say goodbye, but before that, I have a few

more things to finish here." He smiles at me, and I keep on smiling but want to scream.

"What kind of things?"

"Some orders that need to be executed tomorrow, and some things to check that they are done, not something that should interest a pleasant companion like you."

"Is it related to Paris?"

"It has to do with German honor," he answers flatly, removing his military shirt and draping it on the arm of the chair, exposing his pale body while remaining in only a sweaty green tanktop. "We will leave after giving the French nation a present, the same we gave the Communists and the Jews. We will always destroy the ones trying to fight and betray us." He keeps talking, but it seems he is mostly talking to himself as he organizes the few things left in his study, turning his back and ignoring my presence.

"What do you mean? Is it about all the stories coming from the east?" I stand outside the study door and ask, regretting it a moment later.

Herr Ernest stops arranging the papers on his desk and looks at me.

"You think the German army is losing, but we never lose. You just don't know how to view history. The Communists and the Jews did not defeat us. Like rats, they entered the camps we built for them."

"What camps?" I lower my eyes, unable to look at his fingers holding the telegrams and commands.

"What does the name matter? Camps we built to ensure German supremacy against the Jews and their ambitions to rule the world."

My fingers scratch the doorframe of his study, but he continues.

"One day you will all thank us for what we did. Please make me dinner."

We eat dinner in silence, and after that he continues to work, leaving me to nap in the small armchair until the door opens, and he goes to bed, not before he sets the alarm clock next to his dresser.

"What happens tomorrow? When are you going back to the army?"

"Tomorrow morning, we will say goodbye properly." He smiles and sits down on the bed, removing his tank top and lying down to sleep.

I cannot go to bed with him, but I must, otherwise he will suspect me.

The city is quiet in the dark, and the gunfire sounds have ceased, but I cannot fall asleep. My eyes look at the bedroom curtain moving gently in the night breeze, and I think about Auschwitz in the east that he built for my family.

The streetlights are almost all off, and the city outside is dark, as if waiting for tomorrow. What did he write in the study? The pain in my stomach does not stop.

Even though I have no one to pass the information on to, I can't help myself, and I rise quietly, walking barefoot to the study door, gently closing it behind my back and sitting in his chair.

Top Secret

8/19/1944

From: Engineering brigade 7II2, Commander

To: Engineering brigade 7II2 Units

Subject: Destroying Paris monuments

Commencement of operations, starting at 8/20/1944 08:00 after the departure of the main army units from the city, executing according to plan.

Oberst Ernest

7II2, Commander

My eyes quickly go through the destruction order he has already signed, examining his signature at the bottom of the page, and the pain in my stomach intensifies. What to do?

I must hurry, my hands moving quickly between the documents, and my hand accidentally hits his fountain pen's ink jar lying on the side of the table.

Even though I try to catch it, the ink jar slips through my fingers and hits the wooden floor, crashing into sharp pieces of glass that sound like they're shaking the whole apartment.

I freeze in place. What have I done? Did he wake up?

"I'm dead," my lips whisper again and again as I get down on my knees, trying to stop the ink stain from spreading on the floor, moving my fingers quickly around the black liquid, which looks like a stain of dark blood expanding without stopping.

"What have I done?" I speak to myself, ignoring the small pieces of glass scattered on the floor that wound my hands, making me bleed on the parquet, dotting the wood with burgundy spots in the dim light of the candle.

I'm dead. The dark stain has been absorbed into the wooden boards and spreads to the carpet, painting its edges black, which my ink-soiled fingers fail to scratch away. Soon he will wake up and kill me, what will I tell him? I will no longer be alive when the Americans arrive.

The hours pass as I kneel on the rug, hugging myself and holding my aching stomach tightly, ignoring the blood and black paint on my hands, soiling my nightgown, painting it with stains. Soon, before sunrise, the bedside clock will ring shrilly, and he will wake up, get out of bed, come looking for me. I will no longer get to see the morning sun.

What was Lizette doing?

In a quick motion, I get up from the ink-stained carpet and walk out of his study, closing the door behind me as quietly as I can and stepping into the dark kitchen. My hands search for the drawer, and my wounded fingers hold the wooden handle firmly. I'm dead anyway.

Do not stop and think, do not hesitate, walk to the bedroom, be careful in the dark, do not stumble and make noise. I can see Herr Ernest lying under the blanket, and I raise my hand above my head, holding the handle firmly until my fingers turn white.

"You murdered my father," I whisper and lower the knife

with all my might, pushing it firmly against his twisting body.

"You murdered my mother." The knife goes down again, hitting and penetrating more and more, ignoring movements under the blanket as his hands reach out, trying to hold me.

"You murdered my Jacob," my whisper becomes hoarse as I stab his hand and body over and over, managing to wound his hand, which is trying to strangle me.

"You murdered my Lizette," I shout in the dark bedroom, stabbing him again and again.

"I'm Monique Moreno, and I'm a French Jew," I scream, and lower the knife one last time into his twisted and quiet body, throwing it away and running out of the room.

Paris, Eighth arrondissement, August 19, 1944, early morning.

When will he wake up and kill me?

I do not know how long I have been in the bathroom, curled up on the floor, waiting to hear the gunshot. My eyes close when I imagine Herr Ernest getting up out of my bed, crawling to his study where his firearm is waiting for him in the black leather case, and coming to hunt me in the bathroom. I'm too afraid to open my eyes.

The alarm clock starts ringing with a loud whirring, and

my whole body cramps in fear as I cuddle my legs tightly.

"Please stop, please stop," I whispered to the clock, closing my eyes, but it rings for more and more long minutes until it stops.

And the house is quiet again.

The morning's twilight has painted the house in blue, and I open my eyes and examine myself, looking at my hands in disgust and nausea. My fingers are painted with clotted blood mixed with black ink stains, and I have to fight the urge to vomit. I have to grip the sink as I get up and stand, trying to wash and scrub my hands and skin until they become red and sore, splashing water on the nightgown to clean it as well. But I'm not going to my bedroom to change into a dress. He's probably waiting for me, awake, hiding behind the door and waiting to kill me.

But he does not come out of my bedroom.

As the day goes by, I can hear the shots from the open windows, sometimes the sounds are distant, and one time a fight takes place on the street below. The bullets hit the building walls, scattering shards and causing me to crawl on the floor near the sink.

"They're on their way," I whisper when the phone in his study rings and does not stop, but I do not dare to approach and answer. He is waiting to kill me.

Soon they will reach me. Towards noon, I crawl to the front door, kneeling on the floor and listening through the heavy door to the voices on the staircase. Despite the wooden table I dragged against the door. I know that even if I try my best, they will break it easily if they arrive. They will put me in front of the wall and shoot me. This time it will be my turn, and I watch his hobnails boots that are standing by the door, prepared to hit me in the name of their master.

Shouts in German are heard in the street, followed by gunfire. Without thinking, I get up and run to the kitchen, trying to find a hiding place.

Holding a knife, I try to loosen the pantry boards, but the panels do not come loose and the knife slips, scratching my hand and making me scream in pain. I'm too scared to hide in the bedroom closet. He's in the room, waiting for me.

Crawling, I return to my hiding place under the sink, holding my wounded hand and trying to prevent the blood from dripping, this is the safest place to spend the night until they come to pick me up.

"I'm Monique Moreno, I'm Monique Moreno," I whisper to myself over and over as it gets dark outside. I must not fall asleep, but my eyes are closing, I can no longer hold them open.

"Where am I?"

My whole body aches from lying on the bathroom floor as I get up quickly. The house is still quiet.

Morning daylight illuminates the house from the open windows, and the sounds of gunfire are heard from time to time. I must get away from this apartment, it's dangerous for me.

Carefully I enter my bedroom, looking at the wall, and ignoring the crimson stain that paints the blanket and what is underneath it. Walking in small steps, my back to the bed, concentrating only on the closet door, I open it, choosing the first simple dress I lay my hands on, and quickly run out of the room, breathing again only when I'm outside.

What to take with me? I need some food. I haven't eaten anything since yesterday, my hands move quickly between the pantry shelves, putting a chocolate bar into my dress pocket. The thought of him lying in the other room makes me nauseous, and I grab the wooden shelf to stabilize myself. I have to hurry. What about his gun? The leather case hangs in his study. Shall I take his gun? I do not know how to use it, but I can threaten if I have to. Slowly, I pull the handgun out of the holster, surprised by the metal's oily touch, and put it in my bag.

Anxiously I get closer to his dirty hobnail boots, kicking them as hard as I can, and I open the front door. The stairwell is empty, and I hurry out of the apartment, going down the stairs out to the street.

The intense light outside is bright in my eyes when I open the building's front door, and I have to wait a few seconds at the entrance hall and watch outside, getting used to the sun.

A German military staff vehicle stands abandoned near the building entrance, its tires punctured, its upholstery torn. Is this the vehicle I'd been inside so many times? Several people pass me running, and I start to follow them. But then I stop and look at the black vehicle waiting for me at the end of the street.

The black car stands across the street as if trying to block it, with its doors open, waiting to put me inside and take me to the horrible building at 84 Avenue Foch. What to do?

I hear a series of shots from the other side of the block, and I cringe in place. What direction to go? Will they shoot me if I start running? The person standing next to the car is not looking in my direction, and I slowly approach the black vehicle, ready to turn around and run.

One man in a black leather coat lies on the street corner, his face to the pavement, and a wet stain of crimson surrounds him, while another man sits by the wheel, leaning on it as though sleeping between the shattered windows and the bullet holes in the dark doors and seats.

Keep on walking with the people towards the boulevard, get away from the black vehicle, assimilate among them, do not stop, and look at the tricolor flag placed on the black car's hood. Just keep walking.

Near the Champs-Élysées, there are more people and more shouts, some citizens waving guns in their hands, some holding the flag of free France, but in every direction shots are heard, and the crowd is running to take shelter behind tree trunks or advertising columns in the street.

I'm saved. I'm one of them, one anonymous girl in the crowd. I survived, I survived.

Paris, Eighth arrondissement, 20 August 1944 10:30 AM.

"She's German. She's a collaborator." There is a shout in the crowd, and I look around to see who they mean.

"That's her, in the brown dress." I can hear the scream again, and some people stop and look at me. I have to keep walking.

"She licked a German officer's boots," the woman continues to shout, and the people start surrounding me until I have no choice but to stop and turn around, facing the neighbor from the third floor below my apartment. She is standing and pointing at me with a look full of hatred.

"She's a collaborator."

"It's not true. I'm French, like you."

"She's German." And more people crowd around with murmurs of rage.

"It's not true."

"She's in love with a Nazi officer," she shouts, and I feel a thump in my back and fold, almost falling to the ground.

"I'm French."

"Her officer housed her in a Jewish family's apartment. She collaborates horizontally," she shouts to the crowd.

"Please, it's not true." I try to run, but they stop me, and another fist is thrown at my stomach, and hands grip me tightly.

"Look what I found in her pocket." There is a roar of joy when a young man pulls out the package of chocolates and presents it over his head, showing the audience around him the cover with the eagle holding a swastika under the word 'chocolate' in German. "Only the Nazis have such delicacies." And the crowd murmurs in agreement, and I feel spit hitting my face, followed by a kick in my stomach and slaps that send me to the ground.

"Kill the horizontal collaborator."

"Kill her."

"Bullet to her head."

"Please, I'm French." I try to get up and protect my face from the kicks and spitting. "Please."

The gun in the bag, it will protect me, I have to live, please. But my hands looking for my bag on the sidewalk can't find it between the shoes of strangers trying to kick me. I've lost my bag. It fell or was snatched from me by someone in the crowd. I want to live so much.

"We will give her the special collaborators treatment," someone suggests and grabs me by the arm, dragging me down the avenue to the cheers of the crowd that surrounds me, still cursing and spitting in my face.

"Take care of her."

"Engrave a swastika on her cheeks."

"Cut off her hair that everyone knows."

"I've brought you another one." He throws me into the center of a crowd where several other young women are standing in torn dresses, eyes downcast.

"Another one," cheers the crowd, "we'll take care of them all." And through my tears, I see Violette in the center of the circle.

Two men force her to sit on a chair taken out to the street from one of the cafés, a sturdy guy is holding her while another in a white tanktop cuts all her hair off with scissors. The crowd is shouting and cursing her, cheering on every clump of hair thrown into the street.

"Make her a beautiful bald spot."

"Let everyone know what she was doing."

"Do not forget a swastika on the forehead, she will be beautiful."

I cannot look at her like that, and I lower my eyes. Maybe it's better that I'm shedding so many tears and everything is blurred. Why is this happening to me?

"You're next in line." The man tightly holding me whispers as Violette is lifted from the chair and led to a display in front of the bloodthirsty crowd.

"Please, this is a mistake."

"Shut up." He slaps and kicks me again, and I stumble and fall on the sidewalk, trying to stabilize myself and holding the pavement stones with my fingers and fingernails.

A huge hand grabs my hair and lifts me to a standing position, and I scream in pain as he presses me to his body. He is a big man, really big, sweaty, wearing a grey tank top full of stains and smelling of sauerkraut, wearing a filthy beret, and his eyes look at the crowd angrily.

"She is Jewish, no one touches her."

"She collaborated horizontally." Voices from the crowd answer him as he begins to drag me out of the circle.

"She's German. We'll take care of her," says a man who tries to grab my arm.

"No one comes near her." I hear his thunderous voice above the roars of the crowd as he presses me close to his body with his huge hand, and I notice the resistance armband around his thick arm.

"She licked German boots." Another young man tries to get closer to me, but the huge man pushes him away.

"Do not touch her."

"There are no Jews in France, the Germans killed them all. She belongs to us." The young man does not give up as the crowd closes on us.

"Anyone who gets closer will die," the big man shouts and points his rifle at the young man, hugging me with his other arm. And the young man stops and steps back, not before spitting on me, turning to the next young woman waiting for her punishment in a torn dress and with a downcast look.

"Give her to him. We have enough horizontal collaborators."

"We must hurry." He supports and drags me, pushing the crowd to the sides by force and carrying me between the people gathering around the young woman who is forcibly seated in the chair in the middle of the street.

"Run." That's all he says, and we start running down the boulevard. I'm running as fast as I can, getting away from the crowd before anyone else tries to hit me. The pain in my ribs from the kicks does not stop, and it is difficult for me to breathe. Still, I keep running, ignoring the sounds of shooting all around and trying to be careful that my shoes do not fall off while running, but after a while I have to stop. I can't breathe anymore.

"We must go on." He encourages me and holds my hand, does not allow me to stop, but he too is gasping and goes for a walk as we approach Concorde Square.

I'm trying to catch my breath, ignoring the pain in my ribs and my torn and filthy dress. His sweaty hand supports my body as he leads me behind a burned-out car parked on the side of the boulevard. There is gunfire all around, and we have to lower our heads.

I cannot run anymore. The smell of the burnt vehicle penetrates my nostrils and fills them with a pungent smell, mixed with my heavy breathing and my sweat.

"I've been looking for you for three days," he says.

"Who's looking for me?" My voice sounds hoarse, like someone else's. I'm gasping for air, tensing up every time a shot is fired from the direction of Rivoli Street, unable to raise my head.

"They are looking after you," he answers and puts his arm around me to protect me, wrapping me in the smell of sauerkraut while I hold my head tightly between my two hands and try to bury myself in the road, wanting to escape from the round of shots in the square. Who is looking after me? Who cares about me? I'm just trying to breathe and stay alive in all the gunfire surrounding us. I'm so tired of being afraid.

Some people are running hunched towards the barriers and barbed wire fences in the square's center, holding rifles in their hands, but the shots are getting heavier, and their bodies suddenly fold and remain lying on the road. "I can't anymore," I scream and bury my head in his big hand.

"We have to move towards the street."

In front of the Nazi headquarters on Rivoli Street, several German cars are burning, raising black smoke to the sky. Occasionally, an orange flash of an ammunition explosion hits one of them, and the fire lights up again, causing me to tremble and scratch the road.

"I can't."

"You must."

Down the street, there are two German armored vehicles firing machine guns in our direction, and bullets are pounding on the buildings around the square, leaving holes in them, but the huge red Nazi flag in front of the headquarters is thrown onto the street.

"I can't."

"Run." He gets up and pulls me, forcing me to run next to him, and we skip and try to cross the square and reach the garden area, passing the sign at the gate which is punched through with bullet holes, kneeling next to a stone shelter, catching our breath.

"I can't anymore."

"We have to get to the Louvre and cross the river. The Latin Quarter is already ours." He gasps as we look around carefully.

A German vehicle enters the square, driving fast and turning around the fountain, and the big man picks up his rifle and tries to shoot at it, but the vehicle manages to escape towards the bridge while I cringe from the gunfire, holding the big man's legs tightly.

"We're trying to stop them from getting to the bridges. They have a plan to blow them up, but they're delaying. It's not clear why," he yells at me even though we're close to each other.

We hear a burst of gunfire, followed by an engine's rumble and creaking chains around the corner, and the noise gets louder.

"Run," he yells, and we get up together as he takes my hand and pulls me after him towards the garden and the river.

The sounds of gunfire never stop. Even as we approach the river, we hear the whistling of bullets and the rumble of machine guns from the direction of Île de la Cité. But the river flows leisurely, its waters greenish in the midday sun, moving slowly and calmly, indifferent to the sounds of gunfire all around as if it does not care at all about the war taking place in the city. The Pont Des Arts stretches peacefully from side to side, empty of people with only the lanterns along it seeming to me like people walking on it.

"Germans," the big man in the stained shirt whispers and points with his finger at the camouflaged position and the round grey helmets that reflect the August sun, and I feel I can no longer move. They are going to kill us.

"Wait for me here," he whispers, but I grab his filthy shirt and move with him, even though I'm probably hampering his movement. I close my eyes tightly as he lifts his rifle and aims, and my hand squeezes his shirt with each shot fired at the German soldiers.

"Run," he yells at me as he starts running towards the bridge.

"I can't. They will kill me."

"Come with me." He turns around and pulls me, lifts me to my feet, and we start running.

Do not stop running, ignore the soldiers lying in strange positions behind the sandbags, be careful not to stumble on the wide stairs that climb to the bridge, ignore the pain, look forward to the other side of the bridge. Do not stop running.

The sound of my breathing fills all my thoughts, and the bridge is not ending. I feel so exposed as the big man runs beside me, grabs his rifle, with two more rifles from the German position on his back. Another step, and another, and I can hear the strange whistles in my ears. The other side is so close, but suddenly the big man folds and falls on the bridge while I'm screaming and stopping next to him, trying to drag him off the bridge. But he is so heavy, and I'm small, and a puddle of blood appears under his body, and I keep hearing the strange whistles all around us, cutting the air around me and the bullets splitting the wooden boards of the bridge as they penetrate. Suddenly the end of the bridge seems so far away.

"Hold on," I keep screaming at him, "we will soon arrive." I turn him on his back and rip the remnants of the pocket from my dress, shoving it where the blood is coming out and trying to drag him onto the wooden boards which are full of bullet holes, and someone comes from the other bank, yelling at me to keep running. And all I do is grab the big man's hand and shout: "Help me carry him, help me carry him."

Paris, Barricade near Pont Des Arts, August 20, 1944, 12:30 PM.

"Philip, I have two more volunteers. Where should I send them?"

Since the Gestapo raid, we have had a shortage of people, they managed to penetrate so deeply, and now we are already past twenty-four hours of fighting all over the city. The police headquarters in Île de la Cité is already ours, but the people there are besieged, and ammunition is running low.

"Do you have any more resistance armbands?"

"Yes, I do."

"Give them to the new ones and take them to the barricade in the direction of the invalid. They have a shortage of fighters. See if you have some guns to give them."

Since the Gestapo raid, the connection between the members has been severed, even with her, and I have no idea if she is still alive. The chances are that the Gestapo got her. I'm trying not to think about it, even though it's so hard.

"Philip, we got another German machine gun. Where should we place it?"

"Take it to Saint-Michel, tell them to try to pass it to the fighters at Île de la Cité."

"Shouldn't we try to overcome the German snipers firing at us from the Louvre?"

"No, we'll get along here. They're in trouble there."

"Philip, we are receiving information from Versailles that they can hear the American tanks."

"Pass that information to all commanders, tell them they have to hold on for a few more hours."

It is my fault. I led her to the traitor. He must have managed to get enough information out of her. Even though he is dead now, it doesn't make me feel better. Lizette was killed, and the newspaper boy was killed, and they probably killed her too.

"Did you hear anything from the Breton?"

"No, should I replace you here? You've been in position since yesterday."

"No, I'll be here a little longer."

Since the first time I saw her, I wanted to know her better. She was standing scared in front of me, in that old warehouse, afraid but willing to fight for her life. Every time we met, I adored her outbursts of anger, saying what she thought and not what I wanted to hear. But she did not want to see me, and now it probably does not matter anymore.

"Philip, they're running out of ammunition at the barricade in front of Luxembourg Palace."

"They'll have to settle with what they have for now, I'll try to arrange more."

Only her diary arrived somehow. Apparently it's hers, I'm not even sure of that. How much of her handwriting had I seen? I always told her to be careful. One woman from an alley shop in the Latin Quarter passed the diary to someone who passed it on to someone, and he came to us. Since then, we have been lurking near the bridges, hitting the Germans when they try to get closer. But she just disappeared.

"Are you sure no one has heard anything from the Breton?"

"I'm sure. I also checked on the positions in San Michelle."

Only the man from the market, the giant Breton, might be able to recognize her. He is the only one who knows her and is still alive. He volunteered to search for her, but he has been wandering on the east bank for several days now.

"Philip, pay attention, there are shots from the Louvre area, near the German position."

"Bring the machine gun that controls the river here. I want you to place it next to me."

A few gunshots stop for a moment as we tense and examine the other bank, and suddenly two people climb on the bridge and start running towards us, and the fighter next to me asks whether to shoot them or not. I tell him to wait, and the German soldiers in the Louvre start firing at them, and I shout for them to bring the machine gun to start returning fire towards the windows and the Germans.

The people running towards us are already at the center of the bridge, one big and one smaller, probably a woman. It seems like they're advancing so slowly, and the big one suddenly falls, as he's been hit. The woman turns and stops next to him and leans over. She might have been hit as well. I can see the gunshots around them on the bridge, and I yell at the fighters next to me to start firing at the windows with everything they have. I jump over the barricade and run towards the bridge. It seems that another one or two are running after me, and I hear the whistle of the bullets as I approach, shouting for the woman to leave him and keep on running to the bank. Her hands are full of blood as she tries to drag the big man lying on the wooden bridge, and she doesn't stop yelling at me: "Help me carry him, help me carry him."

Epilogue

Monique experienced fear many times in her life, some have been told in this book, and some have not.

Like those long minutes at the barricade next to the Pont Des Arts, when someone gave her a bottle of wine to drink, and she tried to catch her breath and searched for the right words to say to Philip, hoping he would forgive her, and that maybe he could love her someday.

And that day in May 1946, as she walked through Paris City Hall in a white dress, accompanied by a huge Breton who held her hand as if he were her father. She was looking at Philip waiting for her at the end of the aisle, praying he would forgive her for sleeping with someone else before him. The Breton was wearing a clean new button-down shirt.

And January 1950, when her first daughter was born and a second seemed like an eternity until she heard her screaming.

Or 1954, when she received the Medal of Honor and feared the dress she wore was too simple for the event, with the President of the Republic standing in front of her.

And November 2005 as well, when Philip held her hand in their shared house on Rue Georges Bizet while lying in bed and smiling at her, closing his eyes forever.

But on August 8, 2012, when she took her last breaths at the Les Issambres Paris nursing home in the Seventeenth arrondissement, she was not afraid at all. She just looked at her daughters and grandchildren around her, and finally waited to meet Philip, Lizette, Mom, Dad, and Jacob.

In memory of all the Jews of France who perished in the Holocaust

In memory of all the resistance members who fought against the Germans, the few against many.

The End

Author's note: Pieces of History

When I started writing this book, I knew I would write about an emotional period for the French nation: days of living, collaborating, and resistance under German occupation in World War II, and above all, the help given to the Nazis to capture the Jews and send them for extermination.

Operation Spring Breeze, mentioned at the beginning of this book, is the first step of Paris' Jewish deportation. During the surprise operation that on July 16, 1942, the Paris police carried out the capture of Parisian Jews for the Nazis. The captured people, men, women, and children, were held for several days without food and water in the Paris Winter Stadium, south of the Eiffel Tower. (The Stadium does not exist anymore. It was demolished in 1959.) After five days, all the Jews were transferred to the Drancy detention camp north of Paris, and later on to Auschwitz by trains.

The role of the Paris police in this operation is undeniable.

But while according to Gestapo records, the French police had to seize over twenty thousand Jews in this operation, in the end only fourteen thousand Jews of Paris were arrested and sent to Auschwitz. It turned out that many policemen had warned Jewish families to flee ahead of time. There were a lot of policemen that endangered themselves to warn the Jews.

Seventy-seven thousand of France's Jews perished in the Holocaust, most of them sent to Auschwitz, but the majority of French Jews survived the war. French citizens hid Jews in farms and villages outside the big cities, or helped them cross the border into neutral Spain. At the end of the war, it became clear that 78% of the French Jewish population had survived the Holocaust. This is the highest number of Jews who survived the Holocaust of all the countries under German occupation. In the Netherlands, for example, only 29% of Dutch Jews survived the war. Did the French population help the Germans eliminate French Jews? History shows that besides citizens who helped the Nazis, most of the French population assisted the Jews and did not extradite them.

And what about collaboration with the Germans in everyday life?

Paris was not a uniform city throughout the war. Alongside open cafés and clubs on the Grand Boulevards, full of German soldiers and French citizens, poor people walked in wooden shoes searching for food. I tried to show both sides.

Throughout the book, I have touched on several historical events or landmarks that serve as the story's backdrop.

Monique's fictional story about the escape with her parents describes the escape of French civilians from the German army in June 1940. The German forces outflanked Maginot Line from Belgium and were running to Paris. German fighter planes fired on refugee convoys, intensifying the disorganization on the roads and preventing the French army from sending reinforcements.

During the picnic on the Maren River, Fritz mentions the Maren's first battle in World War I. In this battle, French soldiers bravely stopped the German army approaching Paris. Six thousand soldiers were sent from Paris by taxis. All Parisian taxi drivers volunteered to drive the soldiers into battle in an endless convoy. Thanks to them, they managed to stabilize a line against the advanced Germans, and stopped them.

During Oberst Ernest and Monique's first trip, they travel to La Coupole, a village near Dunkirk and the Belgium border. In a hidden site between the woods, the Germans built a huge bunker that would contain the V2 missiles, Hitler's revenge weapon. Towards the end of the war, these missiles would be launched against London, exploding in the city and causing destruction.

The cannon battery mentioned on the second trip to Normandy is the cannon battery near Longues Sur Mer's village on Normandy's shore. This battery controls the areas that later would be called 'Gold Beach' and 'Omaha Beach' in the American code maps for the D-Day invasion.

Slava, the Polish soldier Monique meets at the shore, is a civilian recruit. Despite the German army's uniform image, the terrible losses at the eastern front against Russia forced the Germans to begin recruiting civilians from occupied countries, with promises of monetary reward and often with threats. Since 1943, many German army units were combined with civilian recruits under German commanders. Such companies were also stationed in Normandy, used mainly for defensive battles.

At night, Monique and Ernest slept in the town of Cabourg in a luxurious hotel near the coast. This area was also heavily protected by the Germans in preparation for an invasion from the sea.

When Ernest takes Monique to the Tuileries Gardens on a Sunday morning in the winter, they purchase paintings looted from Jewish families. The works of art were collected in the old tennis hall located on the edge of the Tuileries Gardens, near Rivoli Street, and German officers used to go there and buy paintings at ridiculous prices. After the war, some of the paintings were returned to their original owners or their surviving family members. But some of the search efforts and legal battles for looted paintings continue to this day. The signs prohibiting Jews from entering public parks and museums were hung on the gates after German occupation began in June 1940.

Although it is commonly thought that the Allies did not bomb Paris, this is not true. During the preparation for the coming invasion, the Allies began bombing all over France, with American and English bombers trying to hit railways and industrial factories that supported the German army. The first bombing described in the book, during which Monique and Ernest are in the bedroom, took place at Renault's car factories and complexes in the city's industrial area. The second bombing, in which Monique escapes the apartment and helps her neighbor, is the big bombing on April 20, 1944, in which the eighteenth arrondissement was hit.

The invasion of Normandy began on the night of June 5, 1944. During the night, three paratrooper divisions parachuted in all over Normandy, and in the morning, another six divisions stormed the heavily protected shores. American and British intelligence managed a series of deceptive moves aimed to confuse the Germans, making them believe the real invasion would take place on the coast of Calais near Belgium. During the first hours of the invasion, German intelligence couldn't decide where the American-British main effort was, so they held the German armored divisions in reserve rather than throw them into the battle at Normandy. Therefore, it was only on the afternoon of June 6 that BBC Radio began to publish credible news of the invasion's real location. All those misleading steps, aided by the French resistance disconnecting telephone lines and damaging railways, led to a long delay in German response, allowing Allied forces to establish themselves on Normandy's coastal shore. Throughout the German occupation, listening to BBC was forbidden, and the Nazis would execute anyone they caught listening to it.

The French resistance movements against the Germans contained several groups with different interests, but all had one common goal, fighting Germans. In the first years of occupation, the Communist underground was the strongest and most active among all the movements, working almost separately from the others. But as the war progressed, they began to cooperate, helping British intelligence with information and receiving instructions for actions against the Nazis, assisting in preparations for the coming invasion. The Gestapo made great efforts to infiltrate the resistance. The Gestapo headquarter was at the building at 84 Avenue Foch.

The trap, in which Monique escapes from the vehicle and Lizette is killed, took place on August 16, 1944. Thirty-five Resistance men fell into the trap of a planted Gestapo agent and were executed. This was the last significant action of the Gestapo against the underground before the battles for the city's liberation. Whoever follows the book will find that I brought the event forward by a few days.

The liberation of the city took several days. Despite Hitler's explicit instructions to raze Paris to the ground in revenge for the bombing of German cities by Allied planes, in the end Paris was not destroyed. There are several arguments as to why this is the case. The prevailing opinion is that the Commander of Paris, General Dietrich von Choltitz, chose to defy Hitler's order until it was too late, and the uprising in the city began.

The uprising in Paris began on August 18 with a general strike. The next day firefights developed between the German army and the Resistance members who lacked weapons but managed to occupy the Paris police headquarters at Ile de la Cité. On August 24, the first American division of the Free French Army entered the city, and on August 25 General von Choltitz signed a letter of surrender, leaving Paris almost unharmed.

The citizens hurried to embrace American soldiers and turned their rage against the French women who had surrendered horizontally to the German soldiers. Tearing clothes, shaving hair, and drawing swastikas on those women's foreheads was a common punishment in the eyes of the crowd seeking revenge after four years of German occupation.

I could not be precise in all the historical details, some I changed and others I had to omit, and I'm sorry I can't let them into the story. But for me, writing this book was an exciting experience of learning about Nazi-occupied Paris, trying to imagine life in daily fear through the eyes of a seventeen-year-old Jewish girl fighting for her life.

Thank you for reading.
Alex Amit

Printed in Great Britain
by Amazon